Three Arachnids in a Warship

(to say nothing of the human)

Michael Coolwood

MONTAG

First Montag Press E-Book and Paperback Original Edition June 2020

Montag Press ISBN: 978-1-940233-75-8
Design © 2020 Amit Dey

Montag Press Team:
Project Editor — Charlie Franco
Managing Director — Charlie Franco
Cover credit — Diana Necsulescu
Photo credit — Bryan Morwood

A Montag Press Book
www.montagpress.com
Montag Press
777 Morton Street, Unit B
San Francisco CA 94129 USA

Montag Press, the burning book with the hatchet cover, the skewed word mark and the portrayal of the long-suffering fireman mascot are trademarks of Montag Press.

Printed & Digitally Originated in the United States of America
10 9 8 7 6 5 4 3 2 1

Table of Contents

Chapter One

Two Arachnids in a Warship

(to say nothing of the human)

BEFORE MY FIRST TOUR of duty, I used to visit the doctor infrequently. After I invited a human into my home, I started calling on my physician once every few weeks or so. I suddenly needed to be sure of what diseases I was carrying, how deadly they were, and exactly how long I had left to live.

My sudden drive to know about the precise nature and time-frame of my death was linked to living with a human... just possibly not in the way you'd expect. I wasn't at risk of picking up a deadly disease from her, for example. The human in question was very clean.

On one fateful morning in June, I was prodded and poked and scanned by every implement my doctor could get her claws on. Finally, she announced that it was my brain that was to bring about my death.

"My brain?" I asked. A slight shudder ran through my voice.

"I'm afraid so, my lady."

"Well, what's wrong with the blasted thing?" I enquired, poking a claw at my carapace to see if I could get at the organ in question. I couldn't.

The answer the medic gave me was expansive and I didn't understand most of it. There was one word that stood out: *mindvirus*. We arachnids have the technology to move our consciousness from one body to another. This is very useful when one body dies unexpectedly but it is also useful for other reasons. I once switched bodies because the storage facility containing my spare was on the other side of town and I did not fancy the walk. Anyway, there are mindviruses that can creep in when switching from one body to another. They are very rare, or so I've heard.

The doctor told me about the course the disease was likely to take, as well as my treatment options. I nodded sagely. The thing was, the mindvirus seemed bad but it didn't seem certain. I needed to be certain.

"Do you have any questions?" she asked, after going on about some medication issue which didn't interest me in the slightest.

"I do, as it happens," I beamed. I started running through my pre-prepared list of conditions that I might still have. After the thirtieth minute, I paused for breath. The doctor chose that moment to interject.

"You have none of these ailments," she said.

"But the mindvirus-" I objected.

"Yes, you have the mindvirus, but you do not have any of these other ailments."

"Blast. Are you sure?"

"Yes." She swiped the data from my data panel into her own. "You do not have the right sort of claws to get Aard Sign Wrist, you do not have the right sort of blood to have Antediluvian Vitae Fever... you do not have any of these, except the mindvirus." She double-checked her own list. "And Housemaid's Knee. You do actually have Housemaid's Knee. I'll get you some cream for that."

She dispensed some cream from a hopper in the corner and handed it over. I slopped it into one of the useful pots I keep in my waistcoat pocket.

Usually at this point the doctor starts fussing with her data panel. I'm sure she would like me to think she is compiling notes of our meeting or something, but I suspect it's more of a subtle hint. She wishes to convey that she's very busy and can't spend all day chatting to me. Not being heartless, I usually take that as a cue to vacate the premises. On that fateful day, however... the doctor just stared at me.

"Is there something else?" I asked, vaguely aware that it should probably be the doctor asking this. Maybe there was something other than Housemaid's Knee that I should be concerned about, after all.

"You're having trouble digesting the news about your condition," she said.

"Which condition?" I asked, bringing out my list. "Because I have some thoughts about the Grey Death. Now, I know it was wiped out in 2052 but I think it might have come out of retirement."

"No. I mean the mindvirus."

"Oh, that," I said, disappointed.

"You need to spend some time away from the data links."

I clutched my data panel to my thorax. "But how will I find out what's killing me?"

She gave me the sort of look doctors aren't supposed to give their patients. "I am instructing you," she said, "to take a holiday. Spend two weeks in a cottage at the seaside. No metropolis, no data links. Take some time to adjust to your new living conditions with this mindvirus. Rest and relaxation, that's what you need. Take your medication. Delete that list of conditions you most certainly do not have."

"What? All of it?" I asked, aghast.

"All of it," she said.

I only pretended to delete it at first, but she wasn't fooled. Eventually, and very reluctantly, I really did delete it. She thanked me and then told me to get out of her office.

I mulled over her instructions as I returned home. A couple of weeks by the sea might be a perfectly pleasant way to spend what little time I had left. That being said, I was not sure that I deserved my last days in the universe to be pleasant.

Sarah, my human lodger, wasn't at home when I returned. She works as some sort of... she tried to explain it to me once. It's something to do with stopping humans from being persecuted. I didn't even know you could stop that before she explained it, but there you go.

Oliver, my arachnid lodger, *was* present. Oliver was a dear old school friend. His fur as greying at the temples, and he wore serious suits. Five years ago, the poor chap was having some trouble with his landlord. Apparently, he objected to one or two of Oliver's hobbies. Anyway, it sounded perfectly ghastly, so I offered to put him up for a few weeks.

Well, after that, Oliver found a place... but he didn't like it. So I said he should stay until he found somewhere he did like. Then the housing market shifted and one or two things happened with Oliver's job and then he lost one of his shoes and then – long story short – there we were, still living together.

It could be frightfully jolly to have a friend stay with you. Sarah was a wonderful tenant. She and Oliver were like night and day, and not just because Sarah's positivity and humour brought the flat to life with its light. She was more diminutive than Oliver, standing just over six feet tall. Her skin was the colour of platinum; Oliver's fur was zinc-like. She was rarely seen without a smile, whilst Oliver usually boasted a sort of homely snarl.

Sarah moved in fairly recently, after her last landlord developed a dislike of humans upon finding one rooting through the bins. Sarah was wonderful company and was terribly kind. She insisted on paying rent.

Oliver did not pay rent. I had mentioned it once or twice but he'd said he didn't want to spoil our friendship by making everything about money.

I found Oliver in the dining room, helping himself to a chop. I thought I had mentioned that this particular chop was destined for my consumption but I must have been mistaken. I sat down opposite the chap and his chop, and mentioned what had transpired at the doctor's office.

"Oh really?" he asked, his eyes lighting up. He thought for a few moments and then a thoughtful look crossed his face. "No, no, no. That's no good at all," he said.

"What isn't?"

"A trip to the seaside," he said. "There are fish. And you know what come with fish? The gulls, my dear lass, the gulls. This time of year, they can take your eye out."

I'd always found gulls to be rather cheerful things, and I said so. They flap about the place and steal potato snacks from people in a most amusing manner.

"Ah, but there is also the swell. The swell of the sea. It's devilish! It will make you sick just at the sound of it. You'd feel pretty silly if you were sick at the seaside, wouldn't you, Jay? A silly ass such as yourself would easily wind up sick on a seaside holiday."

He was right, that would make me feel silly. I hadn't considered how horrifying the seaside would be until Oliver brought my attention to it. I began to mull over suitable alternatives, trying to keep the spirit of my doctor's orders alive. Quiet, and far from the datanet.

"What you want to do," said Oliver, "is take a trip in a b-"

"I know! I'll go on a tour of war museums!" I said. "I'll learn, I'll laugh, it will be wonderful!"

"No," said Oliver. "Do you really want to learn how much better at armed conflict everyone else is than you? It would be humiliating. You wouldn't like to be humiliated on holiday, would you?"

He was right. The medals I'd received as a result of my last service had been issued sarcastically. Oliver had said he could tell.

"No, my dear lass. What you want to do is take a trip on a b-"

"I have it!" I said, throwing a claw into the air. "I shall visit the planet's core. It must be fascinating down there."

"No."

"Well, why not, dash it?" I asked. The ninny was really beginning to set my teeth on edge with his objections to every little thing.

"Well, because it's impossible," he said, looking at me like the fool I am. "There are no craft that could stand the pressure and even if there were, you'd cook. Even if you didn't cook and you could stand the pressure, there'd be nothing to see except molten rock. Honestly, Jay, you really can be the most exhausting chump. I mean-"

Oliver was winding up to one of his long speeches. I prepared to grin and bear it but, to my surprise, he checked himself. "No," he said, breathing heavily, "what you want to do is take a trip on a boat."

Now *that* was an idea. I said so. He said he was glad I agreed.

"That's settled. I'm taking one next week anyway. You can come, too."

Well, this was wonderful. "What sort of boat is it?"

"It's an old decommissioned frigate, last of the 66th grand battle fleet," he said. "I picked it up for a song six months ago and I've been outfitting it. It will be frightfully jolly, Jay, you'll love it. We can ride the shipping lane spanwise and then take a merry jaunt through the asteroid belt near the Fields of Zuk. There's a cathedral there that the Reapers built, in tribute to that shepherdess they won't stop banging on about. There are all sorts of monuments and things to look at. We can stay at inns or slum it on the ship if you like. It'll be a lovely trip, just the two of us."

Well that was the best news I'd heard since I found out I was going to die in two years' time. Oliver and I spent the next few hours chatting about the sorts of things we might do on this trip. Sarah came back as the sky was turning citrus and I told her about our plan.

"How wonderful," she said. "That sounds absolutely perfect for you, Jay. In fact, I have some leave I haven't used up. Would you mind if I tagged along? I haven't taken a trip for some time. Oh! We could drop in on my cousin Gertrude and Uncle Angus at Newbury Towers! It's not at all far from the Fields of Zuk! We could nip in to see them once we're done there! Does that sound enjoyable?"

Oliver said something short and snappy in response to Sarah's suggestion, but I couldn't hear what it was because I was busy saying "Of course!"

Oliver rounded on me, a snarl or something on his fangs. "What is it, dear boy?" I asked.

He was silent for a few moments. A slight hiss escaped his mouth. "There is room for Sarah, isn't there?" I asked.

"… Yes," he said, eventually. He didn't seem happy but I couldn't think why. I gave him a moment to get his thoughts in order but this didn't seem to help. Wishing to not make things awkward for poor Sarah, I turned back to her. "We shall be delighted to have you along, dear one."

And like that, it was settled. Two arachnids were to go messing about in a boat, to say nothing of the human.

Chapter Two

Three Arachnids in a Warship

(to say nothing of the human)

THE NIGHT BEFORE WE were to take possession of the boat, Sarah and I spent a few minutes discussing my mindvirus. I admitted to her that I was scared, although I think she thought I was scared of the mindvirus itself.

Sarah had asked if she could do anything for me. I replied that she could. I had accidentally-on-purpose packed my data panel in my bags, in spite of my doctor's wishes. I asked if Sarah would mind keeping it for me.

I had to blurt it out. I did not *want* Sarah to look after it. *I* wanted to be the one looking after it – but I knew I wouldn't be strong enough to resist checking the data feeds. So, I asked Sarah to look after it and not let me near it without good reason.

She said she should probably take it now, before I changed my mind. My reply was a little confused, but it went something like: "No. No. No, no, no, no, no. Yes, probably. NO. I meant no."

She said she'd take my eighth answer.

The next morning, I was awoken by the sound of clumping about the place. Oliver, it seemed, had risen before me. Out of habit, I reached for my data panel to establish what time it was. I then remembered that I had entrusted it to Sarah as my doctor instructed, and cursed my foolish adherence to medical advice.

I rose from my bed and pattered over to the largest of my windows. I peered between the curtains to see if I could make out the city's grand old clock tower through the clouds. Dawn had only recently broken, and both clocks on the side of the tower I could see showed the same time: half past six.

I brought my room's lights up and spent a few minutes splashing water over myself before slipping into a suit. I found my bags where I left them and started to haul them to my door. That was when I saw the note. It had been slipped under my door sometime after I went to bed.

I picked it up and examined it closely. It was from Sarah, although it was not in her usual careful handwriting. The note said that she had to attend to an emergency and she would meet us on board ship. It was most curious.

I pocketed the note and opened my door. Outside, I saw Oliver. He was carrying several long pieces of wood, nails and an electro-hammer. He was walking towards Sarah's door.

"Good morning!" I said, cheerily.

He dropped the hammer on his claws and yelped.

"Oh, my dear chap, I'm so sorry!" I said.

"You incorrigible imbecile!" he roared.

"Well, quite," I said. "I say, do you know what's happened to Sarah?"

"What do you mean?" demanded Oliver. "Nothing's happened to her!" He eyed the bits of wood he was holding. "Yet."

"Oh," I said, "I thought she had some sort of emergency." I handed him the note.

"Hm." He glanced at his pieces of wood. "Can't be helped, I suppose. Well, you'd best be off, Jay."

"I'm sorry?" I asked.

"Come on, come on," he said, having moved from thoughtful to aggravated in the space of only a few seconds. "You'll be late if you don't leave now!"

He took my bags from my claws, made his way to the front door and opened it. I scuttled after him and I was just in time to see him hurling my belongings into the street.

"Er," I said, "aren't you joining me, Oliver old chap?"

"No. No, no, no. I have something to do." He placed a claw companionably on my shoulder before shoving me out after my bags. "I'll meet you at the docks," he said, and slammed the door in my face.

I looked about the place. The sort of people who were awake at six thirty-ish in the morning hurried about, ignoring me. I gathered my bags into a neat pile and set about flagging down a cab, all the while trying to make head or tail of Oliver's dashed odd actions. I failed.

A cab arrived eventually and spirited me to the train station. There, I discovered I had no idea how to go about locating the ten past seven to Bungington. Still, I didn't let that dissuade me. There are few problems that can't be solved by asking questions like my mother used to: in an exaggerated aristocratic accent whilst waving stray bits of currency around.

I reached the docks shortly after nine and instructed a small child to unload my bags. The child asked if it would get paid. I replied that it didn't seem to have pressing engagements and it should be glad of the entertainment. This didn't seem as persuasive as I would have liked, so I provided a shilling to sweeten the proposition.

I sauntered around the docks until I found a chap in a uniform who either worked here or was dressed as a dock worker for some recreational purpose. I enquired as to where Mr Oliver's frigate might be located and he directed me.

I found myself at the foot of the great glass elevator that would ferry me up to the ship moored at dock Oseta 2. There was a pleasant-looking relaxation vault that would keep me in relative comfort during the brief trip, so I took advantage of it. I relaxed. Once this was done, I still had four minutes to wait, so my eyes turned to the miniature telescope that occupied one corner of the elevator.

I put my eye to the telescope. My view was pitch dark. I cursed, fumbled about for a ha'penny and slipped it into the miserly machine. With a mechanical grind, the closed iris that had prevented me from seeing through the telescope flexed open and I was presented with a stunning view of the ship that was to be my home for the next two weeks.

It appeared to be a perfectly standard Mark-IV frigate by design. Oars could be seen lining the sides. These jutted out away from the ship and would propel the vessel using jet propulsion for speed or gaseous emission for fine control.

The deck was open to allow boarding parties to leap across to other ships. The occupants were able to breathe, thanks to an atmosphere shield that stretched from the prow to the stern. The shield was transparent, apart from the occasional rolling blue flash as it refreshed itself.

Two colossal masts sprung from the deck, one at the centre line, one towards the stern. These were used to support particle nets. The nets would collect space debris as the ship travelled through it. This debris would then be ferried down to the reactor, in case the fuel supply was depleted and raw materials were needed as a substitute.

There were marks of the ship having been converted for civilian use. Many of the gun batteries had been removed to make room on the deck. There was even a small crane for the loading and unloading of cargo. I focused on the nameplate on the side of the ship: it was called *The Dancing Cox*.

It was far from pristine. The sky-blue paint had been retouched in places. The masts were a little ragged. There was obvious battle damage along the beams. The anti-ship gun batteries were in need of maintenance and the close-quarter flechette launchers looked like they were on loan from the last century.

It was truly beautiful.

The first thing I saw when I stepped onto the *Cox* was a lifebelt. The second thing I saw was a perfectly pleasant section of wall. The third thing I saw was Sarah. The fourth thing I saw was a gentlenid I didn't recognise. He was as tall as Oliver but lacked the haughtiness of my friend. He was dishevelled and his suit had seen better days. His bearing was aristocratic but, despite this, he was rather easy on the eyes.

"Hello there," I said to Sarah. "I got your note. Is everything okay?"

Sarah stomped up to me. "I'm sorry to spring this on you, Jay, but I'm in a bit of a crisis."

I glanced over her upper leg. The gentlenid behind her appeared to be gibbering to himself.

"Do tell, young one," I said.

"Behind me is an old friend. He's just finished his tour with the Special Operations Unit and he's in a state."

The old friend in question must have heard my gasp at Sarah's mention of the Special Operations unit because he dove to the floor and took cover behind a pile of rugs.

This was surprising but understandable. The Special Operations Unit handled extremely dirty jobs. It was oft said that you needed to be suicidal or insane to join their ranks – and if you weren't before you started, you sure as bells would be after you left.

"He finished his contract today," said Sarah, "and I'm the only person for a couple of light-years around that he knows. Could we bring him with us? He really needs to be around some friendly faces right now."

I could scarcely believe she was even asking. "Of course," I said, strolling over to her old friend and introducing myself. He rose to his claws cautiously and brushed himself down. I shook his claw, giving my full name but inviting him to call me Jay. He stared at me as we shook claws. I began to feel rather self-conscious. He was probably wondering who, exactly, would come out looking quite so scruffy. I was going to explain that I had never managed to get the hang of making myself look presentable, but I decided this would not be the best first impression to make.

The fellow blinked and shook his head, breaking eye contact. He let go of my claw, rather self-consciously. He introduced himself as Bainbridge Lusitania. "I can't tell you where I've been or what I've done," he said, "but it was *horrifying*. It's delightful to meet you."

This didn't seem likely, but one must make allowances for ex-Special Operations personnel. As if to illustrate my point, Bainbridge suddenly cried shrilly, "*What's that?*"

He drew a vicious-looking service weapon from a holster so well concealed I hadn't even realised it was there, and pointed it ten degrees above my head and four to the right. I suppressed the urge to duck.

"No," he said. "No, it's okay. They're not here for us."

I looked up at where he had been pointing his weapon. I couldn't see anything.

"Don't look," he hissed, suddenly standing right next to me. "You'll only draw its attention. Would you like a claw with your luggage?"

"I would," I said, trying not to move.

"Excellent. Pigstick and I have set up on the aft deck for now, I'll put you back there with us."

He scuttled over and hauled most of my luggage onto his back. I joined him and gathered the rest. At his side, I murmured, "One small thing, my dear chap. You just used Sarah's old name. Did you mean to?"

When Sarah was younger, before she found herself, she'd inhabited an arachnid body. In those days, she'd been known by the nickname 'Pigstick', for reasons I was never privy to. When she'd left that life behind, she'd left the name as well. Sometimes old acquaintances of hers forgot this.

Bainbridge struck his brow with a free claw and apologised to Sarah, who waved it aside. She did not mind people forgetting, she said; only when people used the wrong name out of malice or ignorance was it an issue.

I followed Bainbridge towards the back of the boat and tried to ignore his muttering. Occasional words like 'horror', 'despair' and 'death' filtered through. I knew I was going to get along with this fellow.

The aft deck of the ship looked like a fine place to spend a few weeks. Sarah and Bainbridge had slung a few hammocks about the place. They were in an untidy row at the approximate centre of the deck, keeping a good deal of space free to operate the deck-mounted guns if needed.

There were a few neat piles of baggage at the foot of two bunks, and Bainbridge placed my effects carefully down in-between two of these piles. This done, I spent a few hours arranging and rearranging things so that they were in the best possible positions. Once everything was organised to my satisfaction, I realised Sarah and Bainbridge had wandered off. I set out to find them.

I discovered them on the bridge, where Bainbridge was poking suspiciously at the controls as Sarah watched. Sarah had been an engineer in her past life but her transition to human form had rendered her unable to interact with certain arachnid technology. To say enough but no more, she was significantly smaller than the average arachnid and, as such, had to choose between operating the low-level controls and being able to see out of the viewscreens.

I appeared to have interrupted a conversation about our destination, for I heard Sarah speaking about Newbury Towers as I entered. The two glanced up and saw me. Bainbridge looked a little glum.

"Anything wrong?" I asked.

"Bainbridge is familiar with Newbury Towers," Sarah said.

Bainbridge clacked his claws together, softly. "Sarah's Uncle used to care for me after my father… well, the old boy's seen better days. I am in two minds about returning. On the one claw, it would be good to see my father before his condition deteriorates. On the other… I am not sure if I will be entirely welcome. We did not part on the best of terms. Hopefully he will not immediately show me the door."

"We can change destination if you would rather?" I said.

Bainbridge gave this some thought, before shaking his head. "No, no. Best to get to Newbury Towers before anything ghastly can happen to father or myself."

"Are you expecting anything ghastly to happen to you, my dear chap?" I asked.

Bainbridge looked at me with wide eyes. I couldn't read his expression, but I saw a tear start to form in the corner of his third eye. I didn't look away, not wanting to make it look as if I was embarrassed by his unconcealed emotion. I *was* embarrassed, naturally, but I didn't want my embarrassment to embarrass him. Such self-reinforcing cycles of embarrassment have trapped me before. Twice, I have needed to relocate my home to a different planet so as to be free of the things.

Bainbridge smiled, warmly as a single tear soaked into the fur below his eye. His expression was no more readable than it had been, but he didn't seem to be in any real distress. "Ghastly things happen," he said, eventually. "Let us not dwell on them on this wonderful morning."

It was a wonderful morning was it? That was the best news I'd had since learning I was terminally ill. Bainbridge turned back to the controls and poked two buttons, experimentally. "I've familiarised myself with the ship systems. We can set off whenever we want. I say, did you know this thing has a security net around the cargo hold? There's nothing in there, though. It's odd. It must be left over from the last people to use the ship. By the way, neither of you have anyone you need assassinating, do you?"

I didn't think I did but Sarah answered before I had time to fully consider the question. "No," she said, sweetly but firmly.

"Blast," said Bainbridge, flicking a control with more force than was strictly called for. "My apologies, my head is a little loud at the moment. Having trouble thinking in a straight line." He then sang three lines from a comic song. I believe it was the Light Brigade Attack Guffaw, but I might be confusing it with another song of the same type.

"Well, shall we be on our way?" I asked.

"Oliver hasn't arrived yet," Sarah said, making her way to Bainbridge's side and laying a hoof on his upper leg.

"What's keeping him?" I asked. "The vacuum calls."

"We could set off and meet him at a pre-arranged spot," Sarah said.

"Call him. Call the son of a two-horned cad," said Bainbridge. "Find the reason for his delay and subtly imply our displeasure. My dying father and Susan's grumpy uncle await."

"I say, steady on," I said, mildly, but Sarah was already vox-o-phoning the Oliver in question.

She managed to get one or two words out before a flood of communication came back and she had to cease her attempts to talk in order to understand what Oliver was saying. After five or six minutes, the vox-o-phone signal was abruptly terminated without another word from Sarah. She looked at us. "He says he's on his way."

Bainbridge chose to fill the time by telling us a funny story from his first days in the Special Operations Unit. He said that during his first mission, he'd been asked to go to a planet he couldn't tell us about, that was filled with people he couldn't tell us about, that were doing stuff they shouldn't be doing, but he couldn't go into specifics.

He said that his unit had done whatever it was they'd done, that he couldn't tell us about, and had met up with one of the two other Special Operations operatives he'd been working with. They'd chatted about this and that as they waited for their colleague. Bainbridge made it clear that, unfortunately, he couldn't be more specific about the content of their chat but it had been really rather funny.

Anyway, the point of the story, he said, was that after about six days, they'd been forced to conclude that their colleague wasn't going to make the rendezvous because he'd been killed on assignment.

Bainbridge broke into a hearty laugh with just a tinge of mania to it. I joined in, of course; the story had been hilarious. At least, I assumed it had been. Sarah didn't join in the merriment for some reason, but humour can be subjective.

After the third or fourth minute of constant laughter, Bainbridge suddenly shot to his claws and drew a weapon from somewhere about his person.

"Someone's here," he hissed.

"It's probably just Oliver," Sarah said.

"I'll check it out," Bainbridge said, before skittering off at great speed.

Sarah and I looked at each other, concerned. "We'd better follow him," I said.

Sarah shook her head. "We'll never find him. You know these Special Operations chaps. They are shadow. They are void. We never see them unless they want us to."

"You're too kind," said Bainbridge, from behind us. We both jumped.

"Don't *do* that," said Sarah, clutching at what I assume was her chest. Bainbridge apologised.

"Weren't you seeing who was on the ship?" I asked.

"Yes," said Bainbridge. "I've done that, that's why I'm back. It's a smuggler. Shall I take him out?"

"You had better show us," said Sarah.

We followed Bainbridge up onto the roof of the bridge, where we could see Oliver carrying his cases onto the ship. Bainbridge was sighting along his weapon at our encumbered friend. Sarah asked him to stop.

"That's our travelling companion," she told him.

"Are you sure?" Bainbridge asked. "He looks like a smuggler. He's probably just using you to add legitimacy to his transportation of illicit goods."

"Everyone thinks that when they first see him," I said. "He's really not so bad once you get to know him."

Bainbridge seemed to weigh this, and eventually conceded. "If you say so."

I scuttled down to greet Oliver as Bainbridge helped Sarah climb down from the roof.

"Let's go, let's go," he said as soon as he saw me. "We're running late."

"Late for what?" I asked.

"Nothing, nothing," he snapped, cheerily. "Let's just get a move on. Get the ship started, would you? I've untied the mooring line."

Of course, I knew I was supposed to be doing something. At least, I *think* I'd known that. Leaving Oliver to the rest of his luggage, I strode to the bridge and brought the engines to life.

It had been a while since I'd taken a warship out of dock but I managed it after hitting only a dockyard locomotive, a boat that was tugging another ship, a twelve-metre crane, two storage houses and a box for mail delivery. I'm really not sure how I managed to hit that last one. Oliver turned up after that to point out all the things I was doing wrong, which helped immeasurably.

I started drifting towards a couple of sandbanks in orbit a little way from terra firma and Oliver started saying I should turn to port. So I turned to port but that, if anything, brought us closer to one of the sandbanks. Oliver, in his helpful manner, started insisting I turn to port but in a much louder voice. So I had another go and that caused us to slew straight into the sandbank, spraying sand everywhere and making all our collision detection systems spring into life.

At round about that time, Sarah popped onto the bridge to find out what was happening. It turned out both Oliver and I had been labouring under a misapprehension as to what 'port' was. He'd thought it meant roll anticlockwise along the x-axis, and I'd thought it meant turn right.

Sarah was helpfully drawing us a diagram with words like 'roll', 'pitch' and 'yaw' written on it when Bainbridge sauntered onto the bridge and asked if we'd managed to sort the steering out.

"Who's this?" asked Oliver, incredulously, causing Bainbridge to take several steps forward and slip one of his claws behind his abdomen. If I had to guess, I'd say that said claw now held a weapon. I tried to steer the ship and make no sudden movements at the same time, which is difficult with my driving style.

Sarah made a few 'ah' noises before beginning to explain, but she was cut off by Oliver. Oliver, you see, objected to other people coming on the trip. He said that the trip was supposed to relax me and I might find it hard to relax if there were strangers in every cubby hole, ready to jump out at me every time I started reading a nice book or something.

At that point, Bainbridge pointed out that he could hear everything Oliver was saying. Oliver rounded on him and asked what his deal was. He must have approached a little faster than was wise, because in a blur of movement Bainbridge had him collapsed in a corner. Bainbridge stood over him, holding three weapons in as many claws, every spare limb restraining one of Oliver's.

I said something extremely helpful to calm the situation down. I can't quite remember what it was, because I was navigating a tricky region of total vacuum at the time. I'm pretty sure 'I say' was in there at some point.

Sarah spoke gently to Bainbridge for a few moments. Oliver spluttered and demanded that Bainbridge release him. One of these courses of action was more effective than the other.

The tricky area having been successfully navigated, I inputted the command sequence that shipped the oars, allowing the boat to drift to a comfortable halt. I turned to see Sarah rest one of her upper legs on Bainbridge's shoulder. Bainbridge slowly drew back and allowed Oliver to get to his claws. Oliver shot up and started making demands.

An apology was on the list, I know that. Various other less reasonable things were, too, including the immediate removal of Bainbridge from the ship. Sarah objected, saying that Bainbridge had as much of a right to be here as he did.

Oliver rounded on me and demanded to know if I wanted to have Bainbridge about, reminding me that Bainbridge had assaulted one of my oldest and dearest friends.

I didn't really know what to say to this. I liked Bainbridge, and Oliver had acted like an unbelievable cad to him from the moment he laid eyes on the fellow. More importantly, Bainbridge needed a safe space now. He needed our hospitality. If nothing else, depriving a friend of Sarah's hospitality would be completely unthinkable.

The thing was… saying 'no' to Oliver was troublesome. I used to be able to say the word with some confidence, but it always puts the fellow in a dashed unpleasant mood. After a few unfortunate occasions where voices ended up a little raised, I decided it was best to avoid the word entirely.

Now, though, I knew I couldn't agree with him. Friendship be damned; he was wrong. I was just finding it a little difficult. My eyes were locked on the deck of the ship and I found my weight shifting from claw to claw. I opened my mouth but couldn't make myself speak. I willed myself, I demanded that I speak. No sound emerged.

"Perhaps it would be better if I leave," said Bainbridge. Sarah objected but without backup, her protestations felt weak. "I will slip overboard," said Bainbridge, a tremor in his voice. "Do not worry. I'll be fine."

This couldn't be allowed to happen. This was wrong. I needed to speak up. I couldn't. I *couldn't* speak. I heard clawsteps heading towards the door of the bridge. I needed to speak up and I needed to do it *now*.

I formed the word on my fangs. No sound came out but that was okay. If I could form the word 'no', I could put breath into the word 'no'. This, I did. If I could put breath into the word 'no',

I could whisper the word 'no'. This, I did. If I could whisper the word 'no', I could speak the word 'no'. This, I did.

"What did you say, Jay?" Oliver asked. My eyes snapped up to meet his.

"I said no, Oliver. Bainbridge stays."

In the past, whenever I have disagreed with Oliver, he has worked himself up into what could best be described as an argumentative fury. I saw the early signs now: the pursing of the fangs, the twitching of the third and fourth eyelids. I dug my rear claws into the deck and prepared to stand my ground. For Bainbridge. For all of us.

To my surprise, Oliver did not break into a fury. He growled the word 'fine' before stalking good-naturedly from the bridge. Bainbridge turned to me. There was something in his eyes that I couldn't identify. Was it pity?

"Thank you," he said, a slight crack in his voice. "I am not used to those outside of the unit standing up for me."

I couldn't think why this might be the case and I said so.

"I was, perhaps, not the easiest chap to stand up for before I entered the unit," he said. "If you will excuse me, Sarah, Jay, I would like to take a few moments."

He left Sarah and me on the bridge. I turned back to the controls and checked our navigational displays. The Fields of Zuk and Newbury Towers were downstream.[1]

---

[1] When discussing the intergalactic shipping lanes, 'downstream' refers to the direction of the solar winds rather than the current of a river. The shipping lanes are arachnid-made routes designed to allow transport of large freighters or small pleasure craft. They are usually designed to take advantage of the solar winds that radiate across and in-between solar systems. There are buoys that line the routes, allowing for a certain amount of autonomy for the craft that traverse them. This differentiates them from the roads that vacuum-traversing cars travel along. The roads are more complex and require constant control. The lanes do not.

Oliver had pointed out last night that there was a lovely, rustic little planet called Gullup just outside our solar system that belonged to these chaps who had only just discovered faster-than-light travel. He'd suggested we drop in on them and see what life is like down there. I programmed in what seemed a decent route to this planet and unshipped our oars. I felt the *Cox* creak as we picked up speed. I patted the ship's console fondly. I was already beginning to like this vessel.

Sarah coughed. I looked over to her and saw a smile glowing on her face. "Thank you. for standing up for Bainbridge," she said.

Her gratitude embarrassed me.

The *Cox* drifted lazily downstream for a short while, passing through a few locks and the occasional subspace tunnel. Such tunnels ferried us safely under the hyperspace bypass that some clot had run straight through the star system.

The subspace tunnel at the edge of the system robbed the breath from my lungs. The sun from our home system shone from the end of the tunnel behind us, and dim light from the neighbouring system's sun guided us from the far end.

The tunnel was constructed from incandescent materials that had been irregularly maintained. The rectangular shapes fit together poorly and had allowed some unknowable gas to seep into the tunnel from places unknown.

The effect was rather eerie. Our ship drifted through the twilight, sunbeams from either end illuminating the thick gas clouds as they billowed around us. I thought about turning the ship lights on but refrained. The half-light was comforting. On the stern, some wag attempted to make the call of one of those night birds that live in chimneys.

The brightness when we emerged from the tunnel shocked me for a few moments, but it was uplifting too, in its own way. We were nearly halfway to the little rustic planet Oliver had mentioned when I began to tire. Given the lack of lads or lasses eager to take the oars and lines from me, I found a decent-looking post to moor up to. I slid the ship alongside the mooring station and fired the docking harpoon three or four times until I had the knack for it. Thus moored, I sauntered to the stern to see what my shipmates had been up to whilst I was doing all of the work.

I rounded a funnel to see Bainbridge and Sarah chatting at one end of the deck whilst Oliver sulked at the other. Bainbridge turned as I approached. "Why have we stopped?" he asked.

"I am weary," I said. "If one of you would care to take the lines we could push on. Otherwise, we should stay moored until I have rested."

"We are still some way from Gullup," said Oliver. "I shall pilot us on for a while in the hope that we might reach it soon after our sleep cycles. You chaps may as well dig into some vittles'."

This suggestion was a popular one. Sarah remarked that Oliver could be quite sensible when he wasn't being a beast about everything he rested his eyes on. Oliver replied that he prided himself on having his little moments of clarity.

He popped up to the bridge whilst Sarah broke out the potted meat. Bainbridge located some round, red fruits I'd never seen before. I was informed that they were called tomatoes. I, for my part, set up the decently-sized camping stove I'd brought along and started applying heat to the items that were passed to me.

We sat in a circle, which is hard to do when there are only three of you, but we managed it. We ate, we shared stories and we laughed. I ferried supplies up to Oliver so he wouldn't feel left out. I found him staring intently off at our destination, but he took the time to give a grunt of thanks for my offerings.

Once the remains were cleared away, we three who weren't at the helm lit our pipes and stared up at the void above us.

Bainbridge mentioned that he had spent the day composing a poem about our little situation and he wondered if we would like to hear it. Sarah and I must have felt terribly content after our slap-up supper because we positively beamed at the suggestion. The chap was gratified by this and drew out a notebook. He flipped through it a bit before settling on a page, then drew himself up to his full height.

"Death," he began, starting strong. "Death approaches.

"Death approaches.

"Death. It approaches."

He continued in this vein for some time. Sarah started to shuffle about the place when he finished the third stanza.

"Death is, like the cold tide, only meant to drag each of us to its smothering embrace," is how the fourth stanza began. He missed the rhyme on the next line but made up for it with some rather remarkable imagery about a piercing arrow crossed with a bird crushed by bearing the wings of time.

The fifth stanza wound up with some quite powerful stuff about every moment slowly slipping away as inexorably as a tear. He then stopped and closed his notebook.

In the past, I have shown weakness and let some arachnid of my acquaintance read poetry at me. Such efforts were often poorly constructed or sloppily read. Bainbridge's piece, however, was stunning. I had never enjoyed a poem read to me more. It was the sort of thing I wished my mother had read to me on her knee.

Quite without meaning to, I burst into applause. Sarah let out a sigh. I could tell she had enjoyed it as much as I had. Bainbridge made a shallow bow to the group and asked if he should read another poem he'd written a few days before. He said it wasn't quite as polished as the last but he was still quite proud of it.

"Absolutely!" I said.

"No!" said Sarah at the same time. Bainbridge and I turned to her, surprised. "It would just… be better for us to sit and truly digest the work you already read to us, old chap," she said, in a pleasantly strangled sort of voice. "We need a few minutes to really… drink it in."

Bainbridge looked very pleased by this, but I felt ashamed. I'd been rather selfish and shallow. I'd experienced this fantastic piece of art and, rather than give it the consideration it demanded, I'd wished to simply move on to the next poem. I was like those hedonist chaps you read about in the periodicals who want to spend every waking moment experiencing new and better pleasures. With this in mind, I sat very still, closed my eyes and began to seriously think about death.

Not long into my reflection, Bainbridge apologised for abandoning the group but he needed to spend a few hours meditating.

"I'm not sure if you've noticed," he said, twitching on every third word, "but I've been acting a little erratically. This is PER-FECTLY-" (he bellowed that word) "-normal for one in my position… I'm told. The Special Operations Unit provided me with a hypnotherapy programme I need to complete once a day if I want to return to a life… of… normality." He trailed off, and stared out at the stars for a moment. His attention snapped back to us. "Sorry," he said. "I lost myself there. What was I saying?"

We reminded him.

"Ah, yes. So, don't mind me, I have to find a quiet spot to recover for a bit. Don't worry if you hear screams or crying or songs about aardvarks, apparently that's perfectly normal." He stared at Sarah and then moved to me. "Perfectly," he said, "normal." He paused before waving. "Toodles!"

Sarah and I watched him go. "I'm glad they don't just shove those poor chaps out the door with no assistance," said Sarah. "That's what I thought they'd done. I found him at the port with nothing but one suitcase, the clothes he's stood up in and a half-eaten lizard on a stick."

"Where did he get that?"

"He said he found it."

"Well, it's good to know they're looking after him," I said.

"They should be doing more. Giving him hypnotherapy seems like the least they could do, but I might be just being cynical."

I rarely heard Sarah use strong language when describing herself. I rested a claw as gently as I could on her shoulder. "We'll look after him."

Sarah poked at her eyes for a second before embracing me and saying that she intended to retire for the night, as the day had been a little on the long side. I realised fatigue had crept up on me as well, so I followed suit.

The hammock was delightful. I was able to swing myself gently whilst counting the stars. One by one by one. So many stars speckling the vacuum. Points of light, points of hope, each slowly fading. I cannot remember the last time I found myself drifting off to sleep in such a contented mood.

Chapter Three

Three Arachnids, a Human and a Naja in a Warship

We awoke to the sound of some feathered creature chirping. It appeared to have boarded back at the docks, and now couldn't find its way off. The chirping and warbling spoke to me. How sweet it was to be a bird, to have sleek wings that could take you wherever your heart desired. To not be bound to the ground by these eight juddering legs I called my own. To be freed from my armoured poly-alloy exoskeleton.

It was at that point that I realised I couldn't feel my fifth knee. I had not slept in a hammock for some years and I appeared to have lost the trick to it. Sleeping on my back, as I usually did, had ended nearly suffocating me, so I'd attempted to sleep on my side. Apparently, this had not been the best idea I'd ever had. I slipped gingerly from my hammock, my useless fifth leg trailing behind me.

"I say, what's up with Jay?" asked Sarah.

"Most amusing. Did you notice that rhymed?" said Bainbridge.

"Probably slept on her leg funny," said Oliver, groggily.

"Did you notice your last sentence rhymed, Sarah?" asked Bainbridge again. "It really was very funny."

"I haven't slept on my leg in any amusing fashion," I said.

"Perhaps I should explain why it is funny," Bainbridge said, overcome with a somewhat manic tone. "You see, when there is a repetition of similar sounds in two or more words, then-"

"Yes, thank you Bainbridge," said Sarah. "We all found it very amusing."

"Oh, good."

"Must you stomp so?" Oliver asked, placing a pillow over his ear.

"Sorry," I whispered. I was regaining some feeling in my knee now, but I was still far from steady. I was doing my best to not collapse onto the deck. Unfortunately, this meant that a certain amount of stomping was called for. My companions grumbled a little until Sarah swung herself out of her hammock.

"Should we be making a start?" she asked, the sleep slowly edging out of her voice to be replaced with resentment.

"We should," said Oliver. He flung a pillow at me. "You did most of the work yesterday, Jay. I shall carry on where I left off yesterday if that suits the group."

This took me somewhat by surprise. It goes without saying that Oliver is a generous and kind individual. That being said, his self-lessness tends to manifest in ways that are a great deal subtler than simply offering to do his fair share of the work. Those that know him less well than I are completely unable to pierce the occasionally prickly exterior he affects, to see the kind-hearted individual lurking beneath. It is there, though. It is there.

"That would be frightfully good of you, my dear chap," said Sarah, after the fifth minute of uninterrupted, stunned silence.

Oliver narrowed three of his eyes. "Why are you all staring at me like that?" Sarah said she didn't know what he meant.

We filled a pail of water from one of the high-powered water cannons stationed on the port rail and took turns splashing it over ourselves. Bainbridge hadn't had time to pack a towel but Sarah, being an over-prepared sort of human, had packed five. She said Bainbridge had better use her second emergency backup towel for the duration of the trip. Bainbridge thanked her and disappeared to see to his morning routine. He was moving a little more freely this morning and appeared to be gibbering less.

I dried myself speedily before locating a cluster of carrion birds we had in the breakfast hamper. One would do me but I grabbed two for Oliver, as occasionally he liked to overdo breakfast before having a lighter lunch and dinner. This plan often went awry at the lunch and dinner stages but you can't fault a fellow for having a plan fall apart on him, no matter how many times it happens. Sometimes plans just fall apart for no reason.

Oliver was swearing as I entered the bridge. It was not unusual for me to enter a room and find him swearing. He enjoyed swearing. He had a knack for it. I had often witnessed him washing up his bloodied gelatinous plates of a morning. Occasionally, he dropped an item or two, occasionally, he didn't. Whenever he did, I was treated to such a cavalcade of foul language that the air took on a delightfully thick quality.

Often when Oliver was set off by an individual incident (say, the cracking of a prized teacup) he would quickly move on to other topics. Such topics have included the appalling state of the floor; the miserable condition the flat was left in, how awful I was at keeping things tidy, how my parents must have been truly ashamed of me – unable as I was to keep a simple kitchen tidy, how I must have longed for death every day knowing how much of a failure I was, and so on. Oliver's swearing in that moment appeared different. It was directed in a way I was not used to, and it was punctuated with phrases such as 'too soon' and 'early'.

He didn't appear to have noticed my entry, concentrating as he was on the ship's controls, so I spoke. "What's up, chap?"

I had to wait for a break in the swearing, so I was standing in the doorway to the bridge for a good seventeen minutes before I was able to subtly draw attention to my presence. I didn't like to interrupt a pal when he was in full flow.

Oliver jumped before rounding on me. I raised the carrion birds I was still carrying defensively. I'm not sure why. Oliver has never actually attacked me when in one of his little moods, apart from those three or four times, but they don't count.

There was a pleasant yet somewhat aggressive expression on Oliver's face that juddered away over the next few seconds. There was a rather alarming vein pulsing in his neck. This disturbed me as it's usually very hard to make out individual veins under a chap's fur and exoskeleton.

"The planet we were due to visit today?" he snarled. "It's at war."

"Oh, how nice," I said. "We can watch how things go and place bets on the winner."

"It's not a proper war," he said. "The locals are using chemical and biological weapons against the idiots that invaded them. A battle fleet is in orbit to quarantine the planet until the place is declared safe."

That was a bit of a blow. We'd have to find something else to do today. Oliver didn't really react when I mentioned this, which was unusual.

"We need to go down," he said, sullenly.

This seemed like a far from ideal plan. I wondered how to phrase my disapproval without disagreeing with him outright. "What about the quarantine?" I asked. A neutral question should do it. I would appear concerned rather than combative.

"Oh, quarantines!" he yelled, throwing several of his legs into the air. I took a step back. "They're overreacting. We can head down, it will be fine."

"We could, absolutely we could," I said, trying desperately to think and feeling my mental gears grind against each other as I did so. "But how would we do it? Our humble vessel may be many things but it's not exactly subtle."

"They won't bother us!" Oliver said, a touch of froth appearing on his fangs. "Quarantines aren't for arachnids, they're for nosy aliens."

"What about-" I said.

"Aliens that can't mind their own business, I mean," said Oliver, probably not wishing to get bogged down in a conversation about whether aliens who don't have noses can, when all's said and done, be nosy.

"Well," I said, trying to stick with the conversation against my better judgement, "I know how we can sort this out. I'll give the battle fleet a ring and see if they mind us dropping down to the planet."

"No!" yelped Oliver. He rushed to my side, repeating himself as he did so. He started plucking at my sleeve, which made me suspect he was anxious about my suggestion. This confused me deeply for reasons I was not entirely clear on.

"I say, what's up?" asked Bainbridge from the doorway. "Can't a chap stare at his claws for hours upon end in silent terror at the horrors said claws have wrought without getting interrupted all over the place?"

It transpired that Bainbridge's night's sleep had not, as I had supposed, completely washed away his traumatic experiences with the Special Operations Unit. They were simply manifesting themselves in different ways today. I wondered if I could do anything to help but this appeared to be one too many thoughts to hold simultaneously in my brain, what with all the brilliant ideas I'd been having to help Oliver. I closed my eyes and attempted to clear my thoughts.

"My apologies, Bainbridge," I said.

"Go away," said Oliver at the same time.

"I would leave you two in peace," said Bainbridge, his voice taking on an edge that made my exospine creep, "but there's all this shouting, you see, and I can't think straight when there's shouting. I don't think you'd like me when I can't think straight. I tend to take drastic action that seems sensible at the time but can get dreadfully messy."

Oliver rounded on Bainbridge and then kept rounding as he appeared to think better of it. After revolving for a few moments, he ended up facing me and took a deep breath.

"Don't vent your anger upon Jay. Face me, you blister," said Bainbridge.

I had only known this chap for, well, not very long at all, and here he was defending me yet again. I would say I was touched but somehow that word seemed a little… I'm not sure. I stared at Bainbridge, suddenly confused, but pleasantly so.

Oliver was rotating slowly to face Bainbridge. "Very well," he said, with a notable lack of grace. "Jay and I were discussing a trip down to the planet you see ahead of us."

"I see," said Bainbridge. "And what about this little trip caused you to start shouting 'no no no no' all over the place? Honestly, Oliver, you're as bad as the voices."

"Which voices?" asked Oliver, understandably a little thrown.

"Never you mind which voices," said Bainbridge. "What I require from you are fewer questions about what the voices may or may not be saying and more explanations as to your disturbance of my quiet contemplation."

"Well-" Oliver said.

"I say, what's up?" asked Sarah, poking her head into the bridge.

Oliver threw several claws into the air. "Well, this is just *perfect*."

"I'm glad you think so," said Sarah, coldly.

"So am I," said Bainbridge, in the manner of one who has spotted a sleeping bear and thinks nothing would be jollier than ramming a sharp stick into its ribs.

"Can everyone just be silent for two consecutive moments?" said Oliver. His words were more reasonable than his tone but I felt like I must make allowances for that. The poor chap was clearly suffering under some considerable stress.

None of us replied. Oliver glared about the place to make sure he had our full attention and weren't about to start interrupting him again before continuing. He drew a deep breath.

"I say," said Bainbridge, "watch out for that boat!"

I glanced past Oliver's considerable form. He had neglected to bring the ship to a stop when we'd started our little chat. He still had his claws on the lines but as he hadn't so much as glanced at the windows, instruments or viewscreens for the past few minutes, I don't know what he thought he was doing with them. To all intents and purposes, our ship was un-helmed at full speed.

This might not have been an issue, were it not for the small group of fishing boats moored some distance away from the quarantined planet that was currently causing so much strife on the bridge. There were several aliens of crusty appearance in these boats, and each boat had a fishing rod. They appeared to be catching dark matter.

Fishing for dark matter can be a profitable way to spend an afternoon if your area is rich in the stuff. It's also pleasant and peaceful. Generally speaking, few things can spoil your fun; one of the things that definitely *can* is an unpiloted warship barrelling towards you. We would miss most of the group by a large margin, but one boat was directly in our path. The lass on board was waving her tail frantically in an attempt to stop us.

"What boat?" asked Oliver, staring at Bainbridge.

I saw us pass directly under the boat. A shadow blurred over the bridge for less than a second. I exhaled... then, there was a slight crunch.

"Never mind," said Bainbridge, as fragments of fishing boat rattled off the bridge roof.

"What I was trying to say-" said Oliver.

"I'm ever so sorry to interrupt you, Oliver," Sarah interjected, "but could you stop the ship? We appear to have hit something."

"And we're heading straight towards a battle fleet," said Bainbridge.

"And a planet," I said.

"Oh yes," said Sarah. "What's going on there?"

"Fine," said Oliver. He throttled the ship down and lowered the anchor. "Now, has everyone finished interrupting? Might I be able to explain why it's vital that we visit this planet?"

"Please continue," said Bainbridge.

"Continue, please," said Sarah.

The other two having rather limited my options for verbal responses, I settled for making an encouraging gesture.

Oliver took a deep breath. "We need to visit this planet because we're here on holiday. We're here for poor Jay, who is suffering. This planet was always to be our first port of call since we planned this trip six months ago."

Sarah raised a palm. I think they're called palms? They're like claws but there are five of them.

"A week ago," Oliver corrected himself. "I meant a week ago." Sarah lowered her palm. "And for that reason," he continued, thrusting a claw across his cephalothorax, "we must set aside our selfish desire to remain uninjured and uncontaminated by horrifying chemical weapons. We must follow the itinerary, my friends, because without the itinerary we are nothing. You!"

Oliver spun to face me and thrust a claw in my direction. The look in his eyes urged me to take his claw and join him on a magical adventure. Music swelled. At least, I assume it did. It may have been my overzealous imagination.

"Jay, will you come with me on the first stop of your holiday? Or will you be a selfish, stupid and cowardly individual, and let the quarantine remain unbroken?"

I held his claw in mine. The music reached a triumphant crescendo, which was shattered a little by Bainbridge asking if Oliver had suffered a recent serious blow to the head.

Oliver turned on him with fire in his eyes but Bainbridge was already rushing forward and checking the other arachnid's vital signs.

"What are you doing?" Oliver demanded, attempting to shake Bainbridge off. "Desist."

"I am checking," said Bainbridge, "to see if you are in the process of having a stroke."

"I am not."

"Your actions say otherwise."

Oliver spluttered. He is an exceptional splutterer. He has never actually managed to drown anyone as a result of his spluttering, but there have been a few close calls. Bainbridge ignored him, only stepping back when he was satisfied with the results of his examination.

"You appear healthy," he said, before striking Oliver across the chelicera with a claw.

Sarah, Oliver and I all gasped, making a quite pleasant synchronised whooshing noise. Bainbridge, however, refused to be cowed.

"Have you quite taken leave of your senses, Mr Oliver?" he asked, somehow twisting the 'mister' into something resembling the direst of insults. "Quarantines are not issued lightly. For all you know, one of my erstwhile colleagues is on that planet performing feats that would make your fangs chatter. I have wrought horrors on worlds just like this. A quarantine is the perfect cover. We will not visit this world whilst the quarantine is in effect. I have a healthy respect for my life, and I am positively attached to the lives of both Sarah and Jay."

I was quite touched, but eager to mention the obvious oversight. "I say, you forgot to mention Oliver in the least, young sabre."

"I thank you for the reminder," said Bainbridge, still palp-to-palp with Oliver. "But I completed my list when I said your name."

"Oh," I said, not fully getting it. Then, "Ooh," as I did get it.

"But… " said Oliver.

"No buts. Sarah, kindly take the lines and move us on past this accursed place. Jay, would you mind proceeding to the deck amidships and attending to the creature in the boat that Oliver crashed into some moments ago?"

I felt like I shouldn't leave the bridge. The atmosphere was decidedly tense, and Oliver may need someone to defend him. That said, if there was someone who needed a helping claw, that really should be my priority. I shuddered to even think it, but we might have *inconvenienced* someone.

I turned right out of the bridge and clattered down the stairs that would bring me to the deck amidships.

The deck itself, as well as the railings, were painted in the standard gunmetal blue. The mast taking up much of this area of the deck was a muted russet. This made the brown and green planks of the rowboat all the more obvious. There were rudders, gaseous exchange units and harpoons scattered all about the place, along with a few oars. The poor little boat appeared to have avoided being crushed by our gunwale, but had not been so lucky when it came to our mast.

Currently in the process of climbing down the mast was the erstwhile occupant of the boat. When my eyes met hers, I found myself rooted to my position. That she was female was entirely obvious from the colouration of her scales. She was a naja: a reptilian species famous for their venomous cooking. I had never seen one of her species in the flesh (or, rather, scales) and her grace and poise took my breath away. The subtle blue and silver hue of her body merged effortlessly into a glistening gold crescendo around her head. Her body had no limbs to speak of. She consisted mostly of head and tail. She did, however, wear a cybernetic module on her back, from which unfurled a variety of metal appendages. She was a very shapely creature. The shape in question was mostly tubular but it drew in at some point and grew out in soft curves that were most pleasing to observe. I did my best to refrain from observing too obviously.

In a different situation, I would have wasted little time in striking up a conversation. Now was most decidedly *not* the time. She was obviously furious. I could tell because her hood had unfurled, giving the upper portion of her body a rather intimidating countenance.

"Hello," I said, eventually. I never know how to introduce myself when chatting to someone who might have been *inconvenienced*. This is made up for by the fact that I often can't keep my mouth shut around those I know well.

"I say, were you driving this boat just now?" the naja asked.

She didn't put it quite like that, I must admit. I could tell she possessed a great deal of spirit. You may ask how I knew this from one simple sentence. I fear I may not have been completely honest in my description of the scene. The naja did speak the words I quoted, that much is true. I chose to leave out a great many others.

When reproduced in its entirety, the sentence would include about three or four curse words for every normal word.

"No," I said, trying to counter her apparent verbose nature with brevity. "Sorry."

"My parent[2] constructed that boat." My face froze. This was partly because it was awful that we had destroyed something so precious, and partly because of the way the naja was speaking. There was a word occasionally used to describe the speech of the naja. It was a word that began with an H and was an onomatopoeia. I disliked the word intensely as it was dreadfully spiciest but in that moment, the word felt like it might have been appropriate, had it not had such a dreadful history behind it.

"I say, what bad luck," I said. "My friend wasn't looking where he was going, you see, and… well, you know the rest."

"I will skin your friend alive," said the naja.

"Oh," I said. "Please don't."

"Where is he?" she demanded, shimmering towards me.

"On the bridge," I said, without thinking.

"Thank you."

"I say-" I called after her. I must admit to a certain amount of panic overcoming me because it goes some way to explaining what I said next. I suppose I must have been trying to defuse the situation. "You have very kind eyes."

The naja paused, then rounded on me. "I'm sorry?"

---

[2] Culturally, if not biologically, Naja are a single parent species. Like many reptiles they are born from eggs. Unusually, such eggs can be externally fertilised by any member of the species so there is often confusion as to the individual whose fertilisation was successful. As a result, Naja consider themselves born to the one 'parent' who produced the egg from which they were hatched. The person who fertilised the egg was providing a useful service, but not one that required much reverence or respect.

"Your eyes," I said, before realising I possibly shouldn't just repeat myself. "They have a definite generosity to them that I thought I really should mention."

"I am recently shipwrecked," she said. "Do you really think now is the time to be commenting on my positive physical attributes?"

"I might not get the chance later," I said.

She appeared to think about this. "What is your name?" she asked, eventually.

"Call me Jay," I said.

"I am Megan."

"Delighted to meet you, Megan," I said, attempting to forestall the calamity that was about to play out on the bridge.

"Are you trying to calm me down?" she asked, her eyes narrowing.

"Yes." I should probably have kept that particular plan to myself.

"Well, stop it. I'm furious."

"My apologies. I was just hoping to persuade you to give Oliver a chance to apologise in person before you take any action you may later regret."

"I do not think I would regret sinking my fangs into the moron who destroyed my boat."

"The possibility is a remote one, I grant you, but I thought it wise to remind you of how remorse can creep up on you."

Megan seemed to weigh my words, swaying slightly as she did so.

"You think this 'Oliver' can be persuaded to apologise unreservedly and offer full reparation?"

I thought about Oliver. I thought about our time together. I thought about his actions and inactions. I thought about how he had behaved to those he'd wronged in the past. I thought about the sum total of apologies I'd heard him issue. I shook my head and reasoned that, in spite of his past actions, he could be relied upon to do the right thing in this instance.

"Absolutely," I said.

Megan dipped her head. "Very well. Take me to Oliver."

I skittered up the stairway to the bridge with Megan following me. I could see through the windows that Oliver was no longer present. Bainbridge was at the lines. He appeared to be guiding us gently around the quarantined planet. I leaned my head into the bridge.

"Bainbridge," I said, wanting to lead with his name lest Megan assume this was the dreaded Oliver, "do you happen to know where Oliver has wandered off to?"

Bainbridge didn't take his eyes from his route. He informed me that Oliver was checking on something in the hold. He conjectured that this may simply be a pretext for having a good old-fashioned sulk, but I didn't give this any real credence.

I got lost looking for the cargo hold three times, which caused Megan to become incrementally more annoyed each time. Still, we got there in the end.

The cargo hold was largely conventional for a ship of this type. Pillared walls stretched up into the darkness where, theoretically, a ceiling was located. The floor was a smooth metal affair, designed to ease the movement of war machines or whatever curiosities were normally stored in here.

What was stored in here at present was Oliver and an extremely large crate. When I say extremely large, perhaps I do not do it justice; it was fully twice Oliver's size and he is not on the short side of things.

Oliver appeared to be unpacking the crate, or at least trying to. He was fiddling with one of the straps that secured it to the deck as we breezed in.

"There you are, Oliver," I said, subtly hinting to Megan that this was the chap she was after. "I've someone who wishes a discreet word."

Oliver whirled around, looking curiously guilty for someone engaged in such an obviously innocent act.

"What? What is it? Can't you see I'm doing… nothing? I'm doing nothing. Can't you see I'm doing nothing? What do you want?"

"Were you piloting this vessel five minutes ago?" asked Megan, sliding in between Oliver and me.

Oliver started sidling away from the crate. "Yes. Yes I was, as it happens. What of it? And who are you?"

"You destroyed my boat," Megan said, slinking towards him.

"Oh, and I suppose you want me to do something about it, do you?" Oliver said, closing the gap.

Megan stopped the merest fraction away from Oliver's mandibles. "I would very much like that. My planet is under quarantine. I have nowhere to go. I had been planning to catch my quota of dark matter and then rest in my boat until the quarantine was lifted. You have denied me the opportunity to do this. I would dearly like an apology."

"An apology?" said Oliver, as if Megan had demanded the blood of his firstborn.

"An apology is what I said."

"How dare you?"

"How dare I? How dare *you*? My parent constructed that boat when I was still in the egg!"

"A pox on your parent!"

This was starting to get a little ugly, but I could see Megan holding her temper. My joining the fray would probably only cause chaos.

"Do I gather you refuse to do the decent thing?" Megan asked, icily.

"Decency? Ha!" Oliver said. "You slither in here and start talking about decency all over the place? How ridiculous."

I don't know if you've ever been on a ship when some idiot has knocked a hole in the side with a poorly-aimed rugby ball or something. I have, and let me tell you, it is unpleasant. In the moments before the vacuum seals slam into place, everything attempts to evacuate the room through the newly-opened hole.

It felt dreadfully like that was what had just happened. Oliver really should not have used the S-word to describe a naja. When used as a self-descriptor, it can be empowering. When used as a pejorative… well, Oliver should really have known better.

"I'm sorry," said Megan, lingering slightly on the first letter of the second word. "Would you care to repeat that?"

Oliver drew himself up to his full height and stuck out his abdomen. "Don't you hiss at me!"

And that was another word he *definitely* shouldn't have used.

"I tried to be civil," said Megan, very quietly.

I shut my eyes. As a result, I didn't see what happened next. All I heard was a roar from Megan and a cry of alarm from Oliver. There were a few thumps.

I waited.

"You can open your eyes now," said Megan. I did so.

Megan was towering over Oliver. This wasn't particularly surprising as Oliver was flat on the floor. Two large puncture marks were visible at the cephalothoracic junction, where the exoskeleton was weakest. Oliver wasn't moving.

"Now, before you say anything, he's not dead."

"He looks dead," I said.

"Well, he's not."

"Are you sure?"

"He's unconscious."

"Ah," I said.

"He was being unreasonable," Megan said.

"And he said some things he probably shouldn't have."

"That as well, yes."

"But you attacked him!" I said, finally putting a claw on why I felt a little uncomfortable with the situation I found myself in.

Megan shrugged.

"But you could have killed him!" I said. I was trying to be reasonable as, apparently, Megan objected in the strongest terms to unreasonableness. My voice was, nevertheless, taking on a stressed and squeaky quality.

Megan dipped her crown placatingly. "I could have done, but I didn't. I showed restraint."

"You did not! You rendered him unconscious!"

"She did, actually," said Bainbridge, from a corner.

Both of us yelped and leapt six or seven metres into the air.

"Sorry," said Bainbridge, sauntering towards us. He was eating an apple. "I thought my input might be appreciated at this juncture."

"Please, input away," I said, waving a claw at Bainbridge whilst I waited for my head to stop pounding with adrenaline.

"A naja can kill in hundreds of different ways. To subdue someone non-lethally is surprisingly difficult for them. Megan bit Oliver with great care and accuracy. It was a wonderful example of precision retribution." Bainbridge flashed a cheerful grimace at me before popping the apple core into his mouth and chewing happily.

"So… How long will it be until he wakes up?" I said.

Megan waved this question away with the tip of her tail. "Oh, no time at all. About twenty-four hours."

"Well, we'd best make him comfortable in the meantime," I said, grateful that Megan's retribution appeared to have made her forget about her boat.

"Allow me! I saw some hammocks on the aft deck. I'll stick him in one of those." said Megan. She wrapped the tip of her tail around one of Oliver's legs and breezed out. Bainbridge and I waited in silence. All was peace and quiet, except for the repeated thumping sound of Oliver's head impacting with the steps out of the cargo bay.

"I like her," said Bainbridge.

"So do I," I said, although I felt bad to admit it.

We both left the cargo hold but not before casting our worried eyes over the giant crate that Oliver had been toying with, where it loomed disconcertingly over us.

"I say, Jay?" Bainbridge asked, as we climbed the stairs up to the aft deck.

"Yes, young Bainbridge?"

"No-one's called me young for a long time."

"You look young. You have a handsome face. Would you like me to not call you that again?"

"Not at all, I like it. A handsome face, eh? Well, I never."

"You had something you wanted to ask I believe?" I said, after a few moments of strange silence.

"Oh, yes. Do you find our guest attractive?"

I coughed, frantically.

"I thought so," said Bainbridge. "Would you like me to talk to her for you? See if she's seeing anyone, that sort of thing?"

My coughing moved from frantic to desperate. I doubled over, suddenly struggling to get enough air.

"Is that a no?" Bainbridge asked, "or are you giving me some sort of signal. We're not under attack are we?"

My gaze was mostly occupied by the step I was glaring at, but I heard movement and could guess that young Bainbridge was suddenly holding several weapons of one sort or other. I fought down the embarrassment that had swept across every atom of my being like a tsunami of childhood diaries. I looked up at Bainbridge. "No, we are not under attack. Please do not talk to Megan. There may or may not be something in what you say, but I prefer to focus on personal connection rather than other matters."

"But she's got a lovely profile, Jay… "

"She has, but I haven't had a chance to talk to her when she's not been absolutely furious. Let's see if she has any other sates of being before jumping to any conclusions, Bainbridge, shall we?"

Bainbridge seemed to be pleased by this conclusion, although for the life of me I had no idea why. He apologised for any embarrassment he may have caused, and I said no apology was necessary. We resumed our climb.

We reached the aft deck to find Megan stuffing Oliver's limp form into a hammock. By sheer luck, she had picked the one that belonged to him. She asked if there was anyone else on board and we led her to the bridge to introduce her to Sarah.

Megan was a little surprised to see Sarah at the lines. Maybe because Sarah was using a box to see out of the viewscreens. You don't often enter the bridge of a warship to see a human standing on a box.

"Hello," said Megan, in the way you might introduce yourself to a sofa that had suddenly developed sentience.

Sarah introduced herself charmingly, as was her habit. Megan didn't appear to warm to her immediately but perhaps I wasn't yet adept in reading her expressions.

Sarah said she wanted nothing more than for Megan to enjoy her time on board. She then cleared her throat and wondered aloud if Megan knew that every passing moment was taking her farther away from her fleet of dark matter fishing boats.

A range of emotions crossed Megan's face in the space of a few seconds. I'm pretty sure horror was in there, as was confusion. Doubt was there in abundance. Polite interest was the expression she eventually rested on.

"Can I ask what you were doing when you destroyed my boat?" she asked, after her expression was stable.

"Having an argument," said Bainbridge.

"Discussing the relative benefits of breaking quarantine," I said, at the same time.

"Trying to be on holiday," said Sarah, once the incoherent babble of our two answers had dissipated.

Megan swayed a little. "A holiday," she said, dreamily. "Do you know when my last holiday was?"

This sounded awfully like a rhetorical question but leaving such things unanswered can cause my brain to start hurting, so I replied that we did not.

"It was years ago," she said, wistfully. "On the Plains of Trenzalore, at the fall of the eleventh. Many people died that day."

"Well," said Bainbridge, after a silence that might best be described as uncomfortable, "would you like to join us for a spell? Afterwards we can let you have one of our lifeboats, by way of apology."

Megan appeared to think about the offer for a few seconds. "I would love to," she said, gracefully, once a polite amount of time had passed. "It is not as if I can return to my planet with the quarantine in place. Will you be coming?" she asked, turning to Sarah.

"I think so," said Sarah, a little unnerved by Megan's unwavering, unblinking stare.

"Fine. Fine," said Megan.

Megan's behaviour was dashed odd. On my last tour, I had a group of aides who ran about the place fetching things for me. One of these gracious young individuals had behaved in a similar manner to how Megan currently was. To cut a long story slightly shorter than it might otherwise be, this lass turned out to be a spy. I mean, can you believe it?

She was executed for her crimes, then downloaded into a new body so she could go to prison for a bit. I believe she teaches chemistry in a school these days. Anyway, I decided to keep an eye or two on Megan, just in case she turned out to be engaged in similar activities. She might not be a *spy*, exactly, and she only acted suspiciously when talking to Sarah…

I excused myself for a glass of water. I appeared to be tying my brain in knots trying to puzzle out this problem.

Not wanting to use the high-pressure water cannon to fill a glass of water, and not wanting to risk depleting my canteen, I scuttled below decks to the galley. This contained facilities that could clean the cooking and eating equipment for the two hundred standing crew of the frigate but, more pertinently, it also had a drinking water station.

I looked in twenty or so cupboards until I found a drinking receptacle and filled it from the tap. The world suddenly fell away from me.

I had expected cool, refreshing water to emerge from the tap. Instead, it was blood. Thick, viscous vitae poured into the glass. My claws couldn't maintain their grip. The glass fell and suddenly my claws were covered with blood. There was so much blood! I closed my eyes but I could still feel it.

Even though my eyes were shut, I could see the first arachnid I killed with my bare claws. I thought I had managed to forget that horrifying moment. I screamed.

"Ha," squeaked a voice from behind me. "I got you! I got you comprehensively!"

I turned slowly. Sarah was standing behind me, chuckling. A smile cracked across my face.

"Oh, you little scamp!" I said, throwing a dishcloth at her. "Did you set this up?"

She grinned. "Guilty as charged! I re-routed the water tank to a supply of animal blood I prepared earlier. You should have seen your face!"

She laughed and I joined her. I had quite forgot how Sarah likes to let her head-fur down when she's away from the city. She can be quite the practical joker. On the last holiday we took together, she tricked a member of our party into burying one of the others alive for a few hours. Well, as you can imagine, this led to much hilarity when everything was being sorted out.

Sarah and I chatted happily as we worked together to reconnect the taps to the water supply, rather than the horrifying animal viscera. She explained that she'd left Bainbridge in charge of the ship whilst she followed me, hoping I might fall into her little trap. That made sense of why we hadn't crashed into anything over the last ten minutes, I reasoned.

"By the by… " I said, wanting a second opinion. "What do you make of Megan?"

Sarah paused in reattaching a pipe for a moment before resuming. "Why do you ask?"

This was a good question. I didn't have an especially good answer. I certainly did not want to start blathering about spies all over the place. It sounded ridiculous and paranoid. Bainbridge's outrageously forward questions were also something I didn't want to bring up.

"Well," I said, deciding to stick to the facts, "she's behaving a little… oddly, isn't she?"

"It's your holiday, Jay. You can bring who you like on it." She smiled at me. I smiled back, baffled. I wasn't sure how that answered my original question.

"Okay," I said, nodding very slowly.

"Okay," Sarah echoed, nodding equally slowly.

"Is there a problem?" I asked, suddenly unsure as to whether there was or wasn't a little tension between us.

Sarah exhaled, grinned, and patted me on a leg. "No, Jay. There's no problem. I'm sure it'll be fine. Come on, let's get back up on deck."

We reached the deck to find that Bainbridge was in the process of navigating the *Cox* through a lock. The solar winds can be playful in this area of space, and the *Cox* would probably be buffeted all over the place, were it not for locks like this. In the locks, the *Cox* was buoyed gently upwards and would be able to enter into calmer winds once it was in the clear.

Sarah and I leaned on the railings to watch as the *Cox* rose to draw level with the lock-keeper's hut. Specifically, I leant on the highest rail whilst Sarah leant on the middle rail, the one that was most comfortable for her to prop against.

The lock-keeper's hut was a fairly Spartan plasteel affair perched on top of the lock's shielding apparatus. It had a definite minimalist charm to it that I enjoyed very much. I found myself gazing at the window, wondering what it would be like to live and work in such a place.

As the *Cox* rose, I saw that the lock-keeper's hut was far from unoccupied. It had, as I suppose I should have guessed, a lock-keeper inside it. Quite by accident, I made eye contact. The fellow had the most amazing facial fur I had ever seen. He started at me. I stared back.

The *Cox* continued to rise. I found myself unable to look away. The lock-keeper raised a mug to his mouth and drank from it, still staring at me. His eyes were a pale red that quite took my breath away. The fellow lowered his mug and raised his hat.

"Morning, ma'am," he said.

"Good morning!" I said, still unable to break eye contact.

"Who are you talking to?" asked Sarah, who hadn't yet reached the point where she could see through the window.

I was about to reply, but the *Cox* suddenly started to slide out of the lock. I lost my balance momentarily and my eye contact with the lock-keeper was broken. I wrenched my eyes back to where the lock-keeper had been, but he was gone... or maybe he had never been there to begin with...

Now I thought about it, I could not imagine such stunning red eyes existing outside of my own imagin-

Oh, no, wait. There he was. He had just moved. Never mind.

I waved to the lock-keeper and he nodded back before taking another sip from his mug.

"Jay?" asked Sarah.

"Oh... sorry, yes." I thought of those magnificent eyes. "Just a passing phantasm."

"A what?" asked Sarah, either confused or amused. Or possibly bemused, now I think about it.

I was about to explain, but my thoughts were derailed by a cry of "Everybody down!" from the bridge. The voice sounded like Bainbridge's.

"Did you hear that?" I asked, but Sarah was already throwing herself to the deck.

There was an almighty crash and I was pitched into the mast, which happened to be nearby. I slid down the mast to land on the deck. "Ow."

My exoskeleton had taken the sting out of the impact, but I still felt a little rattled. I got to my claws and scuttled to Sarah's side to make sure she was okay. She looked up at me.

"What happened?" she asked.

"I hit the mast," I said.

She got to her feet. "You ask a silly question… "

"Are you okay?"

"Oh, fine," said Sarah, dusting herself down.

"Good. Shall we find out what we hit?"

"I'm agog."

The answer to my question became fairly obvious as we neared the bridge. There was a modified corvette across our prow. It looked like it might have once been a rather proud warship; it had been decommissioned since then, much as ours had. Most of the weapons had been removed and there was a tennis court on the poop deck. Several parts of the boat also seemed to have taken significant damage recently. One part of the boat near the forecastle appeared to be on fire.

It looked like we had hit this ship, or they hit us. As we approached, we saw mooring ropes fire from the *Cox* to a nearby buoy. Bainbridge scuttled out of the bridge, closely followed by Megan. They approached the ship at our prow. Sarah and I moved to join them.

"I say!" called Bainbridge. "I say! Hello there! Is everybody okay?"

"What happened?" I said to Megan.

"This boat was heading straight for us as your chap exited the lock," she replied. "We couldn't avoid it. The occupants may be intoxicated."

Three arachnids burst onto the deck of the other ship. They each held weapons in at least two claws. They were in an advanced state of dishevelment. One was wearing her tie as a bandana. They looked about the place frantically before noticing us.

As one, they pointed their weapons at us. Megan, Sarah and I threw ourselves to the deck. Bainbridge didn't move.

"Hello there," he called. "Do you need help?"

There was silence for a few moments. Gunfire, most notably, did not rend the air like angry steel-tipped hornets.

I poked my head over the rim of the prow. The three arachnids on the other ship were having a whispered conversation. After a few moments, one turned to face Bainbridge and called, "Are you pirates?"

Bainbridge turned to us. "What do you think I should answer?" he asked, grinning.

"I think you should probably answer that we aren't pirates," I said.

"I agree," said Sarah.

"I might be a pirate… " said Megan. "I've always wanted to be a pirate."

"See, Megan gets it," said Bainbridge. "The rest of you don't know how to have any fun."

"Stop teasing them, Bainbridge," Sarah said. "They're armed."

Bainbridge looked back at the three arachnids for a moment.

"They are," he said, "but the lass on the left has no ammunition in her magazines, the chap in the middle doesn't know how to use either weapon he's carrying, and the individual with no obvious gender cues on the right appears to be holding a water pistol that's been painted black and had a kitchen knife strapped to it."

"You mean… " Megan said, "they're trying to look scarier than they are?"

"In one," said Bainbridge, "is how you have got it."

"Are you?" called one of the trio.

Bainbridge turned to face them. "Are we what?"

"Pirates!" cried the same voice, sounding outraged. Although now Bainbridge had pointed it out, I was sure I heard an edge of terror in the voice as well.

"We're holidaymakers. Can we be of any assistance?" Bainbridge called, cheerfully.

"You can give us your ship!" cried one.

"Oh no," Sarah said, and covered her head with her legs.

"Very funny," said Bainbridge. "Can we be of any actual assistance?"

The arachnids put their heads together and had another whispered conversation.

"I am not sure I like these people," said Megan. "I think we should upgrade this holiday to include piracy and take their ship."

"Be kind, Megan. I think they've been through some trying times," said Sarah.

"Well, you'd know all about trying times," said Megan.

"What do you mean?" I asked.

"… Nothing," she said.

I might have been imagining it, but I thought I saw Sarah roll her eyes.

"Can you give us a claw getting into the lock?" called one of the dishevelled group.

This seemed more reasonable than their last request. The poor gentlenids looked exhausted.

"Absolutely," called Bainbridge. He turned to us, grinning. "And to think my C.O. said I was no good at diplomacy."

We held a quick strategy meeting, which resulted in Megan and Bainbridge popping into one of the launches the *Cox* had on standby. They buzzed over to the other ship and asked for a rope to be thrown down to them.

With this done, they crossed to the far bank and made a landing on the towpath. From there, they hauled the prow of the boat into position so that it sat mid-stream.

Whilst they were doing this, Sarah and I pulled the *Cox* over to the side of the lane so we could pass their ship without ramming it again.

Once the ship was in position and we were clear, the other arachnids spooled up their engine and fairly shot into the lock. Bainbridge threw their rope to them as they passed.

I heard him call to them as they entered the lock. "Why did you think we were pirates?"

There was no reply.

"So, we might have to worry about pirates later," Bainbridge said, as he and Megan came back aboard, "but it's probably nothing to concern ourselves about."

"If we do get attacked by pirates," said Megan, "it will result in my owning a boat that is less broken than my last one."

Bainbridge grimaced. "Yes. Sorry about that."

Megan bared her fangs, prettily. "Do not worry. I have had my revenge." This caused Bainbridge to chortle.

"Well," said Sarah, "I think I'll take a stint at the lines if nobody else wants to?"

Bainbridge and I bowed to her. Megan said this was fine by her, as long as Sarah thought she could manage it.

The next hour passed peacefully. Bainbridge brought out a battered deck of cards from his pack and we spent a little time playing with them. None of us knew any of the games familiar to the others but that was okay, as it turned out Bainbridge's cards were missing some twenty percent of those that should have been present.

We ended up playing a variation on a human game Sarah had told me about. I forget the name, but it had something to do with a chap called Calvin. The purpose of the game was chaos and a total lack of organisation, so I was terrible at it. Bainbridge and Megan, for their part, rather took to it.

We tired of the game after a while. Megan asked if anyone wanted tea, which is a question rarely responded to in any way other than with an enthusiastic 'yes!'

Four cups of tea were poured. I said that I would bring Sarah her cup. Bainbridge said he would join me and see if we were heading towards anything interesting. Megan, presumably not wanting to be left out, trailed after us.

"Ah, what luck," said Sarah as we entered the bridge. She took the tea and thanked us. "I'm just bringing us into orbit around a tomb world we might enjoy a little stroll around." She turned back to the instruments. "Would that suit you?"

"Tombs!" I cried, excitedly.

"Tombs!" cried Bainbridge in anguish.

"Ah!" cried Sarah, smiting her brow with the claw that wasn't holding a teacup. "I wasn't thinking. Shall we move on to the next stop, old chap?"

Bainbridge was trembling forcibly in a corner of the bridge. His eyes gripped the floor for dear life, his talons were skittering around in tiny circles. Gradually, though, he calmed.

"I will be calm," he said. "I am free of my past. I have nothing more than the usual to fear out in this calm."

He drew himself together, and then up. He opened his eyes and bowed slightly to Sarah. "We will visit the tombs. It will be a delightful occasion and we will see many interesting examples of gothic design. Nothing could be more pleasant."

Chapter Four

Trans-Exclusionary Naja

We pulled the ship into orbit around the tomb world and took one of the boats down to the surface.

We landed on a rather cheerful-looking landing pad and were met by a human who helped us tie up the boat to a mooring post. Tombs and graves and monoliths of every sort stretched out as far as the eye could see. They were organised in patterns that would make the hearts of jaded mathematicians melt. Come to think of it, I don't think I've ever met any other kind of mathematician.

The landing pad was raised a good few hundred metres above the morass of graves below us. Detail was difficult to establish from this height because mist swirled hither and thither. I asked the human about this and they cheerfully informed me that they had mist generators on standby to add to the ambiance.

Occasional larger monuments jutted from the mist. Here, an enormous arachnid perched atop a pile of skulls. There, a naja curled around a sword, roaring at the sky. I rubbed three of my claws together in anticipation.

The human who was attending on us sold us a guidebook and wished us a pleasant visit. Megan looked far from comfortable until we were away from the landing pad and out amongst the graves. I asked her why, but she said it was silly. This didn't seem like much of an answer but I might have been missing any number of levels of subtlety.

We spent a few hours examining the place as a group before some slight fractures appeared. Sarah wanted to spend an extended period in one of the larger catacombs. Megan, for her part, wished to proceed in a strictly linear manner, without distractions. Bainbridge, meanwhile, was finding the visit slightly harder than he would like us to think. He was getting more and more on edge with every name we read and every date we noted.

I suggested that we divide our efforts for the next hour or so and could meet up back at the boat for lunch. This idea was met with enthusiasm by Sarah and Megan, who scooted off. Bainbridge looked a little too shaken to be left alone. I suggested that we should sit at the foot of an enormous sepulchre and chat a while.

He smiled gratefully at me and didn't so much sit as flop down. I joined him. We spent a few minutes discussing the weather, our surroundings and the horrible disasters I had caused. Poor Bainbridge still seemed edgy in spite of this. I wondered what I could do to help and realised that I knew precious little about the fellow.

I asked him where he hailed from originally. He told me of his home and his father, who was in poor health. He mentioned his family home, which he had not been able to visit for decades, having been mostly raised by a guardian rather than his parents.

He told me of his schooling. No expense had been spared in this area. He had been sent to Blues, the very best school for light-years around. He described his time there somewhat bitterly. His education in the classics and modern languages had been first rate. His education in other matters had been lacking, it seemed.

The place, as Bainbridge described it, fostered something of a superiority complex in its pupils. They were repeatedly told that they were the best and would go on to do great things. This can go to a young arachnid's head. Bainbridge fell in with a group of chums who were absolutely convinced they were the best at whatever they turned their claws to, whether this turned out to be true or not.

When he left school, he described his subsequent choices in desultory tones. A couple of disastrous tours of duty in the armed forces led to his self-confidence growing in inverse proportion to his actual levels of achievement.

I wasn't used to a chap being quite this honest and forthright after only knowing me for a short time. I mentioned this after Bainbridge lapsed into a momentary silence after describing his second tour of duty. He turned to me and smiled.

"I do not make friends easily," he said. "But I like you, Jay. I do not feel the need to be anything less than honest in your presence."

I felt a wash of embarrassment at his candour, but I felt pleased that the chap was evidently calmer now than when he had been poking around the tombs. And I was curious as to how a self-described egotistical layabout could have transformed into the shy, charming and self-deprecating creature that sat next to me. I invited him to continue.

"After my second tour, things came to a head somewhat," he said, his eyes affixed to the ground under our feet. "Many decisions I had made up until that point came back to haunt me. I began and then destroyed the only genuine romantic relationship I'd ever become involved in. And then I was persuaded to join the Special Operations Unit."

I was shocked. People usually join the Special Operations Unit because they wish to serve their species in the most tangible way possible. Either that or they have become weary with life. I have never heard of someone being persuaded to join before.

"Who persuaded you?" I asked, wondering if I should be minding my own business.

"A friend of Pigstick's," he said, before smiting his brow. "Sarah. A friend of Sarah's. My blasted brain is taking a little while to catch up with the facts on the ground."

"And how... why... " I asked, not wishing to pry but being insatiably curious nonetheless.

He smiled, sadly. "It is a long story. It seemed like the best thing to do at the time."

"And was it?" I asked.

"I am not yet sure. I'm in something of a turbulent state of mind. When I think about the actions I took that led me to where I sit now, it seems inevitable. When I think about the person that persuaded me to take that last step, to join the Special Operations Unit, I feel conflicted.

"On the one hand, he is responsible for my facing the most devastating events I have ever experienced. I can barely sleep, I am paranoid, I cannot indulge in relaxing activities such as exploring a tomb world without feelings of rising panic. Then again, I feel I have become a less difficult person as a result of his persuasion. I do not know, were I to ever meet him again, if I would embrace him or attempt to commit grievous bodily harm."

"Is there anything I can do to help?"

"Just your being here with me is an enormous help, Jay. That, and our destination. I feel that I need to visit Newbury Towers, to return to where I started and wrap up any business that yet remains. That being said, it might be wise to not head there directly. I am not yet ready to face the ghosts of my past."

My gasp bounced around the sepulchre and back to us. "You are haunted by ghosts?" I asked, "You have confirmed the existence of life after death? That's *dreadful* news. Is there any way it can be avoided?"

"I was speaking figuratively, Jay."

"Oh, good."

Bainbridge gave me strange look before shaking himself. He stood and dusted himself down. "Shall we look at one or two of these stone slabs?"

I answered that I would be delighted to do just that. We sauntered along the row, looking at the tombs. There was a black one. A greyish black one. Another black one. Another greyish black one. There was a sort of blue black one. There was one which was entirely grey. There was one that I would describe as obsidian. There was one that was a kind of indigo colour. There was one that was bright yellow and in the shape of a duck.

Bainbridge and I were just puzzling over that last one when Megan drifted into the row. "Is that a duck?" she asked when she reached us. We said that if it wasn't, it looked dreadfully like one.

We asked her how her examination of the tombs was proceeding.

"Oh, perfectly well," she said, "but I wish there weren't so many humans about."

I didn't entirely like the sound of that.

"Oh?" I said, trying to sound as if there might be an entirely sensible reason behind her statement. "Why is that?"

"Well, I don't see why vermin should be allowed to just wander around freely. They breed, you know. And they get into the skirting board and chew the wiring."

"Are you sure you're not thinking of rats?" Bainbridge asked, dubiously.

"No, no. That's definitely humans," said Megan, appearing to warm to the subject. "I read about it in my news feed. They carry diseases, as well. Horrible diseases."

This was true, as far as it went. That being said, I was currently the bearer of a particularly nasty mindvirus so I didn't feel selecting humans for special criticism in this regard was entirely fair.

"I meant to ask you," Megan said. "Why was a human driving your ship? Is it some sort of pet you've taught tricks? If so, you must be remarkably clever."

"She's not a *pet*," Bainbridge snarled. "She's my friend."

"Oh yes, yes, of course it is," said Megan. "I had a friend who talked about her Oxyuranus microlepidotus the same way."

"No," said Bainbridge. "I do not mean she's my friend in the way insane people talk about their actual pets. I mean she's been my friend for forty years."

"Forty years?" asked Megan. "But humans never live that long. What have you been feeding her?"

"She hasn't always been human," I said. I then kicked myself mentally, then physically. Susan has given me permission to discuss her past with people, but I try not to. Such disclosure was often neither relevant nor helpful. I had probably just made things worse.

"She was born arachnid," said Bainbridge quietly, in response to Megan's incredulous expression. "She's never been an arachnid, though, she's always been human."

"Oh," said Megan. "Oh, I see. Yes, it's rather silly when people say things like that, isn't it? I had a friend at university who told us about someone who insisted she was a Terminator class star ship."

Bainbridge and I glanced at each other.

"Did you ever meet this person?" I asked.

"No. Why would I want to meet them?"

"It doesn't sound like they're real. It sounds like your friend made them up."

"No, no, she was definitely real. She insisted she was a star ship and insisted everyone call her the N.S. Cerastes!"

Bainbridge and I smote our brows.

"Okay, let's say this person existed. Claiming you're a star ship is still not the same thing," said Bainbridge, clearly tired of the conversation already.

"Oh come on," Megan scoffed.

"No. *No*," Bainbridge said. "People who feel uncomfortable because of the body they were randomly assigned at birth and feel that the only way they can be happy is to change the way they live are *not* the same as people who want to escape into a fantasy."

Megan scoffed once more. She started talking.

The next few minutes were as unpleasant as they were tiresomely predictable. They were followed by a resentful, uncomfortable silence. Megan, it transpired, did not have a problem with the consciousness swapping procedure, she just didn't see why people would swap to a different species. They would never be a *real* member of that species, she explained. And besides, why would anyone want to become human? To be a lesser creature? To be little better than an animal?

We tried to point out that just because someone is born a certain way, it doesn't have to define them. Birth is a random accident, after all. Megan found this very amusing. I believe she thought we were joking. Words like 'unnatural' and 'disgusting' started to drip from her fangs. Eventually, and to my considerable relief, she stopped talking. I felt angry and sad.

Megan's strange attitude since she had first seen Sarah made a lot more sense in light of this conversation. To think I had believed she was a spy! Sarah must have known, or at least suspected. She must have thought me terrifyingly naive when we had that little chat in the galley.

"I wonder if we should take you back to your planet now," said Bainbridge, dully. "The quarantine might well have lifted. We will provide you with a boat to replace the one that was damaged, of course."

Megan looked surprised and a little hurt, but the politeness that had deserted her since the start of our conversation returned. She agreed that it was time she left us. Bainbridge asked me to locate Sarah and explain matters whilst he returned to the ship to issue Megan with a new boat.

I found Sarah in a nearby catacomb. It was dark. It smelled of wet rock. Skulls glared out at me from every nook and cranny. It was the sort of place I would have really enjoyed, were it not for the news I had come to deliver to Sarah.

On occasion, I have felt the need to object to people's comments about Sarah, particularly with regard to the form she occupied previously. After such objections, I usually worry that I have been inadvertently patronising. 'Step aside, Sarah!' my actions seem to say. 'You are incapable of speaking up for yourself! I must leap to your defence! Marvel at how brave and tolerant I am!'

My worry about these words being implied by my actions was in no way helped by the time I accidentally said all that out loud.

That unfortunate incident aside, I have since been advised that I can do as much defending as I want… as long as I'm doing it for myself. If I find something objectionable (and some of the things I hear said of Sarah's transitioned state are *highly* objectionable) then I should say so for that reason, not because I think Sarah would be upset if she heard.

Sarah was understandably a little quiet when I caught her up on recent events. She took some time to herself before returning to me. By then, I was having a nice chat with a cryptographer, who was also a naja, although she seemed to be not quite as generally furious as Megan. I was in the process of asking about the sort of crypts she photographed on the tomb world.

"You don't understand," she said as Sarah walked up. "It's nothing to do with actual crypts. It's about information security."

"How fascinating," I said, not really understanding what she was saying.

"Can we get going?" Sarah asked. "It would be nice to be back on the ship, I think."

We strolled in a companionable silence back through the tombs to the landing pad. I tried to sneak the occasional glance at the stone slabs we passed but didn't like to make it seem like I was being dragged away from the place, so I had to do this subtly.

Sarah asked if something was wrong when I cried out in pain and threw myself on the ground in order to get a better look at an elegantly-sculpted monument for the third time in as many minutes. I assured her that it was nothing.

We reached the landing pad after a short while. Bainbridge was waiting for us there. Megan was nowhere to be seen. Sarah embraced him. Bainbridge knelt into Sarah's embrace, his legs encircling her gently. A few quiet words passed between the two whilst I saw to the boat. There were tillers to be unwound, oars to be unshipped and portable atmospheric generators to be cranked.

Bainbridge appeared at my side as I was topping up the spare atmosphere generator with a few cranks.

"I say," he began, in a surprisingly timid manner, "would you mind rowing back to the ship? It has been a long day and Megan tried to explain herself on the way back, which only made things worse and then she just started going on about piracy and… "

I waved him into silence. I assured him that I would take the controls on the way back. He should stay in the stern and rest.

Bringing a small rowing boat out of orbit is a delicate and delightful task. One has to pull the oars with the right subtlety, one has to adjust one's speed so orbit is broken but not completely obliterated. No one wants to go flying off at altogether the wrong angle away from a world. Folk can get quite dizzy as you row around and around in circles, trying to find the right heading to get yourself back on track.

I rowed with a deliberate slowness but there was a strength to my actions. The feel of the oars' wood beneath my claws was comforting. The enchanting whispers of the Socal thrusters at the end of each oar lulled my senses. I rocked as I rowed and, quite without meaning to, I began to sing quietly.

The tune was one I had known for years. The words were harder to recall but I got most of them right. It was about this woman and she had this car, and she liked the car… or maybe it was a space ship. Or a rocking horse. Either way, she liked it and she wanted to hang on to it but there was this chap… I think his name was Paul or Saul or Orl. Something like that, anyway. And he didn't like the car or space ship or rocking horse and he wanted her to get rid of it. She said she didn't want to and he said that he *did* want her to, so she told him to get knotted. He said he didn't want to get knotted and she pointed out that this didn't matter a fig to her. So he said she was beastly and she said he was an oaf, and he stormed out of the café or classroom or war zone or wherever they were and she never saw him again, for which she was profoundly grateful.

Sarah signed contentedly as I reached the third verse and Bainbridge settled back in the stern and closed his eyes.

I looked ahead to see the *Cox* in the near distance, drifting against its anchor. The magnificence of its blue metallic hull was punctuated by the silver oars that slid out gracefully into the void. It made me think of home. The home I'd left behind and the new home I'd found here. It made me think about death and how one day soon I'd finally be able to rest amongst the stars, much as our beautiful warship was now doing.

The peace and tranquillity I felt in that moment was only slightly derailed by Bainbridge crying in his sleep.

Sarah and I unintentionally woke Bainbridge as we moored our rowing boat to its port on the deck of our ship. Bainbridge sprang to his claws, drew two devious-looking firearms from about his person and levelled them at us.

Sarah and I had grown accustomed to his ways by this time, so we went about our business, although a little more slowly and cautiously than we otherwise might have done. The moment only lasted for a few seconds. Bainbridge apologised, vanished his weapons into his waistcoat and told us of the dream he'd been having. Apparently, in his dream, my singing had been luring people onto rocks as they came to correct the lyrics I was poorly approximating. This amused me greatly.

We made sure the rowing boat was stowed and then went to check on Oliver. He was still unconscious in his hammock, so that was a relief. We discussed his position and decided to roll him over, because nobody likes bedsores.

My third stomach rumbled, as did Bainbridge's second. Sarah only had one stomach but hers rumbled the loudest, possibly trying to compensate for its isolation.

We looked through our packs. Sarah brought out a pie, Bainbridge uncovered a cluster of vegetables and I took out a bottle. We chopped and served and poured. We nibbled, we savoured and we drank.

Oliver still hadn't awoken by the time our meal was complete, so we poured a few doses from the bottle down his welcoming throat in the hope that he would ascribe his condition upon awakening to a hangover rather than the true events of the day.

Sarah expressed her intention to turn in. I was not yet tired, my spirits braced by the company I found myself in, and I said so. Sarah smiled and left to see to her hammock.

I looked out across the deck of the ship, up the rail and over the side. I gazed longingly at the stars and felt the air drift from me in a deep exhalation. I remembered how I had felt as I rowed towards the ship and expressed, more to myself than anything else, that I would like to take our ship on a little further into the quilted night.

Bainbridge said that was a capital idea and asked if I might enjoy his company on the bridge after he had completed his hypnotherapy. I said that I would.

Bainbridge skittered off to find a quiet corner to meditate in whilst I buzzed up to the bridge. Not wanting to rouse the sleepers in the stern, I dimmed the lights across the ship. I initially left the bridge lights on, the better to see the instruments by, but after I'd brought the engines to life, raised the anchor and started slipping inexorably forward into the cold void, I chose to surround myself in darkness. The oars drove us forward.

All was silence for… maybe an hour, until I heard a faint noise. The faint noise became a whisper, which gradually grew louder. I was eventually able to make out the words. They were: "I approach. I approach. I approach."

I frowned. "Death? Is that you?"

"No, Jay," said Bainbridge, patiently, as he entered the bridge. "It's me. I thought I'd try to alert you to my approach, as I didn't want to startle you and cause you to wake the others in your shock."

This was a very wise course of action. I nodded, my form picked out in silhouette by the light of the instruments. I asked

Bainbridge if he felt that his therapy was helping. He said that he felt that it was.

"Did I ever tell you I was once engaged to be married to a human?" Bainbridge asked, after a few moments of companionable silence.

"You did not," I said. "What happened?"

"She never got around to attending the ceremony."

"I'm sorry to hear that," I said.

Bainbridge hummed thoughtfully. "The strange thing is. I couldn't tell you *why* I got engaged to her. At the time, I thought I was in love, which is a strange thing to think about someone you've only met three or four times."

I didn't know what to say to this.

"If I had to examine my motives," said Bainbridge, apparently not minding my lack of reply, "I would have explained my actions with the following: delight at having a creature find me attractive, petty rebellion against social norms, impulsiveness, bloody-mindedness and a slight amount of sociopathy."

"I say… " I objected. Marrying a human was something that was rarely done but it wasn't necessarily indicative of sociopathy.

"Oh, there was a great deal of other stuff going on at the time which I needn't get into now," Bainbridge said. "Let us just say that my attraction to this human was complex and not as pure as I would have liked to make out at the time. The reason I bring it up, Jay, is that it was the first time I'd really interacted with a human in a way that wasn't connected to stopping them from harming themselves or each other in some way. I had no idea that there was anything other than self-destruction in their tiny little heads."

"And many of them don't even have that," I said. "Sarah has introduced me to several humans who aren't in the least bit self-destructive. They abstain entirely from hunting their fellow kind for sport, they abandoned killing creatures for food and they even bathe in water. It's remarkable what can be achieved under the right conditions."

"But we only know this about humanity because we have a personal connection to humans. What can be done with the arachnid about town, who only sees... what we used to see? Sorry for making assumptions about your past, Jay."

"No, you're quite right," I said, remembering the times when, as a youth, I would see frightful things happening to humans and consider it perfectly usual instead of tragic. We were all young and stupid once. There was also the occasion when... but I did not like to dwell on that.

"There must be a way to present humanity to other species as something other than it appears," said Bainbridge. "I mean... how did you come to live with Sarah?"

I told him.

Chapter Five

On Humans and Why It's Not Easy Being Blue

The first time I'd met Sarah, she had been sitting on the end of my bed. She was neatly dressed and her head-fur was tied back behind her head, leaving her obviously intelligent features as the first thing I saw.

Seeing her like this was strange for me as, like many of my kind, I sleep on my back, my legs curled until my claws touch my thorax. This meant her bizarre human torso stretched upwards and her tiny, piercing eyes bored into me as her face met my ceiling.

At the time, The 17th Grand Battle Fleet had been at war with a set of blue people who lived on some planet in the rough part of the antipodal spiral leg of the galaxy. The blue chaps had been buzzing about the place, assimilating other species into their culture. I say *assimilating...* it was more like a large-scale kidnapping effort, but there isn't really a succinct word for that. Species-napping? No, not that. That's a terrible term for it.

Anyhow, one of the planets the blue fellows purloined belonged to some humans and Sarah happened to be living there. The humans hadn't enjoyed being assimilated into the society of blue people. This wasn't because the people in question were blue, as far as I understood it. The humans would have objected if anyone had invaded them. Goodness knows they make an awful fuss any time we need to kick them off a planet that is about to explode, or fall into a black hole or something.

The humans didn't like being kidnapped but they were armed with sharp sticks and primitive firearms, whereas the blue fellows had advanced pulse weapons and smart missile systems, so the humans had to put up with being subjugated.

The blue chaps got on a bit of a roll after a while and ended up attacking one of the ships of the 17th Grand Battle Fleet. This ship had belonged to a scatter-brained arachnid called Jeremy. Jeremy should have been with the rest of the fleet, on manoeuvres on the other side of the galaxy, but had got lost.

For the blue chaps, attacking Jeremy was a mistake. The 17th Grand Battle Fleet arrived the following day and started attacking anything blue, or that looked like it might be thinking of turning blue, in revenge for the slight. I had been the strategist attached to the flagship. It had been my job to make sure that we were engaging in an efficient, devastating war that would remind certain young species that you just didn't go around attacking people's spaceships all over the place. It wasn't polite.

So, it had been decided by our commander that we were to invade some planets in this blue empire, ignore some entirely (allowing the blue fools a safe haven to retreat to) and wipe certain others from known space. This was because the commander of the battle fleet had been enjoying the manoeuvres the fleet had been on and therefore deeply resented being called away to sort out Jeremy's mess.

I had decided that the planet that had been under human control until recently was to be destroyed utterly. I had assessed it as having no significant life to preserve.

Our fleet pulled into orbit and started broadcasting a fair warning message. The message simply gave any sentient species one planetary rotation to remove themselves from the vicinity. I considered it reasonable at the time.

Anyway, some blue space craft pinged away at our battleships for a while after we broadcast the warning but it turned out that they had no way to shield against our Devastation Strength weapons, so that little annoyance didn't last long. The attack was to proceed in the morning so I went to bed with a mug of slimy rumen and a book.

I woke up in the middle of the night to find the light of my bed chamber on. I was confused by this, certain I had turned it off after becoming bored by a chapter about my book's main character demonstrating how amazing she was by competing in a combined pie eating contest/martial arts tournament. As my vision came into focus, I saw Sarah.

I opened my mouth to cry for help. I believe my rationale for this at the time was that nobody liked to be surprised by vermin in the middle of the night. Such thoughts were not uncommon for me at that time.

Sarah behaved quite differently from any human I had ever seen before. She leant forward and placed a foreleg gently to my jaws. This shocked me into total silence.

Prior to this instance, I had lived something of a sheltered life. I had rarely seen humans in the flesh. I had seen some in the occasional nature documentary. Nature documentaries are fine things but they tend to sensationalise or romanticise, showing humans burrowing into the ground to create dens or freezing their food. This human on my bed was obviously very different.

"Hello," said Sarah. She spoke in my language, the arachnid tongue. Her voice was crisp and pleasant. There was breeding behind it.

Aristocracy, I should say. There is breeding behind a great deal of human voices. As I understand it, the real trick is to get humans to *stop* breeding for five minutes. Yes, aristocracy is a much better word.

"I would very much like it," said Sarah, "if you would refrain from obliterating the planet you are orbiting. Ask me why."

My eyes shot from side to side. "Ffry?" I mumbled. Sarah's palm was still pressed to my mouth, which meant my elocution was suboptimal.

"Because there are millions of innocent lives at stake. Make an outraged noise."

I had been in the preparatory stages of making an outraged noise when Sarah made that second request. Being explicitly invited to do just that threw me a little. I did make the noise (I had been asked to, after all) but it didn't quite have the same vigour as it might have had otherwise.

"I am not talking about the blue fire cadre, I am talking about the humans. Scoff."

That time, I remained silent. It was becoming increasingly obvious that the human was someone I should be listening to. After a few seconds of silence, Sarah leaned towards me. She bared her fangs.

"I said… I want you to scoff."

"But… why?" I asked.

"Because I want you to know that I know *everything* about you. I want you to know that I can predict how you will react before you know yourself. I want you to know that I am permitting these reactions. For now. If you react in a way I do not permit, there will be consequences. Now. I want you to scoff. Please comply."

I scoffed, somewhat half-heartedly.

"That's better," she said. "Humans are sentient. They do not deserve to die because another species attacked you. Especially not when there are much better ways of accomplishing your goals."

She sat back and removed her claw from my mouth. "Speak," she commanded.

"May I move?" I asked. I'm not entirely sure why I asked. I could have crushed her human body using only two legs. I was captivated by her words and the sinister yet delightfully vague threats she'd made moments ago.

"You may," said Sarah.

I rolled upright, disentangled myself from my bedclothes and skittered over to a chair in the corner of my quarters. Sarah rotated to face me.

"How else might we accomplish our goals?" I asked, suspicion attempting to edge its way into my voice but being batted away by curiosity.

Sarah's mouth widened in what appeared at the time to be a death rictus. I later learned that this was called a grin.

"Arm the humans. The 17th Grand Battle Fleet has enough weaponry to destroy a sizeable part of the galaxy. Give a tiny fraction of the most horribly imaginative weapons you can to the humans and they'll take care of the fire cadre. You may speak."

"It would be much easier to just kill everybody," I said. This was a dreadfully silly thing to say, but I was tired.

Sarah inclined her head, graciously. "It would, but think how humiliating it would be for the fire cadre. Your commander wants to express her displeasure at them, correct? Imagine how horrible it would be for an advanced race to suddenly lose to humans."

This was a particularly well put point. We discussed the possibility for an hour, the plan gradually growing in my mind until

I could feel every tendril, every ripple of consequence that would result from such an action clearly. I finally agreed.

That moment of clarity having passed, I suddenly started to wonder again who, exactly, this human was and what she was doing in my room.

Sarah explained her past. She explained that she was wise to the security of arachnid fleets, having served on one, and knew how to slip through unobtrusively when necessary. I asked, agog, if she'd once been part of the Special Operations Unit. She said she hadn't, she'd just enjoyed slipping away from her ship to visit local bars and gambling saloons.

Her history was how she had anticipated my every move in our early conversation. She explained that she'd visited five or six other officers before me and the conversations with those individuals had been less productive. They had asked why, they had made the outraged noise, they had scoffed. When they had been given the chance to speak, they had said nothing helpful.

Had I not been captivated by Sarah's intelligence, I would have ended up like the other arachnids Sarah had visited: sedated and, presumably, having rather embarrassing dreams.

There was one final point I needed to raise. "The humans on the planet. What will they do after they are free of the blue people? They'd still have all those weapons… " I let the implication hang in the air.

Sarah explained that this would, usually, be a concern. She informed me that she had a cabal of like-minded people stationed on the planet who were working with community leaders to try to moderate the humans' darkest instincts. When the time came, Sarah assured me, the humans almost certainly – *probably* – wouldn't immediately turn on each other.

This was good enough for me. I woke my commander up, which was a dangerous opening gambit, but when I explained why

I had done so and how deliciously humiliating Sarah's idea would be, the strategy was accepted.

There was one slight niggle: I was sent down to the planet's surface with Sarah to co-ordinate matters. This was apparently because my commander didn't want to just hand advanced technology over to the humans and hope for the best, no matter how persuasive Sarah was. Even if we translated the user manuals into the human language, who knew how many of them would be able to read them? Would they use the manuals for food? Would they use them as sanitary items? Would they bury them in the hope they'd grow into trees? I didn't know the answers to any of my commander's questions, so I kept quiet.

My commander insisted that arachnids must be present if we weren't just going to wipe out the planet. We'd need to explain how to use the weapons and then, when the humans forgot what we told them, we'd have to explain again. This was the stated reason. The unstated reason, the reason that was written clearly across my commander's face, was that this was my brilliant suggestion and if it went wrong, I was going to be in the middle of it when it blew up.

My commander really resented being woken up before her eight REM cycles passed. I selected a team of twenty trainers, logisticians and bodyguards. We took three shuttles down to the planet: one for the twenty arachnids, to say nothing of Sarah, and two for the weapons.

The plan went smoothly, after a few minor accidents. The humans really didn't get the concept of an overcharge setting. We explained over and over again that our most powerful weapons would overcharge and explode if treated poorly. Two or three cities were reduced to their component elements because a human forgot what they were doing in the middle of a firefight and held down the firing stud on their weapon for too long.

The blue chaps fought back. Of course they did, but the humans were determined. More than that, they had the technology to back up their determination. A platoon of blue chaps would lay into a strategically important location, but humans would pour from windows, rooftops, out of sewer grates and air ducts, from every conceivable hiding spot and rain down vengeance upon anything blue.

Unfortunately, the sky on the planet in question was blue, so more than a few flying creatures were unnecessarily culled. But every war has unfortunate casualties.

More and more blue chaps arrived. The humans eliminated them with a complete lack of style but a certain admirable determination. I stayed with Sarah because she was the only person who could persuade the humans to not run away from me. Together, we managed to co-ordinate things so that human casualties were high but not tragically high.

The planet smelled and I kept getting my claws muddy. That aside, the challenge was enjoyable. Trying to organise humans is a little bit like trying to herd Arthonian Mecha-Crocodiles – the trick is getting them to understand what you want whilst stopping them from biting their own legs off in boredom. After a certain amount of trial and error, not to say consultation with Sarah, I found myself making headway.

To my surprise, after the third month, I found myself warming to the squishy, odourful mammals. There was just something so ·fiercely tenacious about them.

The blue chaps couldn't keep up their war forever because my battle fleet had obliterated their presence everywhere else in the system. The humans took a little longer than I would have liked to mop up the stragglers, possibly because they heard me use that term and thought I was encouraging them to be hygienic.

Those humans, it seemed, did not enjoy hygiene. It did not speak to them. I showed some of them soap, once, and they stared blankly at me. In my claw, they saw mere animal fat scented with gentle fragrances and carved into an amusing shape. I knew what they were thinking: 'Why do you wish to apply this to my flesh? What good will it do? It may improve my condition in the short term but the next time I see a muddy puddle, I will not be able to resist the urge to roll in it. Thus, the good work will be undone. Far better to not waste the effort'.

Once it had been repeatedly explained that mopping up stragglers was merely an expression and they did not actually need to clean themselves or their surroundings, the humans finally took to the idea. They drove the blue chaps from their planet and established a government.

Watching this step was fascinating. History tells us that whenever humans establish a government, they include self-defeating rules at every stage. They self-sabotage. They take a fundamentally decent idea, like democracy (far from the best governmental system but it has the benefit of being easy to understand), and seem to pick the least effective possible system. First past the post is the option humans usually go for, rather than single transferable vote or even mixed member representation.

'Why?' they are asked. 'Why would you pick the most unrepresentative and inefficient democratic option possible?'

There are many possible answers. Status quo bias, appeal to tradition, sheer bloody-mindedness... personally, I believe that the humans are historically plagued by self-doubt. They give themselves the system they feel they deserve. The poor chaps don't deserve first past the post democracy, of course. Nobody deserves that... but that's self-doubt for you. It does horrible things to a person.

First past the post would likely have been the system these current humans ended up with… were it not for Sarah's little cabal. They had grown close to many of the senior humans on the planet and, when the humans formed a government, Sarah's group were the ones they turned to for advice.

It was Sarah's cabal that advised the humans form a government based on a more solid and representative system than democracy. I forget what system they ended up using because, sadly, it didn't last long.

The thing about giving humans weapons is that, after the things have ceased to be useful, the weapons themselves persist. They sit on shelves and languish in cupboards. Humans cannot abide objects of power that go unused and so, despite the hard work of Sarah's friends, the humans began to tear each other apart.

I had remained on the planet as part of my fleet's efforts to get the star system into something close to working order after kicking the blue chaps out. I was there when the first cities were vaporised. I was there when Sarah's cabal were turned upon. Sarah was the only one I was able to save. The planet was all but lifeless two months after the last blue creature had been removed from its surface.

Sarah took some considerable time to recover. She was badly wounded during the insurrection and it was only the medical facilities on my ship that saved her life. Even after she had physically recovered, the fate of the planet she had called home for some years and the humans she had known there weighed heavily on her. She barely spoke, she barely ate, she barely moved.

My fleet left the system and, not knowing what else to do with her and not wanting to simply cast her to the winds, I requested that Sarah be allowed to stay with us.

Sarah came back to herself slowly. We had medics on our ship who had seen people in such a terrible state before. They gradually helped her find herself again. At first, it seemed that Sarah neither wanted nor appreciated my company, but this changed. She started asking to see me. We would talk of this and that... and gradually, an idea formed in my brain.

Ranan, the planet I live on, had a large human population. That is how I now describe it. Before meeting Sarah, I described it much as the local council did: that there was a pest problem.

The river that winds across our planet had uncountable tributaries and offshoots. Where there were rivers, there were riverbanks and where there were riverbanks, there were humans. They combed the beaches for shells, bones and dead birds. They built primitive huts that were obliterated by the rising tide. Numerous pest control measures had been attempted over the years, but no permanent solution had ever been found. I mentioned this to Sarah, in more sympathetic terms, and wondered out loud if there might be someone kind enough to help with the situation.

Sarah did not take to the idea. It caused anxiety attacks that, I'm told, set back her recovery several months. I did not mention it again.

Sarah *did* mention it again, however. Her recovery progressed and she started working in logistics on my ship. Two years after we first met, we were celebrating the end of my tour of duty with a few friends in a cabaret club. During a lull in the conversation, she brought up the idea that I had steadfastly not mentioned for some considerable time. She said she thought it might be just the thing for her.

The next week, once bags were packed and goodbyes were said, we travelled back to my planet together. I helped her find a flat and she started working with human community leaders. She even found a small, secretive group of people who, like her, had not always been human. She told me that this wasn't uncommon. People of similar mindsets tended to seek each other out, after all.

I remained deeply disturbed by my actions concerning humans, given that it was a chance encounter that had caused my change of heart, rather than reading a well thought out article in a news feed or a rationalist debate with some chap at the club. I did not like dwelling on the sort of person I would have continued existing as, had I not met Sarah.

Chapter Six

Bainbridge Establishes That 'It' Is Done

I slept surprisingly well, after relaying this story to Bainbridge, only occasionally being awoken by the handsome chap's moans. It was dawn by the time we, as a group, were woken by Oliver swearing at us.

What he actually said was a bit garbled. Presumably because he was still feeling the after-effects of Megan's venom. He was behaving chaotically, running between our hammocks and screaming unintelligibly before staring out into the void, clutching at his head-fur and screaming again.

The reason I initially described him as swearing is simple: the only words I could understand in between the more or less constant screaming were ones I would hesitate to use around my mother. Unless she used them first and I was absolutely certain of what they meant.

Sarah wasn't fazed by this behaviour, it being not particularly unusual, other than the garbled nature of Oliver's actual problem. She heaved a spare pillow at him but missed due to Oliver's erratic movement.

I reacted to Oliver's rage as I normally did, by curling my legs to my chest and feeling my consciousness collapse in on itself like a terrified cave system.

Bainbridge, for his part, wasn't used to Oliver's little ways. He leapt from his bunk, weapons bristling from three of his legs, and swarmed up an electrical discharge pylon. He swung around the pylon a few times. He was either getting his bearings or indulging in a brief moment of childish hijinks, the way many of us used to before the pressures of the real world intruded upon our lives.

Whatever the explanation, Bainbridge stopped sharply on his fourth rotation. A spyglass emerged from the side of his skull and whipped into place over his two rightmost eyes. He peered into the distance for a few seconds. Then, with no warning other than a slight tightening of the jaw, he leapt from the pylon and landed on top of Oliver.

Oliver reacted well, all things considered. He grasped at the legs that Bainbridge wrapped around his throat and attempted to flip the other arachnid off his back by tipping himself forwards and stamping his rear legs into the deck of the ship. I was impressed by Oliver's quick thinking, but what was more impressive was Bainbridge's reaction.

He didn't resist Oliver's attempts to throw him. Instead, he allowed himself to be thrown. Bainbridge landed on the deck with a juddering crash but broke his fall with two spare legs. As he did this, he used his momentum to pull Oliver down into a choke hold.

Oliver suddenly found himself lying on top of Bainbridge, his legs tangled uselessly. Bainbridge lay on his back, every leg wrapped around Oliver except one... and that one held a sizeable energy weapon to Oliver's head.

"Who are they?" Bainbridge growled. "And what do they want?"

Sarah looked from Bainbridge to Oliver, and then to me. I felt my thoughts uncurl now that the weight of Oliver's rage was lifted. As the seconds passed, it became more and more obvious that something sinister was happening. Something more worrisome than one of Oliver's little moments of indiscretion.

"Speak," said Bainbridge. Oliver simply gibbered.

"B," said Sarah, approaching him with caution, "what's up?"

"Look what's approaching to aft," said Bainbridge, placing the barrel of his gun mere millimetres from Oliver's eye.

Sarah and I looked.

There were ships approaching. Several of them. They were heavily armed. They were heading straight for us. They didn't carry the markings of any military organisation I knew of. They did, however, fly flags. They flew the most terrifying flag to those who brave the interstellar lanes: the solid teal flag of the cut-throats and vagabonds that indulge in piracy.

That flag sent a shiver through my exoskeleton. There is a reason why teal is seen as a somewhat uncouth colour... and I was staring at that reason.

"They're sending a message," said Bainbridge, who was still immobile.

"What does it say?" Sarah asked.

Bainbridge didn't reply. Instead, he tapped into our ship's internal broadcast channel and played the message through the speakers that were placed around the deck.

"OLIVER!" boomed the speakers. "OLIVER!"

Sarah and I looked at Oliver. Bainbridge looked at Oliver. Oliver looked at the deck.

I felt cold. I could feel myself shutting out all information I didn't need. I could feel myself focusing on what would be needed to resolve this situation. I felt time begin to slow.

This had happened frequently during my tours of duty. When a mission had taken a distinctly unpleasant turn, or we had been ambushed. I needed to *think*, to work through our options and establish a course of action.

I had questions. Why did the pirates want Oliver? This was irrelevant. The fact was, they wanted him. I wondered who they were but, whilst this would be useful information later on, it didn't help at this stage.

I looked out at the pirate ships.

There were four of them: one behemoth, which was probably a troop carrier, and three smaller ones. The three smaller ships were arranged in a line directly underneath the troop carrier. It looked like they intended to fly beneath us, possibly to latch onto our hull and pin us in position. The troop carrier would move alongside us, and we would be boarded.

These pirates had enough crew for a flotilla of four ships. To board a ship like ours with our skeleton crew, they would only need a small boarding party. That meant these pirates had resources to spare. We were outnumbered and outgunned.

Judging by the speed of the pirate ships, they would be launching their attack in two minutes. We could not bring our ship's main battery online in that time. There were anti-personnel weapons at points around the deck. We could defend our position for some minutes using those until a more permanent solution could be found.

We could head below deck and hide, but that would mean abandoning the bridge to the pirates. We would lose the advantage of our deck weaponry and have fewer places to retreat to.

We needed to make our stand here. Our chances were less than good. Bainbridge would be an asset, but Sarah's body was not built for combat and I had never been comfortable under fire. I'd just never got the hang of it.

Oliver could fight. Whether he would stand with us or not was another question. I shook myself mentally. That was ridiculous. *Of course* Oliver would stand with us. We had 100 seconds.

"Attend to the guns!" I cried.

Bainbridge didn't move. Sarah started running around in circles.

I grabbed Sarah's pathetically small shoulders and pointed her in the direction of the twin-linked pyroblasters stationed on the port side. They were the smallest and easiest to use of the weapons. I strode to Bainbridge and laid my hand on a free leg.

"We must defend ourselves, Bainbridge. Will you stand with us?"

His eyes snapped up to meet mine and I could see he was insulted by any suggestion that he would not. Good. Far better for him to be indignant and focus on the matter at hand than keep trying to extract information from Oliver.

He paused for five seconds we could barely spare. I could hear Sarah cranking frantically at the charging station of the pyroblasters, trying to bring the ignition flares online. Something clicked in Bainbridge's expression and he flung Oliver to one side.

"You have a plan, Jay?" he asked, bounding to his feet.

Calling this set of actions I had decided on a *plan* might be exaggerating things slightly, but still… I nodded and indicated the weapon placement that would cause most damage in the hands of someone like Bainbridge.

I scuttled over to Oliver, hearing Bainbridge cry 'yoiks!' behind me. I lifted Oliver to his feet and dusted him down. "Take your position next to me, old chap," I said. "We won't let them take you."

There were two guns on the starboard side where we would be most useful. I didn't have the time to retrieve my service weapon from my pack, so I hurried to the emplacement on the left and removed its dust cover. Underneath was an elegant barrel leading back to a flechette hopper. I hooked the ammunition belt from the hopper to the ignition chamber that would superheat the shards of metal. I checked the connection between the ignition chamber and the barrel and found it free of obstruction. The gas canister at the base of the weapon was nearly full, but I fumbled the connection between it and the mechanism and wasted precious seconds making sure everything was correctly connected.

Once I was satisfied, I sighted at the nearest ship, the one that was approximately fifteen seconds out of firing range. "Test fire!" I cried, and squeezed the firing stud. A burst of superheated metal shards flew harmlessly into the void. My weapon was ready. I heard shouts of "Test fire!" from the others and jets of fire and super-concentrated acid jetted from the guns of my companions.

I took a moment to reflect. What a feeling it would be to stand next to Oliver in battle. We had served together before, we had even taken part in the same battles occasionally… but I had only once before had the honour of fighting side by side with my old friend. The thrill of that long-past moment soared through me and a smile ghosted across my jaw.

What a battle this would be. My oldest friend Oliver, my great friend Sarah and noble Bainbridge. We might not all live to see tomorrow, but given my fate otherwise would be a slow and painful death to the mindvirus… I could not think of a better way to die than standing and fighting with my three comrades.

"Hey," said Sarah, bringing me out of the rather pleasant moment I was having. "Where's Oliver?"

I looked to my right, at the other flechette gun that was allocated to Oliver. He wasn't there. I looked around. I couldn't see him anywhere.

"Hey!" said Bainbridge. He pointed.

Oliver had taken a lifeboat. He was rowing towards the pirate troop carrier with as much speed as he could muster. He was waving his free legs. What was the blighter doing?

The smaller ships had been readying harpoons but paused at the sight of the approaching rowboat. Sarah, Bainbridge and I held our breath, along with our fire. Oliver's lifeboat drew up alongside the deck of the troop carrier. I could see him being hauled out by several figures. Some were arachnid, some I didn't immediately recognise and I was pretty sure I could see a naja whose colouring was similar to Megan's.

Oliver appeared to be shouting something, but the airless void of space swallowed his words before they reached us. The pirates didn't seem particularly interested in what he had to say. One of them swung a nasty-looking object into Oliver's abdomen and he crumpled.

The three smaller ships appeared to reach a decision and retreated from us, back to the carrier.

"Er… " said Bainbridge.

The carrier spun on its central axis.

"Are they… " said Sarah. Yes. They were. The carrier and the other three ships throttled up their engines and sped away from us at full speed, back the way they had come.

"Well… " said Bainbridge. "That happened."

We stared as the ships retreated.

"Should we… go after them?" Sarah asked.

"Their ships are considerably faster than ours," said Bainbridge.

"Ah."

"A pity, really."

A pity? Did Bainbridge revel in understating the case? My friend of forty years had been kidnapped by pirates and I was powerless to do anything about it. This was a tragedy of monumental proportions.

"About Oliver?" Sarah asked, her voice also lacking the grief-ridden sobs I would have expected.

"No," said Bainbridge. "I was looking forward to seeing if I could defend our ship to the last, as I would have liked, or if I would crack under the pressure and run away to hide."

Sarah approached me. "I say, are you all right, Jay?"

I realised I was shaking.

"It's okay, dear one," she said, placing her tiny human claw on my leg. "They've gone. We're safe."

I felt my legs give way beneath me. I slumped. First onto my abdomen, then onto my side. The deck darkened half of my vision. The other half began to blur.

I felt claws on me.

As I believe I may have mentioned, it was a shock to find out that my mind was the thing that would eventually end my life. I had always expected it to be my liver that would get me.

I find this all very amusing. How could I not? We are nothing but a pinpoint of light living in something that could self-destruct at any moment. A body can be crushed by falling lumber. A sudden decompression event can whisk one out of a star ship, leading to asphyxiation.

And we can always be placed into a new body, this is true. Replacements can be found. One's consciousness can be scraped out of whatever receptacle it was languishing in and stuffed into a new body. So, what are we left with? This thing that lives in bodies, that thinks and feels… that is apart from everything. It's a joke. A pleasantry.

Worry gets the better of me from time to time, I am sorry to say. There are days when I can do very little other than worry. On other occasions, I can feel overcome… not by what shape my doom will take, but what actions I took to make the extinguishment of my consciousness seem attractive. On these occasions, I do not find the jollity in my situation.

I thought of Oliver, fighting for his life on a pirate ship. We were unable to render assistance. All was lost.

No.

I lifted my head from where it lay, causing Sarah to jump back. There was something we could do. How foolish I had been to not see it before! We must inform the authorities of his situation without delay. That was the only course of action we could take.

The authorities must be aware of the pirates. The ship that we had bumped into by the lock yesterday would have made sure of that. That meant they would be quick to act.

The pirates were unlikely to take Oliver's life immediately. He was a man of means. He would no doubt inform the pirates that I would pay a considerable sum to have him returned safely. That was what happened the last three times he got himself kidnapped, after all.

I leapt to my feet.

"Oh, hello," said Bainbridge. "You're back. Shall we have tea?"

"There is no time for tea!" I announced, after spending ten or eleven minutes ruminating on the merits of Bainbridge's suggestion before dismissing it on the grounds of how terribly urgent our situation was. "We must act immediately!"

"Golly!" said Bainbridge, looking up from the cup of tea that had appeared in his claws. "What are we going to do?"

"We must inform the authorities at once!" I cried, pointing in the direction of the ship's communication apparatus.

"What about?" asked Bainbridge.

"Oliver's kidnapping!" I cried once more, maintaining my gesture towards the communication apparatus.

"Why?" asked Bainbridge, sipping gently from his cup.

"Oh, give me strength," I said. I did not need the approval of my compatriots. I stomped towards the apparatus. I could hear Sarah scuttling after me.

"You're right, of course, Jay," she said. "We should try to find what happened to Oliver… but he did appear to make his way to the pirate ship willingly. We cannot be sure that he is in danger."

I brushed this aside, being careful not to brush Sarah aside as I did so. Human bodies are dreadfully fragile.

I grasped the communication horn and dialled into the emergency assistance line.

"Good morning," said a pleasant voice. "How may I be of assistance?"

"Good morning," I said. "I say, sorry to bother you."

"Not at all," said the voice.

"Glad to hear it. Well, this is dashed difficult, but my friend has been kidnapped by pirates."

"Oh, what bad luck!"

"Isn't it? Can you help?"

"Me? No, not at all. I've got all this filing to do, you see."

"Ah," I said. "Is there anyone else there who can help?"

"Yes, you know what, I think there might be," said my new friend. "I'm pretty sure we have one of those special task force things to deal with pirate kidnappings. There are a few of them happening at the moment. What's their number?"

"I'm afraid I'm not sure… " I said.

"My remark was purely rhetorical," said the voice. "Here we go. Please hold the line whilst your call is transferred."

There was a whirr.

"Hello," said a new voice. "And thank you for calling the pirate kidnapping task force. All our operatives are currently busy. You are being held in a queue. Your call will be answered as soon as possible."

Music emerged from the communication horn. I glared at it.

I do not like using new-fangled apparatus such as interstellar communication hubs, and this experience was doing nothing to modify my opinion.

"What's up?" asked Sarah.

"I am being held in a queue," I said.

"I don't understand," said Sarah. "There's just the two of us here."

"I mean my call is being held in some sort of virtual queue."

"I don't understand," she repeated.

I didn't fully understand either, honestly, but I attempted to explain to Sarah what the various voices had said to me. No light dawned in Sarah's eyes, even after I'd been over everything twice. I was winding up for a third attempt when Bainbridge stuck his head onto the bridge.

"I say," he said, "I've hit on a promising line of inquiry that might shed some light on this situation. I suggest we investigate what it is that Oliver has locked up in the hold. It may be that was what the pirates were after."

"No," I said, "No, no, no, we couldn't possibly do that. That would involve delving into dear Oliver's personal property. That sort of thing's just not done."

Bainbridge appeared to consider this. "Isn't it? Let's find out, shall we?" he said, exiting stage left. Sarah followed, having to scamper to keep up.

"Find out what?" I heard her calling.

"Find out if it's done!" was the last I heard of Bainbridge's voice. He sounded rather pleased with himself.

I blinked three or four of my eyes. I checked the communication horn. Music was still emerging from it. I looked through the bridge windows at Bainbridge's rapidly retreating back. I was confused.

I attempted to route the communication signal to my data panel and then remembered that Sarah had stashed it somewhere. I blustered for a few moments, then found a remote communication access device stashed in a supply box on top of a flare gun and a magazine depicting gentlenids of many walks of life engaging in… sporting activities. There were a few rowing, several playing tennis… some were wrestling… quite a few appeared to be wrestling, actually. I didn't know it was the fashion to wear that style of clothing whilst wrestling, if I was honest. When I was at Hounders, my college at Oxenfurt University, we'd worn something completely different.

I was beginning to feel a little warm under the collar, so I grabbed the remote communication access device and made a mental note to come back and thoroughly investigate just what was going on with this sporting magazine.

I then immediately lost my mental note, but I was pretty sure I'd remember having made it, so that would probably lead me to remember what I had written on it.

I scuttled downstairs to the cargo hold as I routed the communication frequency to the remote access device. I could hear Bainbridge and Sarah struggling with something. What were those two up to?

Upon entering, I found the cargo hold was different from how I remembered it. It was still dank, it was still a little under-lit. There was still the enormous crate in the centre. Bainbridge and Sarah were there. The tentacles were new. I'm pretty sure I hadn't seen them before.

There were about fifty of them, and they looked mechanical. Most of them seemed remarkably sharp and those that didn't were armed with whirling blades or pyro-casters. They appeared to have sprung from the crate for some reason, and were in the process of attacking Sarah and Bainbridge.

Bainbridge had two sleek, black firearms in his claws and was blasting for all he was worth at the tentacles nearest to him. A thin, silver sliver snaked behind him and struck towards his thorax. Bainbridge sensed it and dodged, causing the tentacle to skewer one of its fellows instead.

"I say!" I said.

My attention was drawn to Sarah. She had her service weapon drawn but she, being human, was significantly slower than Bainbridge. A blade sliced towards her head. Sarah snapped off three quick shots that ripped the tentacle to shreds, as well as two others that had been preparing a similar attack. Sarah took a step backwards and turned to face another tentacle. This one was bearing down on her with some sort of drill. Sarah shot at it, but it swooped to the side at the last moment.

Sarah took another step backwards. Her weapon was now dry. I saw her reloading whilst she kept her eyes on the tentacle. She wouldn't be able to bring her weapon to bear in time. She just wasn't fast enough.

I threw myself forwards. I didn't have my weapon, it was still in my pack, but my form was armoured in a way Sarah's wasn't. I snatched the tentacle from the air as it made a fresh stab for Sarah. The blasted thing appeared nearly at the extent of its reach, so there was plenty to grab. I hauled it taught and heard the tell-tale click of an ammunition port sliding shut. I stepped to the side, leaving only empty air between my form and the tentacle. There was the sharp slam of a gunshot and the tentacle was suddenly light in my hand. It had been severed halfway along its length. I tossed it aside and stepped out of Sarah's way, so as not to block her aim.

"I've got it!" cried Bainbridge cheerily.

"Got what?" yelled Sarah, before taking a shot at yet another tentacle. This one appeared to be wielding a cricket bat, but it was reduced to its component parts before I could be sure.

"The security protocols! One second!" said Bainbridge. One second passed. "There we go!"

The tentacles froze... and then retreated back into the crate.

Sarah exhaled for what seemed like a very long time. Her eyes were locked on the crate. I saw her fish two ammunition canisters from her waistcoat and load them into her service weapon. Her little human hands didn't shake. My claws most definitely did.

Bainbridge was fiddling with a panel on the side of the crate. He appeared to be making progress. I was about to join him, as I was sure there was something I was supposed to be asking him, before I paused. A thought struck me. I sidled close to Sarah.

"Sarah," I hissed.

She didn't look up at me. Her eyes were locked on the crate. "What is it, my dear?" she said.

"Did I patronise you just now?" I asked.

Sarah blinked a few times. "Because you intervened with that drill... thing? No, no, that was very nice of you, thank you."

"It's just, I saw you were reloading," I said.

"Exactly. You would have done the same for anyone else, yes?"

"Just so."

"And you'd like anyone else to do the same for you?"

"I would."

Sarah turned to me and smiled. She has quite a lovely smile. "Thank you, Jay. I appreciate you being so quick on your claws."

I have always been absolutely terrible at taking compliments. I was also rather embarrassed to discuss such subjects. The adrenaline was still pumping through me, making it extremely difficult to think calmly.

I did, however, remember why I'd come down to the hold in the first place.

"Bainbridge!" I said, stepping forward and almost falling as I trod on a loose piece of tentacle. "Did you find out?"

Bainbridge didn't look away from the panel on the crate. "Sorry?"

"You said you were finding out whether something was done. Did you?"

"Oh, that. Not yet. Give me a moment."

I waited for several moments whilst I tried to remember what it was, exactly, that Bainbridge had been talking about. I was still mortified after my conversation with Sarah and a claw continued to hold the remote communication link to the local police service. I checked that I was still on standby. I was.

I realised what Bainbridge was talking about just as he said, "And it seems like it *is* done, that's good to know."

There was a beep from the crate. The sides fell away, leaving a mechanical chrysalis that towered seven metres tall. It was breathtaking, but I had no time for awe. The chrysalis was opening. It cracked down its length and yawned open in a lazy, yet decidedly menacing movement.

The walls of the chrysalis were thick and heavily armoured. What could be inside that would need such protection? Thick gas bellowed from within. A claw reached out of the smoke and gripped the side of the chrysalis, buckling the smooth surface. Another claw followed, then another.

I realised I might have been asking the wrong question. What could be inside this chrysalis that would need such heavily armoured walls to *contain* it?

A creature unfurled from the chrysalis. It towered over us.

It was covered in spiked, red armour, with dark blue fur visible in its few unarmoured areas. It had six legs in total and stood upon three of them, the other three ending in small clusters of deadly-looking claws. As we watched, portions of the creature's armour slid aside and weapons unfolded into the creature's grip. The pieces of armour that had moved then returned to their original position, sealing themselves tight. The creature's triple heads were seated on thick, cabled necks. Each head featured one cluster of fifty or so eyes in its centre, and several mechanical sensors implanted into the sides. A huge mouth ran from one side of each face to the other. If this creature was to fully open its jaws, it could swallow me in three bites; one from each head.

"Hello?" said the remote communication device in my ear. "Anti-Piracy Squad, how may I be of assistance?"

The creature roared.

"I'm going to have to call you back," I said.

Chapter Seven

The Lower Biggleswade Alcohol and Crumpet Society

Bainbridge had his weapon trained on the creature.

Sarah had her weapon trained on the creature.

I did not have a weapon. I felt a little left out. And terrified. The creature roared again. Bainbridge shifted his grip and drew two more guns from parts of his clothing I wouldn't like to speculate about. Sarah was sweating. The creature roared once more and then doubled over, coughing.

Sarah, Bainbridge and I looked at each other.

"It's okay, it's okay," screamed the creature. "I've got some blasted dust in my lungs. Right. Where do you want me?"

It looked around blearily. It stood up and cracked one of its necks from side to side. The other two heads appeared to focus on the door that led from the cargo bay.

"Don't tell me, don't tell me!" it said. "I'm going out there."

It stumbled towards the door, ignoring us completely. Bainbridge and Sarah moved out of its path, keeping their weapons trained on it all the way.

"Where are they, then?" I heard it roaring as it crashed up the stairs. "Come hither, fools. I have something to show you!"

"I'm confused," said Sarah, after the echoes died away.

We were silent for a short time. Thunderous cries drifted down from the upper decks.

"We'd better see what it's up to," said Bainbridge after a while.

I looked at Sarah and she nodded. We followed Bainbridge out of the cargo hold. When we reached the deck of our ship, we found Bainbridge standing quietly twenty metres or so behind the creature. The creature was screaming defiance. It was also standing at the stern of the ship, firing its weapons into the empty void of space.

"Take that, you swine!" it screamed at one point, and, "Have at you!" at another.

One of its heads flick for a moment to look at us, after which its shouting became louder and it fired its weapons with greater ferocity. This went on until Sarah, clearly bored, walked up behind the creature. She tapped it on an exposed patch of fur by its knee, the highest point she could reach.

"Excuse me," she said. She then had to say it again, louder. She then had to say it a third time, still louder, during a point when the creature wasn't screaming defiance at an enemy we couldn't see.

The creature froze. A head whipped around to look at us and then went back to staring out into the void. A rumble emerged from the creature's thorax. It spun around to face us, causing Sarah to jump back. The legs that supported its massive form bent, bringing its heads to our eye level. Three claws came up to rest next to three bowed heads.

"What are you doing?" Sarah asked.

The creature spoke in a noticeably quieter voice. It was very nearly what your average gentlenid might consider a normal speaking volume. "I am bringing death and destruction to your enemies, my… " It paused. An eye cluster focused on Sarah and then went back to staring at the deck "… Mistress."

"What enemies?" Sarah asked. "There's nobody here."

"Yes, I thought that was odd," said the creature, shaking two of its heads. "I mean," it said, its voice slipping back into a roar, "I shall seek and destroy your enemies! Simply indicate where they may be found! Please don't put me back in the box!"

"I understood those first two things it said," I said, sidling next to Bainbridge, "and I understood that last thing it said. How is it that I'm still baffled by this situation?"

"We're not going to put you back in the box," said Sarah, ever the diplomat. "Why don't you tell us your name?"

"Yarl," it said.

"I'm Sarah. That is Bainbridge, and that is Jay. It's a pleasure to meet you."

"Look," said Yarl, still not looking up. "Who are you people? Because you don't seem like the selection committee to me."

"Why don't you sit down?" Sarah asked.

"I would *love* to sit down," said Yarl, collapsing into a many-legged heap. "Thank you." I

"What's the selection committee?" asked Bainbridge, approaching.

Yarl laughed. "Oh, come on, you can't get me like that. I wasn't born yesterday! Ha. No, no, no. Nice try. I was born… what year is it?"

We told it. It moved its fangs for a few moments.

"Seventy years ago," it said. "Do you have any tea?"

I scuttled off to make tea whilst Sarah and Bainbridge fussed around Yarl, trying to establish just what was going on.

All I heard as I pulled the tea-making supplies together were repeated statements on behalf of Sarah and Bainbridge along the lines of: "We are not the selection committee."

I found some biscuits and arranged them in a shape that was pleasing to the eye. That took maybe twenty minutes. My fastidiousness was fortunate; By the time I re-joined the group with the supplies, Yarl appeared to have only just got the idea that, whoever the selection committee were, we weren't it.

"Look," said Bainbridge, snagging a biscuit I'd rather had my eye on. "Would you mind telling us what's going on? We're thoroughly confused, here."

"Well, look," said Yarl, "I'm not really sure I should. I mean, if you're *not* the selection committee… and you're *sure* you're not, correct?"

"Yes," said Sarah and Bainbridge in unison.

"Then I probably shouldn't be telling society secrets to outsiders."

"What society?" I asked.

"The Lower Biggleswade Alcohol and Crumpet Society," said Yarl.

"The what?" asked Bainbridge, sounding incredulous.

"The Lower Biggleswade-"

"Sorry, sorry, forget I said anything."

"But what sort of society is it?" I asked.

Yarl beamed. "A secret one!"

"I've got it," said Bainbridge. He had been tapping away at one of his implants. "The Special Operations Unit have a file on them. They're an organised crime outlet who prey on people with more money than sense, the intoxicated and the easily exploitable."

"Oh I say, hang on now," said Yarl. "That's not right, dash it."

"I think," said Sarah, softly, "that the only way we'll be able to understand is if you explain to us. Would you do that? For us?"

"Mmmm," Yarl said. "Mmmmmmm-well, okay. But only if you *promise* not to tell anyone about this!"

We all promised.

"Okay," said Yarl. "Well now. Where to begin? I was in my second year at Jerome College, Biggleswade. I was studying classics, you know, Tis Pity She's Got High Standards, Love's Scarface, The Spanish Gallipoli, all those things. Do you know them?"

"No," I said.

"Yes," said the other two, at a much higher volume.

"Well," said Yarl, "my friends were all signing up to clubs in our second year. One joined this society where she ran around pinching things. Another joined a society where she stole things. Anyway, I got approached by this lass who was in my Art History class. She said that I'd come to the attention of the master of her club because I'd managed to sink seventeen measures of the finest cordial in forty minutes at the students' union the night before. She said she could arrange for me to be interviewed by the selection committee for the most amazing club on campus: The Lower Biggleswade Alcohol and Crumpet Society."

"What does this club do?" I asked.

"You know," said Yarl, "I'd meant to ask that myself, but I never got around to it. Something about alcohol and crumpets, I suspect."

"They're loan sharks," said Bainbridge sipping his tea. "They also run gambling dens, conduct smuggling and are suspected of people trafficking."

"Oh," said Yarl. "Really?"

Bainbridge shrugged "That's what the surveillance reports say."

"Oh. Well, anyway, I said it sounded marvellous and so I got interviewed by this committee, you see. They asked all sorts of questions about how wealthy I was-"

"And how wealthy are you?" asked Sarah.

"I had this inheritance, you see... " said Yarl. "And a title came with it, along with some land, and they seemed *dreadfully* interested in all of it."

Sarah smote her brow. "I see. What else did they ask you?"

"They asked if anyone would notice if I went missing suddenly."

"And what did you say?" I asked, getting the hang of this interrogation lark.

"I said probably not," said Yarl.

I tried to sound intelligent. "I see."

"And anyway, this all went on for a few hours, then they told me I was going to be put up for selection. I'd need to get into a box and when I got let out, I'd need to do whatever the committee told me."

"And when you got let out of the box," said Bainbridge, "what did the committee tell you to do?"

"Well, they told me they needed me to destroy a military installation and kill everyone inside."

"And that didn't seem odd to you?"

"Well, I say, good old Reginald 'Numpty' Telgrim had to stand in a pond for forty-eight hours for the selection committee for his club," Yarl said. "This didn't seem strange compared to something along those lines."

"And what happened the next time?" asked Bainbridge.

"Oh, you know. Much the same thing. And the time after that. And the time after that, actually."

Sarah held her head in her hands. "How long have you been doing this?" she asked.

"About forty-five years, now," said Yarl. "Give or take."

It looked around at us, a little affronted.

"Now, I say, look here. You're all wondering why I didn't think anything was odd, I can tell. Well, I must say – I mean, I *will* say – that's a bit thick. I *did* think something was dashed odd as it happens but, you know, I didn't like to say anything. I mean, I probably would have if this had all gone on for, I don't know, another twenty years or so, but... I mean... well. One doesn't like to be rude, does one?"

"Have another biscuit," said Sarah, eventually.

"Gosh, thanks," said Yarl. "I say, you're being dashed pleasant given we've only just met. I'm most awfully grateful."

There was a chorus of 'not at all's from everyone who wasn't a three-headed, heavily-armoured, aristocratic war machine.

We were left with one complex and challenging question: Did Oliver know that he was smuggling Yarl into a war zone to commit unbelievable slaughter in a thoroughly illegal manner, and was merely using his friend Jay's presence to add a front of legitimacy? Or... had he been duped? Did he think that, for example, he was transporting lifesaving medicine to be delivered to homeless, unemployed orphans?

Sarah and Bainbridge were very strongly of the opinion that this last option was unlikely but some very strong points were made for it, I must say. There was a lot of back and forth across the group, but without compelling evidence either way, the discussion ended in a stalemate.

"Well, why don't we go and ask him?" I finally asked, feeling a little frustrated.

Sarah and Bainbridge looked at each other. Yarl drank its tea. Light appeared to dawn in two sets of eyes. I couldn't think why, unless two of the people in the discussion enjoyed being proven wrong.

"That's a wonderful idea, Jay!" said Bainbridge. "We shall head out at once!"

He leapt to his claws and started heading to the bridge. This surprised me... until I remembered that the reason Oliver hadn't stood up for himself much during the conversation was because he'd been kidnapped by pirates.

"But dash it, we can't!" I said, following Bainbridge. I heard the sounds of Sarah and Yarl following me, presumably not wanting to be left out. "He's been kidnapped, remember?"

"No, no. It was a brilliant idea, Jay," said Bainbridge, not slowing down. "We were swayed by the strength of it." He reached the bridge and started checking the fuel reserves. I shifted from claw to claw, not really knowing what to say.

"But... " I said.

"No, it's okay, Jay. We'll track the pirates down, kill them all and ask Oliver what exactly he thought was in Yarl's crate. It's brilliant!"

"There were an awful lot of pirates," I said.

"Ah, but this time we have the element of surprise," said Bainbridge. "And Oliver will be ever so eager to get away from them, he'll probably help."

"Well," I said, trying to formulate my objections in a coherent manner.

"You mustn't worry, so, Jay," said Sarah. "Everything will be fine."

"I forgot to ask," said Yarl, as Bainbridge started running ion trail traces using the ship computer. "What are you all doing on this ship?"

Bainbridge yelped in triumph and plotted a course. He turned to face Yarl as the ship started to move. "We're on holiday!" he said, beaming.

"Ah," said Yarl. "You know; I haven't been on holiday in forty-five years."

"Would you like to join ours?" asked Sarah.

"I think I would," said Yarl. "What sorts of things do you people do on holiday?"

"We visit sites of historical interest," I said. "We chat about things and sleep out under the stars. We meet interesting people and eat interesting food. We occasional indulge in a little light dinking. That sort of thing."

"But our itinerary for the near future," said Bainbridge, drawing a gun and checking its magazine, "involves tracking and eliminating a gang of ruthless pirates and then interrogating a ne'er-do-well about his smuggling operation."

"Ah," said Yarl. "Well, it's good to start with what you know, I suppose."

Chapter Eight

One Scheme Too Many

I can't for the life of me think why I thought chasing down the pirates was a good idea.

I must have thought it was. Bainbridge and Sarah kept congratulating me on the proposal. Still, as it was my idea, I decided that we should probably come up with some sort of strategy before we tracked the pirates to their dastardly lair.

I suggested we needed a set goal from this mission. One was immediately proposed. There was a little quibbling over semantics at that point. Someone – who, exactly, was a mystery – needed a little convincing that 'capture and interrogate' was, in fact, a synonym for 'rescue', but they were assured by everyone else that this was indeed the case. That having been done, we started discussing how we should go about capturing and interrogating Oliver.

We had located some deckchairs left in a cabin below decks by a previous occupant of the *Cox*. We arranged these in a rough circle so that we might relax as we discussed plans. We had pulled the *Cox* into a mooring bay to the side of the lane to have our conversation. Stars shone down upon us. Off in the distance, a shivering spiral of green gas was illuminated by a nearby star. The light reflected on the deck. I could not have imagined a better environment for plotting.

I, you will be unsurprised to hear, wished to spend a good week in this environment, planning out a complex scheme that would involve either minimal or maximal loss of life, depending on how we all felt about the matter. I tentatively proposed something similar to what had been attempted in the Chartal system during my second tour and, whilst that had led to the entire system being stripped of all non-essential life, I was pretty sure I knew what had gone wrong on that occasion.

That plan was rejected, so I suggested a variant of my Otavia strategy. That plan had been flawless and I was very proud of it. Bainbridge asked how long it would take to execute; I replied that, if everyone did their part to the best of their abilities, it should only take a week or so.

Bainbridge dismissed this, saying he didn't plan to live that long. This saddened me. He saw my expression and hastened to assure me that he was joking. He clarified that his attention span was not all it should be at the moment. A week was a long time to do something that could be done in an afternoon under ideal circumstances.

Slightly fed up with my plans being poo-pooed every way I turned, I threw the question open to the group. Bainbridge, of course, wanted us to infiltrate the pirate flagship and massacre everyone on board one by one. As he described it, I gather the point was for the pirates to discover their slain comrades one after another and for fear and paranoia to set in until the coup de grâce, where we would slaughter the remaining few pirates as they cried for their loved ones in whatever boltholes they had crawled into.

The rest of us rejected this, as it sounded dreadfully messy.

Yarl said it would far rather just board the pirate ship and kill everyone normally. We raised a few eyebrows at this. Yarl was a curious fellow. For someone who, it seemed, had been tricked into a life of slaughter and violence, it seemed to have taken to the life remarkably well.

Sarah broached this subject as delicately as she could. Yarl said that once you've been doing that sort of thing for a while, you get quite good at it. It's nice to be good at something. Yarl had never really been good at anything before encountering The Lower Biggleswade Alcohol and Crumpet Society.

"But you know that slaughter and mayhem aren't activities that should be pursued indiscriminately, don't you, my dear chap?" I asked.

"Oh yes," said Yarl, "oh yes. One mustn't catch innocent people up in the violence unless the Selection Committee demand it."

We glared at it.

"Oh, I see what you mean," it said. "Right, yes. Not even if the Selection Committee demand it. I say, life has become complicated since you let me out of that chrysalis."

"We'd need some way to get into the pirate base," I said, attempting to move the conversation along a little. "We're rather outnumbered."

"That," said Yarl, "is what *this* is for." It thumped its amour.

"Does it provide complete protection?" Sarah asked, poking at a spot where blue fur emerged from between armoured segments.

"Not complete, no," Yarl said, "but by the time chaps get close enough to me to take advantage of the gaps in my armour, they're in for a bit of a grilling." As if to demonstrate this, a head of Yarl's that wasn't talking breathed a rather lovely jet of white fire into the air.

After we'd extinguished the resulting blaze on the cabin roof, Sarah pointed out that this left the rest of us surplus to requirements.

"We're supposed to be on holiday, after all," she said. "It would be a shame for one person to have all the fun whilst everyone else languishes about, feeling useless."

Sarah suggested that she could reach out to the pirates as an ambassador. "I'm not one for actual combat these days. I'm rather fond of this body, but one of the few things in need of improvement is the lack of an active countermeasure system.

"I shall discuss the terms of Oliver's release with the pirate chief. Whilst I do this, Bainbridge can infiltrate the ship and start a campaign of sabotage and murder. You, Jay, will accompany me as my bodyguard and, to keep your strategic muscles toned, I would very much like you to pick a time and a place where Yarl would be usefully deployed if negotiations break down."

We ruminated on this plan. Bainbridge commented that it suited him as well as any other. Yarl agreed on the understanding that it would be allowed to rampage, even if just a little. If there was time afterwards, it said, we could scour the place for alcohol and crumpets. After forty-five years, the scamp more or less felt like it was owed some. This was agreed upon.

I was less than confident in this plan. I have never been one for action in the field. I mean, I could shoot straight if given a decent pair of optics. I was able to hold my own in claw-to-claw combat... but I've never been keen to get stuck into the meat of things. Not least because the meat will insist on flying off in all directions and getting lodged in my fur.

My specific concerns in this instance regarded the well-being of Sarah. Her puny human form was not one that I was happy to put in harm's way. I was far from convinced I would be able to protect it from damage, which would be most distressing for Sarah. She had become rather attached to her form over the years.

I wondered if I should vocalise some of these thoughts, but I refrained. Sarah had, after all, been in some pretty serious scrapes since acquiring her body. I should really trust that she can look after herself, even without my help. There is as much cunning and guile residing in that brain of hers as there is kindness and sympathy. It's a wonder there's room for anything else, really.

If I had been a smarter lass, I might have thought something like 'it's better to judge someone's situation based on the person they are and not the body they inhabit'. This would have been a wonderful phrase to bring to mind at the time. Unfortunately, it's a phrase that I read some time later on the back of a cereal box.

My concerns remained relatively unresolved, therefore, but I had the constant nagging suspicion that I was either worrying over nothing or being dreadfully patronising. Or perhaps both, you never can tell with me.

I chose to abstain from the subsequent vote as a result and the motion was carried three to zero, with one abstention. That left us with one question: How does one go about locating the lair of some nefarious swashbucklers in such an unfamiliar area?

Sarah and I both shared knowing glances when this question was raised. We both knew that Bainbridge's Special Operations Unit information hub would allow such information to be accessed in seconds. We could ask him to access this information... but we didn't necessarily want to. The poor duck had been through a lot recently, and the last thing we wanted to do was remind him of his ties to the Network at every opportunity by asking him to interface with its systems.

This only left us with the options available to your everyday gentlenid about town. We could try to trace the ion trails left by the retreating pirate ships. We could scour the newsfeeds for any reports of pirate activity in the area and attempt to divine the location of their base by analysing the pattern of the attacks. We could broadcast our location on an open channel, and try to tempt the pirates into attacking us by openly discussing stashes of valuable artefacts and high-class pornographic material.

The array of options available, coming so quickly after our last discussion, led to a certain amount of frustration. It quickly turned into what my old drill sergeant would have referred to as 'a full and frank exchange of views'. Strong opinions were expressed. People's judgement was called into question. Eventually, things started to get devious.

Someone, at one point, attempted to wheedle me around to their proposed course of action by reminding me that I had been at school with them, in an attempt to play upon my finer feelings. It took me half an hour before I remembered that I had been at school with precisely none of those present.

The argument was thankfully stopped before someone said something they might regret when the ship started to move. We were shocked by the sudden rumble of the engines. I looked around, curious as to who could be piloting our vessel. That was when I realised Sarah was missing. My shock was reflected in the faces of Bainbridge and Yarl.

"She's trying to enact her plan!" howled Bainbridge.

"Which one was that again?" asked Yarl.

This caused Bainbridge to pause. "I can't remember," he said, then rallied, "but we must stop her! She's enacting the wrong plan! Probably!"

Well, as you can imagine, this battle cry got us pretty well fired up. We all ran to the bridge, where Sarah was at the lines. She glared at us as we stormed in.

"What?" she asked, as Bainbridge bayed like a wounded archaeopteryx.

"What are you doing?" I asked, trying to establish myself as the voice of reason, even though all I wanted to do was snatch her pathetic human claws from the lines.

"I'm going to ask a local," she said, curtly.

"Well... no," said Bainbridge, quite reasonably in my opinion.

"What do you mean, no?" asked Sarah, not looking at us.

"Well, that wasn't one of the options," Bainbridge said

"That is rather the point. Now please, cease your prattle, there is a schooner coming up that might contain someone helpful."

The schooner that we were approaching was, as the name implies, a two-masted sailing vessel. It was an unassuming ship. Rather than being powered by oars, as the *Cox* was, it used electrostatic fields from its masts to harness the solar winds. It was a method of propulsion that required tremendous knowledge and patience. Sarah might well have found us the perfect person to ask about the local area.

Sarah drew us alongside the schooner and sounded the horn.

"Did you have to do that?" asked Yarl, after we all stopped clutching at our various auditory sensors.

"What did you say?" asked Bainbridge.

At the prow of the schooner, an eyestalk shot up and peered in our direction. This was quickly followed by a horrifying, blue seeping liquid attached to the eyestalk. It moved with a disturbing slickness. Every slimy centimetre of the creature oozed with menace.

"Can I help you?" the creature asked.

Yarl and I were frozen to the spot, half hypnotised by the disgusting nature of the creature before us. Bainbridge was wiggling a claw in his external audio sensor, possibly trying to reboot the thing, all the while looking in entirely the wrong direction. Only Sarah seemed unfazed.

"Yes!" she said. "Do you happen to know if there is a lair of dastardly pirates nearby?"

The horrifying ooze puffed at a pipe that was half submerged in one tendril. I couldn't fathom how Sarah was able to interact with this person without having her brain lock up. I was completely unable to move and Yarl was making a constant high-pitched whine that hinted that it was in a similar state.

"Pirates?" said the gelatinous horror. "Pirates… We had some brigands pass through last spring, but they're long gone. There were some young chaps trying to start up a new gang, but they spent so much time inventing a gang sign that their mothers put a stop to things before it could get serious. Pirates, though… "

How was Sarah coping with this? Every moment in this person's company made me want to eject my lunch from my digestive tract and hide under a table. Preferably a table that was quite far away from the erstwhile contents of my digestive system.

"You know; I think I maybe heard of some pirates setting up a base nearby… Do you mind my asking why you're interested? Not hoping to join them, are you?" The creature howled a chuckle. The noise thundered into me like a wall of white-hot needles.

"Oh no!" Sarah chuckled. "You caught us!"

The two laughed. I heard Yarl collapse next to me at the cacophony. I felt like I was watching this all happen from a very long way away indeed. The agony and the horror had completely overwhelmed me.

"No, seriously," said Sarah, "someone we know was kidnapped by pirates, you see, and we're keen to find them so we can get him back."

"Oh, what bad luck," said the creature. A jet of foul smoke erupted from the pipe it held in a tendril.

"I say," said Bainbridge, who had apparently managed to reboot his audio system. "That was unpleasant. Can you not do that again, please, Sarah?"

Bainbridge turned. Bainbridge saw the Ooze. Bainbridge froze. That was how I knew it was serious.

Sarah turned to him. "What are you doing?" she asked. She turned to Yarl and me in turn. Yarl was collapsed on the floor, making bubbling noises. I was standing, but only just. "You're all being very rude," she said. That was true. The agony of our obvious rudeness was second only to my terror in the face of the secretion that Sarah was asking for directions.

"I have it!" said the focus of my terror. "There were some thoroughly uncivilised individuals who made a little home for themselves in an asteroid belt near here. Might they be the ones you're after? They fly that teal flag. And they never pay the milkman on time. *And* they didn't help out with our village fete. Did you ever hear of such a thing?"

My perception was beginning to darken. I had a vague impression of Sarah's voice, the only reassuring thing in a world whose horrors were constricting around my very being. I had only one slightly coherent thought:

Sarah's primly human salads must be serving her. Our arachnid wisdoms, sundry of which remained comprehensively antagonist, were not holding us from the umpire. It was too helpful. Sarah must select…

I blacked out.

Chapter Nine

The Importance of Getting
A Good Night's Sleep Before
Mounting a Rescue Operation

I woke, my limbs stiff, terror still clinging to my brain, on the deck of the bridge.

My head was resting companionably against Bainbridge's waist. I shifted away, hoping to preserve my dignity and my reputation as a respectable individual who didn't throw herself at unconscious people.

I was still a little bleary, but I was, after much trial and error, able to establish what had been going through my mind in the moments before the darkness affectionately smothered me. Sarah's primitive human senses must have been saving her. Our arachnid senses, many of which were heavily augmented, were not hiding us from the unsettling otherness of that creature's form. It was too horrifying for us, but Sarah must have just seen a perfectly respectable and polite ooze creature.

Had she not realised the danger she was in? Or was she the only one out of us three not behaving like a perfect cad? That last thought was deeply troubling. The rudeness we three had displayed was shocking.

I could hear Sarah making a strange, airy sound with her human face hole. It wasn't unpleasant, but it was pretty consistently out of tune.

I must have made some sort of noise because Sarah looked around at me.

"Oh, you're back," she said, cheerily. "Did you have a nice nap?"

I attempted to riposte with some witty phrase or other, but I could only groan. I tried to get up… but my limbs weren't obeying me.

"Ssmsm," I said. "How long have… this?"

"You've all been out for three hours," said Sarah. "Another six or so and I would have thought about calling a doctor."

I became aware of pain in five or six of my limbs. I looked down.

"Did you do this?" I asked.

"Well, you were all being rude and then you left me to do all the hard work," said Sarah. "So yes, I had a little fun at your expense."

Sarah had been through our belongings. She had been through the items left behind on the *Cox* by the previous owners. She had also apparently brought a few specialist items with her.

Yarl, Bainbridge and I were now dressed in different clothing. I was wearing an admiral's uniform. Yarl was dressed as one of those Ghostbusters the humans revere. Bainbridge had been eased into a one-piece ostrich costume.

I investigated as much as I could, given the circumstances, and found that only my top layer of clothing had been removed in order to facilitate this little pleasantry from Sarah. I should be grateful for small mercies. Things could have been much worse.

Then, it occurred to me that they might be.

"Do you have an image recorder?"

"Me?" Sarah asked, innocently.

I decided not to press the matter. If there were images, no doubt they would surface eventually. If there were not, it would be best to not go about accusing humans left and right until I had enough feeling in my limbs to extract myself from this get-up.

I will not detail what happened over the next half hour. We four that were present agreed that it would be best not mentioned again, although I noticed that Sarah had two of her smaller claws crossed over each other when she agreed to this, for some reason I couldn't quite fathom.

Twelve hours later, after two slap-up meals of cold pie and some reptile eggs Bainbridge had brought with him, everyone's embarrassment had faded to the everyday background level a gentlenid expects of life. Once we all felt a little better (or 'less pathetic', as Sarah described it) we were able to establish a plan for our immediate future.

Sarah had been able to establish rough co-ordinates for the pirate base from the horrifying creature who had given her directions. She insisted on referring to the fearful individual as 'charming', which was met with stunned silence from the rest of us. The being's name was unpronounceable by human or arachnid vocal cords, but Susan insisted on referring to them as 'Claire', which I'd previously considered rather a jolly name.

Sarah had exchanged numbers with Claire and issued a standing invitation to drop into the flat if they were ever in our neighbourhood. This was good news, as I'd been hoping for an excuse to move to a new building. Possibly even a new city.

Seeing our pained expressions, and understanding that we wished her to move the conversation on as quickly as possible,

Sarah spent the next twenty minutes talking about how wonderful it was to meet someone like Claire. Apparently, it was the first intelligent conversation she'd had in months.

Had I the wit, I might have pointed out that this time frame encompassed conversations she'd had with her fellow humans before we'd embarked on our voyage. I'm sure something devastatingly humorous could have been formed from this idea. Trying to work out a way to construct such a quip without sounding dreadfully offensive towards Sarah's non-arachnid friends proved too taxing, however.

Once Sarah became bored with tormenting those privileged enough to call her 'friend', she smoked a contemplative anti-allergen tube and stared out into the void of space in calm silence. Bainbridge and I exchanged looks, wondering who would be the one to ask where exactly Sarah had taken us to. Were we mere moments away from encountering the pirates? Yarl exchanged looks with us as well, although it looked more baffled and shaken by events than we were. It was possibly hoping someone would give it instructions as to what to do next.

I couldn't help Yarl without getting information from Sarah about the pirate base. The question, if poorly phrased, might bring Sarah's mind back to Claire, which could not be allowed to happen. After much cogitating, racking my brain for the absolutely perfect turn of phrase, I decided that I had it.

"So… " I said.

Sarah looked around at me. I felt suddenly very afraid. Had my brilliantly chosen sentiment been less apposite than I'd hoped? Was she going to start talking about Claire again? The terror lasted only a second before I recognised a memory being jogged in Sarah's inscrutable human eyes.

"Ah, yes!" she said, snuffing her anti-allergen tube and tucking it behind her external auditory sensor flap. "I knew I neglected to mention something. We're half a day's sailing away from the pirate base."

There was a great deal of exhaling from we three previously unenlightened individuals. Yarl even made a blustery 'hurrah' sort of noise.

"I must say, though," said Sarah, "that I do not feel that proceeding with the attack today would be wise. I find myself weary after piloting this craft for most of the day."

She glared at each of us in turn. 'Would it have caused you considerable harm to help with my toil on the bridge?' her expression conveyed. It would not have caused me harm, I had to admit. It might have caused the boat harm, as my muddled brain would have led us straight into every craft, buoy and errant satellite in a six light-year radius, but I did not feel strong enough to point this out.

"With that in mind," said Sarah, "I have located a planet that we might orbit around. We will eat, drink and be merry for a few hours and then consign ourselves to the old dreamless. Tomorrow, when we awake, we can go and play with the pirates."

"As one does with food?" asked Bainbridge, still a little confused.

"That's right. Very well done, Bainbridge," said Sarah. There was something of a schoolmistress tone in her voice. I decided a prudent course of action would be to wear an expression of approval and keep my mouth shut. I didn't want to be given extra homework as a result of a thoughtless comment.

Bainbridge nodded. His claws twitched a little. I turned to him. "Are you not fully recovered, young Bainbridge?" I asked. "Would you prefer to proceed to the slaughter? Would that perk you up a little?"

Bainbridge thought about this for a moment. He absently drew a gun from a pocket and started disassembling it. "I want nothing more than to drench my claws in the blood of those who have wronged arachnid society," he said, "which is making me feel a little on edge. I think I wouldn't be able to enjoy assaulting a pirate base if we did such a thing now... how sad that is." He looked up at Sarah. "I consider your plan wise."

Sarah smiled, and indicated the planet we were sailing towards on the ship navigation systems. It was only a little way away from both the pirate base and the Fields of Zuk, the place of natural beauty we had intended to view on our way to our final destination. What luck! We could drink in the sights before assaulting the pirate base!

We were only a few minutes away from the planet we were to moor at, so it seemed churlish to question Sarah's plan. It later transpired that we should have been a little more assertive.

The planet Sarah had chosen for us to orbit was far from ideal.

There are these planets that have a certain fascination with ancient technology. You know the sort of thing: solid rocket motors, satellites, liquid coolant. These things are very quaint, there's no doubt about it, but they don't self-destruct or degrade naturally. They just hang about the place, getting in everybody's way.

Over considerable time, this detritus can turn into what the broadsheets call a debris field. Apparently, Sarah's people had a considerable problem with this on their home planet. They kept sending space ships up into orbit but lacked the technology to clear up the bits and pieces the space ships left behind. What they were left with were a billion pieces of debris, mostly under one centimetre in size. This led to their primitive space craft being corroded if they attempted to maintain orbit for too long.

Luckily for the humans, they eventually worked out how to clear such debris away. Other planets either lack the will to clear their debris fields regularly, or they feel (wrongly) that such a field lends a certain rustic charm. This was the case with Dessan, the planet Sarah had chosen for our rest stop.

Normally, this would not be a problem. Arachnid space craft, even the ancient models, are designed to repel debris of this sort. *The Dancing Cox* was not outfitted with such a field; it had been removed when the ship was decommissioned. The *Cox* was currently only protected by an atmosphere field. Atmosphere fields are not designed to keep out debris.

"Ow," I said, as I was struck in the head by a frozen lump of coolant.

"Ouch," said Bainbridge, as an engine piece impacted with his thorax.

Yarl roared an ancient battle cry as part of an old missile collided with one of its reproductive organs.

We were attempting to rig up the ship's soft covering of electrostatic fields. Unfortunately, the generators required to sustain the field had not been used in some considerable time, judging by their condition, so the task was difficult.

"Hold up your end, won't you?" Bainbridge said, the field collapsing around our ears for the seventy-fifth time.

"I'll hold up my end," I said, "if Yarl will do the decent thing and stop thrumming the tussle fittings!"

"I will *not* stop thrumming," roared Yarl, "because Bainbridge said the blasted field of… whatever this thing is needs to be stretched and fondled into position, otherwise the entire thing will explode and kill every last one of us!"

"Oh, come on!" I said. "That hardly ever happens!"

There was then another full and frank exchange of views that resulted in everyone rotating positions one step to the left.

To ensure we were all on the same page with regards to the operation of the electrostatic field, I decided now would be a good time to explain, very loudly, what actions I was performing and my reasons for performing them. That way, my dunderheaded colleagues might realise the mistakes they had been making throughout this process.

An electrostatic field, you see, forms around objects that are electrically charged with regard to its surroundings. The flow of electrons is key. If an object is negatively charged, then it will have very few electrons. If it is positively charged, it will have a ton of the things.

With this in mind, the positioning of the generator pylons needs to be precise. We needed to create a field using the pylons that would create a safe area for us by manipulating the field so that both negative and positive effects were applied to any debris attempting to pass through, thus repelling it.

I spent some considerable time instructing my colleagues as to the correct installation of the field generators about the deck of our ship. It was hard work, as we were consistently pelted by debris. Poor Sarah needed to excuse herself from this work, given that one piece of debris hitting her in the wrong spot could maim or kill her and we didn't have any human spare parts on board.

We three eventually managed it. We had the very dickens of a time with the generators on the port side of the ship. The blasted things just didn't want to fit into their sockets, but some work with a lever and a large hammer that Bainbridge kept in his bunk (for 'close up work', he explained) got the silly things in place eventually.

It would have been prudent, at that point, to buzz about a bit ensuring that all the generators were properly in place and ready to be activated. I am ashamed to say, however, that a particularly large piece of satellite struck me above my third eye just after I'd slotted my last generator into place, and so I threw caution to the winds. I called for the generators to be switched on.

We moved from generator to generator, activating them. Things didn't seem to work quite as planned. In fact, an even greater concentration of debris seemed to strike us. Nevertheless, we persisted, until Bainbridge came to turn the last generator on.

There was a fizz, an almighty bang and then, to my surprise, Bainbridge was running about the place, yelling unpleasantries. Activating the last generator appeared to have caused a feedback event that led to some pain on his behalf.

We thought about this, our thoughts occasionally difficult to keep track of thanks to the regular stinging blows from errant fragments of rubble. Yarl eventually rumbled into life to say that it had worked out what went wrong.

It explained that I hadn't been quite right about the workings of the electrostatic field. The positively-charged terminals generated a low-density electron field, whilst the negatively-charged terminals did the opposite.

Now that this was all cleared up, Yarl took charge. It explained that it remembered the sort of equipment we were attempting to use from its youth. A distant relative had once demonstrated how to use generators of a very similar type.

Yarl gathered us around the ship's aft-most available socket and demonstrated how the field would probably work, if everything went according to the plan it vaguely remembered from fifty years ago. During this demonstration, Yarl activated the generator.

The generator sprung to life as Bainbridge and I were still clustered around, listening to Yarl's explanation. More pertinently, we hadn't been around the ship to deactivate the already-stressed generators that had been calibrated wrongly.

An electrostatic field was generated. Unfortunately, it was spun around a far tighter area than we had intended. It arced between Yarl's generator and the ones around the ship. The problem arose when the field started arcing back to Yarl's generator in order to complete its full loop. This shouldn't have been possible; there are safety measures built in. However, these field generators were old, and did not function as they once might have done.

This would not have been a problem at a safe distance. It turned out that poor Bainbridge was not at a safe distance at all. He ended up trapped in this unstable field. He was being repelled and attracted by the field in the same instant, causing his entire form to vibrate violently. He cried out for us to disable the blasted fields.

I tried to deactivate a generator, but it transpired that activating the field was much easier than deactivating it. Bainbridge tried to assist but every movement resulted in the field constricting around him tighter. This left him being tossed and tumbled by the vibrations, but also having his airways constricted by the ever-tightening field.

It was at this point that Yarl took matters into its own claws. Or rather, its own jaws. It inserted the nearest generator into one of its imposing maws and bit down. The field died immediately, and Bainbridge was flung some thirty metres towards the bridge.

"I think I know what went wrong," I said.

Bainbridge emerged from the pile of crates that he had landed in. "Oh no," he said, "I'm not letting you people try this again. I know what went wrong, everybody listen to me."

The first thing we needed to do, he explained, was make sure we'd inserted the generators along the port beam correctly. He had been sure, he said, when I'd been insisting we get them into place by any means necessary, that something might be up.

I wasn't sure this was entirely fair, but Yarl and I watched as Bainbridge demonstrated how to remove one of the generators in question and replace it properly.

I'm a little unclear on subsequent events. One moment Bainbridge was wrestling with a generator, trying to extract it from its socket, the next minute one of his legs had been torn from *its* socket. We may never know exactly what happened.

We rushed to his aid, naturally, but his automatic medical systems had activated long before we reached him. Bainbridge decided to deal with the situation by clutching at his leg and screaming 'why?' over and over again.

I wrested the leg from him and plunged the business end back into the hollow where it belonged. Bainbridge screamed, but I did not let go. I felt the tendons at the damaged end of his leg begin to wind around the joining tendons in Bainbridge's body. Suddenly, his leg was jerked sharply inwards. I felt it click into place. Bainbridge screamed again. Then he flexed the leg in question.

"Ah," he said. "Well. I think I'm okay now. Thank you, Jay." Then he said, "Ow!" as another piece of debris struck him on the bonce.

Sarah's voice came from the bridge: "Why don't we give up and try to find an inn or something down on the planet?"

My first response to Sarah's question was to reply that we couldn't give up on getting the electrostatic field in place as we'd only just started. Bainbridge, to his credit, got in ahead of me. "Yes!" he said. He repeated this several times and occasionally punctuated these exclamations with wails of pain.

I wasn't quite ready to give up so easily. I began objecting, but Bainbridge rounded on me.

"Jay, I am trying to hold my temper, but I must warn you that if you delay us for *one* second more your body will be exhibited in eight separate display cases around the ship as a warning to the others," he said.

"Sorry to be unpleasant," he added as an afterthought.

With that in mind, everyone present decided we should leave our ship to the elements and try to find an inn down on the surface.

Chapter Ten

Six Little LARPers and Four Little Baffled Onlookers, Totalling Ten

The planet Dessan was pretty much what you'd expect from a place that couldn't find the will or the technology to keep its upper atmosphere clear of debris. It was a place dedicated to living the simple life.

There were no planet-spanning conurbations, no archologies, no aquariums… There were no museums, no rowing clubs, no gentlenid's clubs… There were no grand monuments, no gin palaces and no grand stately gardens.

Cottages were present in abundance. They were cottages so picturesque and pleasant to behold that they'd make your eyes bleed without the appropriate filters.

There were a lot of them. An awful lot of them.

There were more than any one planet could possibly need. Village after village of the things dotted the horizon as we dropped through the atmosphere in our skiff. What, I wondered, did all these people do all day?

An answer was easily forthcoming, because there were spaceports of every size and description littering the landscape between villages. I claimed earlier that there were no museums on Dessan. I may have been wrong. The entire planet appeared to be a museum of spaceflight.

As we descended further, I was able to make out the public houses that lay at key points in the closest village. This should have been comforting, but I have heard about places such as Dessan. Such public houses would probably be closed before sundown and only carry stimulants sufficient to intoxicate, rather than give pleasure through taste or texture.

As we landed and began our delicate enquiries, we discovered that the *other* thing Dessan possessed was an inn. One single inn. We asked for directions and it transpired that it was located on the other side of the planet.

After a certain amount of muttering, we hopped back into our skiff (except for Sarah, who finds hopping difficult with only two limbs upon which to walk) and set off for the co-ordinates we'd been given.

The co-ordinates led us to a swamp.

At first, we thought we had suffered an attempt at humour on the locals' part… but then we noticed the village in the middle of the swamp. Well, it might have been a village. It looked more like a collection of outhouses with a taller, less ramshackle building in the centre.

We cast a few glances around the place but didn't see anywhere else that might house us for the night, so Sarah pulled up our skiff at the landing stage and Bainbridge secured it. As he did so, I took in my surroundings a little more clearly.

The outbuildings seemed to be mainly for storage. They were rickety reconstituted metal affairs, but each had a sturdy padlock, an anti-intruder disintegration security field or – in some cases – both. A worn stone path led towards the taller building, which loomed over the island like the spectre of death that follows each of us everywhere we go.

The inn, assuming it *was* an inn, was a traditional looking three-storey affair. It had a red roof, a small garden and roses around the door. The windows had been set into wood frames for some reason and, as we approached, we saw that there was a doormat inviting us to brush our claws before entering.

There was a vacancy sign on the door, hanging from a nail. Taking this as a signal that this was indeed an inn and not some-body's house, we entered the building.

The interior was dimly lit, but we could make out armchairs dotted here and there, several doorways leading to other rooms (unless they contained space/time portals, in which case they might all lead to one another) and a large mahogany reception desk.

There was an arachnid behind the reception desk. She was asleep.

I coughed. She didn't move. Yarl coughed. Sarah coughed. Bainbridge slipped past us and rang the bell next to the desk clerk's ear. The arachnid's eyes clacked open. Slowly, she stood. First, she straightened her legs, bringing her head off the desk. She straight-ened her back, bringing herself up to her full height. Then, she raised her head and inclined it in our direction. Finally, her eyes focused on us.

"Good evening," she said. "May I be of assistance?"

"We'd like a room, please!" chirped Sarah, whose mammalian voice box can occasionally forget what species it's supposed to be representing.

"Of course," said the clerk. "Are you guests of Mrs Rios, as well?"

"I don't think so," I said.

"No, we're not," said Bainbridge.

"I might be." We all turned to look at Yarl. "Well, Mrs Rios might be a member of the selection committee," it said, defensively. "Maybe she invited me here to apologise."

The clerk cracked her head to the side and stared at us. "Very well," she said, before returning her head to its upright position. "Most of the rooms are filled by guests of Mrs Rios, but there are some rooms in the… " The clerk trailed off as she scanned her info panel. "Ice house… no. Wood shed… no. Chamber of horrors… no… . Ah, there are some rooms on the top floor next to the morgue."

"Why is your morgue on the top floor?" asked Bainbridge.

"It's not actually a morgue," said the clerk. "There's some party or other happening tonight for Mrs Rios' guests and we've been told to designate one of the larger rooms as a morgue."

"Is it going to be used as one?" I asked, wondering if it wasn't too late to go back and sleep in the skiff.

"Goodness me, no," said the clerk, fixing me with a cold, piercing stare that chilled my blood and made my stomach turn around to try and find somewhere to hide. "I believe this is all part of a Live Action Roleplay."

I nodded at this. Some gentlenids enjoy dressing up in costumes and pretending to be great warriors or historical figures. They drank, they argued and they failed to solve puzzles. Crucially, they maintained character at all times. Such a pastime was not for those not easily frustrated.

The clerk handed keys to each of us in turn, although it seemed to me that she lingered over mine. Our claws touched as she handed over the decryption code cube and our eyes met. I didn't think I'd ever been quite so sure of someone's character in my life. What stared back at me was menace personified.

"Dinner is at seven," she said, before I looked away.

"Does anyone else think something entirely odd is going on?" I asked as we climbed the stairs to our rooms.

"They're Live Action Role-players," said Bainbridge. "They're supposed to be odd."

I tried to voice my concerns but I found I didn't have anything specific to say. All I had was a feeling. A feeling that doom was hovering over us, waiting to strike at any moment. I couldn't say this out loud, though. Sarah would, not unreasonably, point out that I *always* feel like that. My assertion that 'this time I really mean it' would probably not be persuasive.

Seven of the clock approached, so we located our chambers. I had brought a valise from the ship, anticipating the possibility of dressing for dinner. Thankfully, my formalwear had not been too badly creased by its sojourn in my luggage, so I had no need to resort to my tweeds.

I was the last to arrive at the dinner table, due to getting lost several times on my way downstairs. The stairwells of this inn seemed to curve in on themselves or split themselves in two between floors. I could make neither head nor tail of them. Nevertheless, I made it to table before the soup was served so I was spared any social stigma.

The dining hall was brightly lit and pleasantly outfitted. Portraits stared down on the diners from the elegantly panelled walls. The ceiling was painted with a charming mural depicting a black hole swallowing a planet. A rectangular table occupied much of the room. Seated at the table were Bainbridge, Yarl, Sarah and four other arachnids that I did not recognise.

There was a space next to Sarah, so I slid into it gratefully. She looked positively elegant in a gown of some sort. My other two companions didn't look quite so chic. Bainbridge, having left the Special Operations Unit with only the clothes and weaponry on his person, was in the same clothing he had occupied for the last few days. Yarl had… well, Yarl had made an effort. There was a bow tie latched around one of its necks but the fellow itself appeared to be locked into its battle armour. There is little you can do to make battle armour suitable for the dinner table. It had, at least, combed its fur.

This seemed strange, considering the chap was titled. I asked it about this during a lull in the conversation and Yarl explained that, whilst it had attended many social events in its youth, nothing more formal than a massacre at a palace had befallen it in several years.

The four other gentlenids dining with us introduced themselves over the soup. Present, aside from the four of us, were the following:

Colonel Isabella Smythe, a retiree who had been decorated for her time in the military. She didn't say who had done the decorating or what the decorations consisted of. Tinsel, possibly. She spoke with a gruff, clipped accent and appeared to dislike talking about her time in service. Her eyes flicked hither and thither and had an aspect I can only describe as… haunted. She had apparently been invited by Mrs Rios, who had served under her some years previously.

Lady Susan Fletcher was a surgeon who had once operated on Mrs Rios, although the details Lady Fletcher could recall were vague at best. She appeared a little too fond of the meagre selection of alcoholic stimulants her host had provided, but perhaps she was simply letting her fur down for the occasion. Her eyes, though… there was something about her eyes. They appeared haunted.

Arthur Dabat was the leader of his village's temperance movement. He had received a letter from an M. E. Rios saying how impressive his organisation was. He had been invited to dine with like-minded individuals on today's date. This made me wary, as I have never been one for those who counsel temperance; thankfully, Mr Dabat was alone in this conviction. The lack of allies to his cause made Mr Dabat seem ill at ease. His eyes switched from side to side throughout the early courses. They seemed almost… haunted.

Finally, there was a young lady who introduced herself only as Myst. She was charming and companionable, and spent some considerable time getting to know the three gentlenids I outlined above. She didn't act quite so cordial with the four of us, however. She kept shooting us odd glances. Her eyes seemed quite… suspicious.

The desk clerk (whom everyone referred to as 'Sally') and an elderly lass by the name of Ms Wobol attended on us. The food was perfectly lovely, particularly when compared to the meals we had cooked for ourselves on board ship.

When it came time for the port and walnuts, Sally and Ms Wobol stayed behind. Sally creaked into life, extracting a letter from her sleeve.

"If I may beg your indulgence, gentlenids and other honoured species present," she creaked, "Mrs Rios sent instructions that I read this letter at the conclusion of the meal. May I proceed?"

"Carry on, my dear," said Colonel Smythe, gruffly.

Sally slid a claw through the security seal and opened the envelope. Inside was a data visualisation, which she uploaded to her visual sensors. She began to read in a menacing voice.

"Gentlenids present, please attend. You are hereby charged with the following indictments:

"Arthur Dabat – that on the twenty-ninth of Jorne, you brought about the death of Anthony Sibil.

"Sally Fungicide – that you caused the death of Theresa Stewart and Sandra Stewart on the fifth of Pidge.

"The individual known as Myst – that you caused the deaths of five individuals in Marb of this year.

"Isabella Smythe – that you brought about the death of seventeen of your fellow officers on the fortieth of Peas.

"Susan Fletcher – that on the nineteenth day of Tubbs, you killed Adam Tibbit.

"Agatha Wobol – that you caused the deaths of Arthur Wobol and Edgar Wobol in Trees of last year.

"Every one of you is charged with murder," Sally intoned. "How do you plead?"

There was a shocked silence.

Bainbridge raised a claw. "We weren't mentioned," he said, indicating Sarah, Yarl, himself and me.

Sally blinked one eye, then another, then the other two and then looked back at her data visualisation.

"The letter doesn't mention you four. Have you murdered anyone?"

"Yes," said Yarl.

"Yes," said Bainbridge.

"Arguably," said Sarah.

"It depends what you mean by murder," said I.

"It probably applies, then," croaked Sally, after some thought.

There was a commotion.

"I say," said Colonel Smythe, who was clearly a little put out. "What do you mean by accusing us of these ridiculous things?"

Sally blinked. "Sorry, was I not clear? I was reading a letter. I'm not accusing anyone. To the contrary, I was accused as well."

"I say," said five or six people.

"Is there any more port?" asked Yarl. We found some more port for it.

Certain barriers between the classes appeared to have broken down as Sally, Mrs Wobol and the other four began to cluster in one corner of the room.

Sarah leaned and whispered in my external audio sensor: "Do you think this is part of the LARP?"

There was a brief moment of confusion, during which Sarah had to explain that LARP stood for Live Action Roleplay.

"It could be," I whispered back, once that was straightened out, "but if it is, it's terribly bad manners to not at least *try* to involve us. Sally could have improvised something."

Suddenly, something incredibly shocking happened. Something I do not think I'll forget for the rest of my (rather limited) days. Someone used... harsh language.

"I never agreed to any bloody Live Action Roleplay!" cried Arthur Dabat, his voice cracking under the emotional strain. The room fell silent.

"This is ridiculous," said Colonel Isabella Smythe. She broke away from the group and sat in a free chair next to our little party. "I will take no part in these proceedings. I have no idea what that letter is talking about. I was involved in the deaths of seventeen people, as it happens, but it was nothing more sinister than a tragic coitus accident! The military tribunal cleared me of all wrongdoing!"

"We didn't actually ask... " said Bainbridge.

"Well, quite." Colonel Smythe drained her glass. She shifted from side to side for a moment. "Blast," she said.

"What is it?" I asked.

"Actually... I was mistaken. For a moment, I thought some bounder had poisoned me, but it is nothing."

"Are you sure?" I asked. "You appear to be shaking."

"And losing colour," said Bainbridge.

"And blood is pouring out of your mouth," said Yarl.

"And you've fallen off your chair, rolled over and stopped moving," said Sarah.

"Do you know, I think maybe she has been poisoned?" I said.

Everyone else called me thick-headed.

Myst let out a piercing shriek and fled the room. Lady Fletcher scurried over to the body which Colonel Smythe used to occupy. "Step aside!" she cried, although I could have sworn nobody was actually in her way, "I'm a doctor!"

"You're a surgeon," Bainbridge said.

"Surgeons have a wide range of skills!" said Lady Fletcher. She set about fiddling with various parts of the late colonel's anatomy. I averted my eyes. There were several squelchy noises before Lady Fletcher confirmed that the colonel was dead. There were a few glances about the place before Yarl put the body in a corner of the room; a task that nobody else wanted to take care of.

"Perhaps we should retire for the evening," said Sarah. "I don't want to get too deeply involved in this."

"Does anyone know if the colonel had her backups up to date?" Bainbridge asked, ignoring her. Nobody was able to furnish information regarding the colonel's backups.

As you are no doubt fully aware, most people these days back up their consciousness regularly, in case of an unfortunate life-threatening incident such as the one just suffered by the colonel. This consciousness could be downloaded into a new body at a later date. This technology had been utilised by all of us at some point, apart from Yarl (as we discovered upon later questioning) who'd never been close enough to death to discover the benefits.

"I haven't backed up in some time... " cried Ms Wobol. "Oh dear... "

"How very... unfortunate," moaned Sally, fixing Mrs Wobol with a piercing stare.

"Please don't worry," said Sarah, "you can start a backup going now."

Mrs Wobol nodded, and wondered out loud why she hadn't thought of that. She initiated the backup procedure. Sarah asked if everyone else was up to date. It transpired that they were. Even Sally confirmed this to us, after she'd stopped piercing people with stares all over the place.

The motives of the murderer were then called into question. It was possible that Colonel Smythe's death was a random act of cruelty, but the letter Sally had been instructed to read suggested a degree of planning.

With regard to the specific accusations set out in the letter, everyone rigorously denied any wrongdoing, apart from Sally, who denied wrongdoing in a thoroughly sinister manner.

The lights were lowered and conversation started to flow again. Lady Fletcher absentmindedly poured herself some port and she failed to suddenly die after drinking it. This was a relief for her, and we concluded that Colonel Smythe's glass had been poisoned, rather than the port itself.

We had started to drink rather more liberally throughout the subsequent hours, and tongues became a little loosened as a result.

"I believe the accusations in that letter were absolutely unthinkable," said Bainbridge. "We've all killed people, though, haven't we?"

A few people drew themselves up in their chairs, but there was an embarrassed silence rather than a series of outright denials.

"Okay," said Bainbridge, slurring slightly. "I'm just going to go ahead and say this: if anyone who was accused in the letter doesn't know what the letter is talking about, raise a claw. If you're completely, one hundred percent innocent of what the letter says, just raise a claw. That's all."

There was silence and utter stillness. Slowly, Mr Arthur Dabat started to lift a leg. Without looking at him, Bainbridge added: "And no lying."

Mr Arthur Dabat lowered his leg.

"Myst isn't here," said Lady Fletcher. "She might be innocent… "

"She hasn't been seen since… " I said, before trying to recall when she'd last been seen. Then a vile thought struck me. "You don't think something nasty has happened to her, do you?"

We all looked at each other. As one, we rose from the table and set out to search for her.

Myst wasn't in the smoking lounge, the billiard room or the indictment parlour. We checked outside and she wasn't there, either.

"Perhaps she's legged it," said Ms Wobol.

"I wouldn't blame her… " said Lady Fletcher.

"I would," hissed Sally. I glanced at her, feeling a shiver run through my exoskeleton. Everyone else ignored her.

"We should search the inn from top to bottom," said Bainbridge.

"Can I just retire for the night?" Sarah asked.

"No, you can't," said Bainbridge. "The game is aclaw."

"Oh please," said Sarah. "Look, B, I'm very tired and we all need a good night's sleep."

"Yes, yes, we do!" cried Bainbridge. "But we can't get a good night's sleep if someone's missing! That sort of thing preys on a person's mind!"

"I think I'll be fine," said Sarah.

I yawned. It occurred to me that, after being struck by quite so many pieces of debris some hours before and having consumed a remarkably pleasant meal, seeing to my sleep arrangements might be a thoroughly civilised idea. There was something intriguing going on, but was it worth being separated from my bed?

I concluded that it was not.

"Don't listen to Bainbridge," said I. "Please, do go to bed. I think I might, as well."

"But what if Myst is hiding in either of your rooms?" Bainbridge said.

"We'll notice," said Sarah. I hadn't thought of that; it was a very good point.

"She'll be hard to miss," I said.

"Oh, go on, Jay," said Bainbridge. "The evening won't be the same without you present."

I had no idea what he meant by that, but if he felt so strongly on the matter…

"Oh, fine," I said. Bainbridge smiled at me.

We divided the house into sections between us. I was given my room, as well as the morgue and the attic.

I wanted to search my room first, but Bainbridge pointed out that we might as well take Colonel Smythe's body up to the morgue as I was going there anyway.

Hauling corpses around the place isn't the most delightful of activities when you're supposed to be on holiday, but Bainbridge was right. It did need doing. I held Colonel Smythe's body whilst Bainbridge held her legs. Together, we made our way up the stairs.

There was a rather tricky set of turns on the staircase, and Colonel Smythe's body didn't quite want to bend in the right way to allow us to get her through whilst maintaining her dignity. We ended up having to stand her up in one particularly difficult section and tip her over onto the next flight of stairs in order to get her past. In another section, we had to nearly fold her in two in order to proceed.

This meant that, by the time we made it to the morgue, both Bainbridge and I were a little out of breath. This was fortunate as the morgue would have taken our breath away, had we any to spare.

Whoever had decorated the place had really... well, *clearly* had a great passion for their work. Six metal tables were arranged in two rows across the room. Every surface had been scrubbed clean and plastic sheeting lined the walls, floors and ceiling. The plastic sheeting was white. Very, very white.

It was a long time since I had been in a room that was so... Spartan. There were no homely touches. No paintings, no decorations... the light fittings that had presumably once been there had been removed, replaced with exposed bulbs set into the ceiling that gave off a cold, calculating white light.

I felt dreadfully uncomfortable and a little afraid.

Bainbridge and I heaved Colonel Smythe's body onto the nearest table and left the room in a hurry. Myst obviously wasn't present. It was my fondest wish to never set claw in that room again.

Bainbridge and I parted company at that point. I had to search my room and Bainbridge had to search his. I started checking my room, but my heart wasn't really in it. Myst clearly wasn't hiding anywhere and I wasn't clear on why she even would be. My bed was right there. It was calling to me. Still, Bainbridge had wanted me to help.

I heard a cry from the floor below me. Something was up. I scuttled down one level, finding a corridor much like my own above. This one had Lady Fletcher standing in it, pointing at an open door.

"Mr Dabat!" she cried. "He's been murdered!"

Bainbridge rushed past me with a cry of, "Yoiks!"

I followed, feeling rather dejected at the sudden loss of life that was occurring.

Mr Dabat had apparently been searching his room. He had been drowned in his bathtub. Some vagabond had filled his bath with wine, which I dare say would have irritated someone like Mr

Dabat, who was involved in the temperance movement. I dare say the murderer hadn't considered that. They were dreadfully inconsiderate, they really were.

Bainbridge was working himself into something of a state at this point.

"We'll catch the bounder who did this!" he cried, a grin splitting his face. A thumping noise caused me to look down. One of his legs was shaking.

I was getting slightly worried about Bainbridge. This sequence of events had little or, more likely, nothing at all to do with us. He was throwing himself into matters because… what? He found things exciting? Was he feeling like he was back in the Special Operations Unit?

Another cry sounded from outside the inn. Bainbridge started bolting for the door, but I lay a claw on his shoulder and he spun to face me.

"What? What is it, Jay? There is something to investigate!"

Lady Fletcher was out of the door already. Bainbridge looked after her and then back to me, then after her again and finally back to me.

"Bainbridge," I said. "Is it not time for your hypnotherapy? It's late."

"What?" asked Bainbridge. "What? No. No, it's fine. We have things to do, Jay! Things to do!"

He looked down at my claw, expecting me to remove it. I did not.

"You usually meditate by now, Bainbridge. Your recovery may suffer… "

"Blazes to my recovery!" he snapped, causing me to gasp. He shrugged free of my grip and sprang from the room.

I heard his sprinting clawsteps fade as he raced down the corridor… but then they stopped. Slowly, I heard Bainbridge return. He poked his head around the doorway.

"What did I just say?" he asked me.

I smiled, sadly. "You said 'blazes to my recovery'."

"Blast," he said. "I thought so. You don't think I might be getting a little carried away, do you?"

"I'm sorry to say that I think you might."

He shifted from claw to claw. "But they might have discovered another body outside… "

"We will go out and view whatever it is that has caused alarm outside together," I said. "But before we do so, I would like you to complete your daily therapy."

Bainbridge shifted a little more but then shook himself. "You are right," he said. "You are right, you are absolutely right. Thank you… Thank you… I say. Would you mind… dreadfully… if you accompanied me to my room?"

I nearly gasped. Bainbridge waved his claws, frantically.

"Not *inside,*" he said. "Not *inside* my room, I just worry that… I worry that if someone does not escort me to my room and then… stand outside… my excitement will get the better of me and I will abandon the therapy once more."

We climbed the stairs together, unspeaking. The inn was silent by this point. We left the peace unbroken as we climbed.

Bainbridge was in his room for an hour or thereabouts. Without my data panel, keeping track of time was difficult. I paced the corridor outside his room, attempting to not let the fatigue overtake me. Eventually, Bainbridge emerged. His appearance was much calmer. His eyes did not dart hither and thither. His legs did not shake. He did not chew his lip.

"Thank you, Jay," he said.

"Do you wish to see what happened outside now?" I asked.

"I do."

Outside, Yarl, Lady Fletcher, Mrs Wobol and Sally were deep in conversation. They stood under the lamp at the front door of the inn, long shadows were cast out into the darkness that surrounded us. The smell of swamp, which I'd almost managed to forget before returning outside, struck me forcibly.

"Hello there!" said Bainbridge to four figures, apparently able to ignore the swamp smell. "What's up?"

"Mrs Wobol found Myst," said Yarl.

"Oh, that's good," said Bainbridge. "So, what was the cry about?"

"She was hanging by her neck from a tree," said Mrs Wobol, a tremor in her voice. "We placed her in the morgue… "

"I say… " said Bainbridge. "That's unfortunate. So, what's everyone doing out here?"

"We are discussing what to do next," said Lady Fletcher.

"I think we should find the murderer!" cried Yarl.

"We've been through this, Yarl," said Lady Fletcher. "We *all* think that. The question is, how?"

I held up my claws. "If nobody objects," I said, "I would dearly like to retire for the night."

Bainbridge turned to me. He didn't respond for a few moments, but then he smiled. "Of course, Jay. Thank you for staying with me."

I wondered if I should stay by his side in case he returned to his pre-therapy state. He appeared to anticipate this thought. "I will be fine," he said, smiling. "Please do not worry. Go on, give your pillows a good seeing to."

I smiled gratefully and excused myself from the group.

Once in my room, I prepared for bed and settled down. I hadn't brought a novel with me, to my chagrin, but entertained myself by speculating about how much progress the mindvirus had made since taking hold. Probably a lot, I concluded.

My room was dark and comforting. I missed the stars. I had been able to see so many of them from my hammock on the *Cox*. There was a window set into my wall; I twitched the curtains aside so I could get just the tiniest bit of starlight glimmering into my room.

I sighed. My bed was warm, it was soft and it was comfortable. If it wasn't for the smell of swamp that seemed to permeate the entirety of the inn, things could be said to be very pleasant indeed. I closed my eyes.

Chapter Eleven

And Then There Were Some

I was awoken several hours into my blessedly dreamless sleep by a cry. I wondered if I should do anything about it. I was pretty sure it hadn't been the cry of somebody I knew. I had never heard Bainbridge or Yarl cry like that but, I was less concerned about their welfare than I was certain other members of our party. I had heard Sarah make such a cry before. I had not enjoyed it.

I lay there for a few moments. Something was wrong with what I had just thought. I knew it. I wondered what? I was starting to feel guilty… then extremely guilty… then utterly wretched.

Then, it hit me. My brain had worked, as brains do (even one such as mine) without my consent. I had dismissed the possibility of Yarl or Bainbridge screaming by thinking they were capable of looking after themselves.

The implication being that Sarah was incapable of looking after herself.

I knew this to be untrue. I had been present when Sarah had expressed her displeasure towards people. I had also seen her defend herself, which she was able to do even against members of my species, thanks to a fantastic selection of weapons she kept stashed about her person – not to mention her considerable reserves of cunning.

I tried to justify my thought to myself. I tried to rationalise it. Sarah's form was more fragile than that of an arachnid and I felt somewhat protective of her, because of our history. Even though that was all true, I couldn't escape the fact that I had, however unintentionally, considered Sarah a bad luck magnet. A victim. Someone who needed my help. My attitude had been different from the one displayed by Megan, but there were points of similarity which made me deeply uncomfortable.

I moaned and rolled over. I thumped my pillow, more out of frustration with myself than anything else. Sarah didn't need my help… and if she did, she was more than capable of asking for it.

Furthermore, was I not being callous towards Bainbridge and Yarl? They may be formidable warriors, but they're just as capable of being surprised as anyone. Well, that wasn't quite true in Bainbridge's case… and it was probably *extremely* untrue in Yarl's case. The point was, I had grown fond of them as people and would not like to see them harmed. Should I not have been as concerned about them as I was about Sarah?

I tossed and turned for some considerable time, alternately resolving to remedy my attitudes to my friends and despising myself. Eventually, I returned to sleep. I dreamt about people who desperately needed my help. All I could do was dither.

Dawn was thinking about maybe, possibly breaking when a scream woke me. I drifted back to sleep after a few moments, but another scream rent the air a short while later.

I grabbed the blanket and pulled it over my head, hoping the outside world would go away. A few minutes later, a piteous moan fit to chill the heart of any living creature crawled through my door, dived under the blanket and demanded my attention. I gave in to the inevitable.

With the limited facilities available to me, it took nearly an hour to prepare myself to meet the day. My fur needed combing, my claws needed sharpening and my lapels needed straightening. I found Sarah, Yarl and Bainbridge in the breakfast room when I descended to the ground floor. They were feasting on cold cuts, it appeared. Tins and pots littered the table.

"Good morning," said Sarah.

"Guess who survived the night!" said Bainbridge. He appeared cheery rather than manic, which pleased me.

His question felt like it had a rhetorical edge to it, but I hazarded a guess that we four had.

"Not only us four!" Bainbridge said, happily. "Lady Fletcher and Sally also survived."

A scream came from upstairs. My three companions looked up momentarily before returning to their breakfast. I slid into a chair next to Yarl and reached for a napkin with one claw, a pot of jam with another, a butter knife with another, the butter with another and a hunk of bread with another.

Sally burst into the room. "Lady Fletcher!" she croaked, "has been stabbed!"

"You owe me a fiver," Bainbridge said to Yarl.

"You poor thing," said Sarah. "Have a sausage roll."

"Have you any idea who's been committing the murders?" I asked.

"We've narrowed it down to two suspects," said Bainbridge. "And one of them was Lady Fletcher."

Everyone looked at Sally.

"You can't possibly think it was me!" moaned Sally. Her eyes rolled from side to side and I could swear there was foam forming at the edge of her mouth.

"Looks like it. Sorry about this," said Bainbridge. "Yarl, would you mind?"

One of Yarl's heads looked up from its ham snack and nodded at Bainbridge. It raised an arm from which a terrifyingly large weapon unfolded. Sally barely had time to widen her eyes before an energy blast tore a hole in her carapace, flinging her backwards into a wall where she slumped to the ground.

"I say," I said. "Was that really necessary?"

"Nothing else to be done, I'm afraid," said Bainbridge. "Nobody else could have committed these crimes."

Clack. Clack. Clack.

Clawsteps sounded on the stairs, along with the slow clacking of someone applauding.

Sarah leaned across the table and whispered to me, "Don't worry, this is the interesting bit."

A claw entered the room, followed by a leg and finally, the entire figure of Myst.

"Myst?" quavered Bainbridge. "But… you're *dead!*"

"Not so!" said Myst. "That was simply a ruse to throw you off my trail." She started to pace around the room. "You know… I was furious when you four intruded on my plans yesterday, but now I realise your purpose. You are here to witness my triumph! You are here to be eyewitnesses to the greatest crime of this or any other century!

"My story starts when I was but a child," Myst began. I tuned out a little at that point. I half listened through some stuff about how she'd always been a youngster obsessed with justice, how she'd always felt betrayed when someone else had spilt the cream or stolen a teacake and landed her with the blame.

There was then some tale about a persistent thirst for vengeance but needing to fulfil this without violating her sense of justice. It all sounded a little far-fetched, if I'm honest. Apparently, Myst ran away from home to live in a cave for twenty years as she gathered information on people from her planet who had, in her view, committed crimes but not been punished for them.

I started listening a little more closely at this point, as there were several parts of her story that couldn't possibly be true if she was indeed sane. Then I remembered that this person was confessing to the murders of five people to four complete strangers eating their breakfast. I decided that quibbling over the details wouldn't enlighten me.

Myst went into some detail about how she'd selected her victims, then spent nearly an hour explaining how she'd gone about killing her five targets over the last fifteen hours. She appeared to have relied on a combination of cunning and blind luck, but she'd managed it, so… well done her, I suppose. Apparently, she'd faked her own death halfway through the proceedings to throw people off the scent. What a strange lady.

"You don't mean… " said Yarl, who appeared to be getting into the spirit of things. "*You're* Ms Rios?"

"The very same!" cried Myst. "And that name was a clue that would have given me away from the start, had any of you the brain to put the pieces together!"

She cackled. I sipped my tea.

"And now I must say farewell," said Myst, when she'd finished cackling. "I'm sure you will wish to tell the police everything you saw and heard but let me assure you, they'll never believe that someone could have planned and executed such a brilliant scheme! You're all going to spend the rest of your lives in prison!"

She started stalking towards the exit, cackling loudly. Bainbridge coughed. Myst cackled even louder.

"Excuse me," said Bainbridge. "There's one thing that has apparently slipped your mind."

Myst froze. She turned. "I'm sorry?"

Bainbridge rose and placed his napkin delicately on the table. He clacked his claws together three times. "Your scheme was elegant," he said. "But you appear to have neglected to take into account consciousness transfer."

"Consciousness what?" Myst asked.

"When you left home," said Bainbridge, "had your parents explained to you about the uploading and downloading of consciousnesses?"

"My parents barely taught me my times tables!" Myst said. "I had to teach myself all the important lessons, like justice and murder and... hang on, does consciousness transfer mean what I think it means?"

"The very same!" said Bainbridge. "None of your victims have actually died! You have simply inconvenienced them. At this very moment, they're being downloaded into new bodies!"

"Oh," said Myst. She covered her eyes with her claws. "Oh *come on!* You have got to be kidding me! You cannot be serious. You!" she said, rounding on me. "Is he being serious?"

"He is," I said, in between mouthfuls.

"Oooooh," Myst said. "So that's why you just killed Sally... "

"Precisely!" said Bainbridge "We knew Sally couldn't possibly be the murderer, so we asked her if she wouldn't mind us executing her current body in order to draw the real murderer out of hiding!"

"Very clever," said Myst, "very clever indeed. But you've forgotten *one thing!*"

There was a pause.

"And what is that?" asked Bainbridge.

"I'm not sure," said Myst. "I was really hoping if I said that, something would occur to me."

"Shall I call the police?" I asked.

"Please do!" said Bainbridge, staring at the withering Myst.

"You'll never take me alive!" cried Myst, bolting for the front door.

Yarl was out of its seat like a shot. It tackled Myst as her claw reached the door handle and wrestled her to the ground.

"I say," it said, "it's nice to know that life can be interesting even when you're not running around, slaughtering people."

"Could you pass the bustilion?" asked Sarah, indicating a tin just out of her reach.

I passed it to her with one claw whilst I located the local police frequency on a nearby dataslate with two others.

"Do you know, I think I made a mistake?" came the rather muffled voice of Myst from next door. "I think it wasn't actually me that did all those murders. It must have been somebody else… "

"You've already confessed," Sarah said, "and you did the slow clack. And you did the self-satisfied confessing voice."

"Even so… " Myst said, plaintively.

"Oh hush," said Sarah.

The police arrived an hour later. They brought Colonel Isabella Smythe and Ms Wobol with them, who had already been downloaded into their new bodies and were extremely curious as to what had happened.

We filled them in but by the time we'd finished, Sally turned up. I explained everything to her, as her behaviour was subtly different post-mortem; her voice was less sinister and her eyes less full of menace. I was curious as to why this was. It transpired that her letter from M. E. Rios had instructed her that the integrity of the LARP relied on her behaving as ominously as possible.

Mr Arthur Dabat turned up as I was exchanging contact information with Sally, who was pleasant company when she wasn't trying to intimidate me. Rather than fill someone in on recent events for a third time, we decided that we were long overdue to return to our ship. We said our goodbyes and trusted that Mr Dabat could be caught up by the twenty or so other people present at that point.

There was a crowd of feral humans outside the inn as we emerged. No doubt they had been drawn by the sirens, like hyper-moths to a flame. One saw Sarah and made a sort of barking noise. Soon, they were all clustered around her, sniffing at her coat tails or shying back, only to lunge forward and try to sniff her, nose to nose.

Sarah handled it all very well. She didn't overreact, she didn't give any of the humans a reason to run away or get aggressive. I wondered if I should start laying into the other humans with my stick, as I didn't want them attacking her. You can never be sure of the temperament of unfamiliar humans.

The thing was, I knew Sarah liked to interact with her own people, however briefly, and I knew she definitely didn't like it when I started hitting humans with my stick. I had, in the past, pointed out that coming up and sniffing at her without invitation was extremely rude, but Sarah had explained that I must make allowances. I let the humans be.

Yarl, I saw, was less than pleased to have a pack of humans scurrying everywhere and clustering around a companion, but it took its cues from the rest of us and ignored them. We made our way down to the skiff which was, thankfully, still tied up where we'd left it. A trail of humans followed Sarah down to the landing stage, and they howled a fond farewell as she stepped into the boat and we started rowing towards the upper atmosphere.

I wondered out loud if we should pick up supplies from one of the countless villages before leaving entirely, but the others were hesitant. Dessan appeared to have left something of a bad taste in my companions' mouths. They were suspicious that if we stopped off at a butcher's shop, for example, we'd stumble onto a meat smuggling operation or a body harvesting ring. I thought this was unlikely, but not so unlikely that I was willing to press the point. Besides, we could always raid the pirate lair for supplies.

We found the *Cox* considerably less ship-shape than when we had left it. The place was heavily dusted with debris. It was also being pelted by detritus as mercilessly as when we'd left, so we hurried up to the bridge and left orbit with all possible haste.

Once we were clear, Bainbridge and I set out to survey the damage our belongings had suffered. We'd neglected to stow our hammocks away, so they now more closely resembled nets. Our packs, thankfully, were rugged enough to weather the damage.

We reported this to our two compatriots after we'd checked on everything that needed checking. After a couple of remarks from Yarl and Sarah along the lines of 'can't be helped' and 'there's precious little that can be done about that now', we remembered about the Fields of Zuk.

We were clear of Dessan's debris field by this point, so Sarah set a course for the fields whilst Yarl, Bainbridge and I crowded around the prow of the ship to try to catch a glimpse of the spectacle. We saw nothing at first, but as Sarah corrected our heading the *Cox* yawed around to starboard – and *there* were the fields.

Bainbridge and I hollered to Sarah, who fired the mooring harpoons and scampered out to join us. We four sat, gazing at the fields.

The fields were gas clouds. They hung in space, drifting without a care in the world. They were remarkable not just because of their beauty, which was considerable: Colours within the fields blended together in ways so sublime they could cause fits of ecstasy or artistic melancholy, depending on your temperament. The furthest field from our position was mostly a glorious golden colour, with occasional flutters of silver and darker patches that only made the gold glow all the brighter. The next field saw purple and green gas swirl together. The next was made up of elegant patches of crimson.

The other aspect that made the fields remarkable was their age: they were the oldest thing known to civilisation. The fields had been here, in that spot, for longer than arachnids or humans or naja have existed… and they would probably be there long after our species ceased to exist.

In that moment, I felt a strange… something. I wanted to feel a claw intertwined with mine.

We stared, transfixed by the fields for some hours. Eventually, we had to break away and set off on our mission. I knew I would return here one day, if I lived long enough.

I exhaled, feeling the flow of air from my lungs up through my thorax, through the array of poison filters and nutrient strippers, into my mouth, between my fangs and out into the cosmos.

I made my way up to the bridge with Sarah. Together we plotted a course. The pirate base was a mere hour away.

The peace I felt deep within me couldn't last. I didn't want it to. I felt determined. I knew we must rescue Oliver as soon as possible. He had been denied the glory of the fields. This would not stand.

Chapter Twelve

The Attack Begins

The pirate base was slightly more ramshackle than I expected and small sections of it appeared to be on fire, which is quite the feat for a base located in the cold vacuum of space.

We'd approached the pirate base slowly. It wouldn't have done to approach it any other way. Whilst the Cox was heavily armed, we didn't have the crew to operate the armaments well enough to combat fully-crewed pirate vessels. We ran up the flag of parley and drifted into visual range of the base.

The base had a cobbled together look to it; bits of old space station made up the bulk of it, whilst pieces of dock sprouted here and there to grant access to the six ships currently in residence. As we drifted closer, we saw that an atmosphere field had been rigged up around the base, which explained the dozen or so arachnids lounging on top of one of the ships. It also explained the fires, which seemed to be confined to parts of the base nobody cared too much about.

For a short while, I thought they hadn't spotted us, which would imply the pirates were all spectacularly unobservant or remarkably inebriated. I was proven wrong when we drifted a little closer. I saw that most of the pirate ships had their guns trained on us. It seemed as though they were happy to let us come to them as long as we weren't being obviously aggressive.

To put it another way, the pirates were just being lazy.

We drew alongside what looked like the pirate flagship and waved.

"What you want?" slurred one pirate, who was bigger than the others and wore a more impressive hat. She was waving a bottle at us with one of her claws, several guns resting comfortably in three or four others.

"You borrowed our friend!" said Sarah. She and I were alone on the deck. Bainbridge was, as we spoke, infiltrating the pirate base by means better left un-speculated about. Yarl, for its part, was lurking below decks waiting for my signal to unleash its wrath. Sarah was playing the role of the diplomat and I was masquerading as muscle.

"What of it?" asked the pirate.

"You're going to give him back!"

"Are we, now?" the pirate said, clambering to her claws, staggering and then steadying herself. "You've got some nerve coming here and demanding things left, right and-"

I shot her.

This was something of a risk. There was the worry that every pirate watching would take this as a sign to start attacking us. However, our plan required me and Sarah to get into the same room as the pirate chief as soon as possible. That required us to get the attention of the buccaneers immediately.

For a moment, the pirates stared. "Ow," groaned the pirate I'd shot, before keeling over and starting to bleed. There was a great cry and rattling of claws, and suddenly there were fifty or so guns trained upon us. Many of them were swaying.

"You will take us to your chief," said Sarah, "or my associate will take a dim view of the matter."

Mere moments later, we were being escorted through the dingy corridors of the pirates' base. Two pirates were ahead of us and two pirates were behind. One pirate was on either side of us and, briefly, one pirate was underneath us. The hapless fool had passed out in the corridor and we'd stepped over her. I say over. Several of us accidentally stepped on her. What clumsy people we were.

The corridors of the pirate base became more resplendent as we approached our destination. There were more flags and more trophies adorning the walls. I saw several arachnid skulls displayed upon spikes, although our pirate escorts wouldn't answer when I asked who they'd belonged to. I saw more than a few war trophies – elegant and deadly-looking firearms or chests of electronic currency.

We finally reached a set of huge, wooden double doors. The designer, it seemed, had been given a very simple brief: Skulls. Every imaginable type of skull had been carved into the door. Arachnid skulls, naja skulls, human skulls… complete skulls, broken skulls… sinister skulls, playful skulls, skulls with bunches of flowers sticking out of their mouths. I got the feeling the designer had really been running out of ideas for varieties of skulls by the end. I could see a set of skulls playing poker in one corner.

One of our pirate escorts knocked on the door before slipping inside. There was a conversation within, inaudible due to the thickness of the doors. Then, with impressive majesty, the doors swung open.

I don't really know what I had been expecting from the chamber of a pirate chief, but I found this particular lair rather surprising. Not because of the contents. The banquet table, the trophies lining the wall, the thick, blood red carpet (that had probably once been a nice shade of cream)… they were all roughly what you might expect. No, the really surprising thing in the pirate chief's lair was the chief himself.

He was human.

He was reclining in an enormous wooden chair at the far end of the banqueting table. The sight should have been amusing, given that the chair was clearly designed for an arachnid twice his size… but it wasn't. His gaze burned through Sarah and me in turn. I felt as if my inner being had been exposed to this creature in a matter of moments.

Our escorts knelt. Sarah and I did not, though I badly wanted to. It would not have been wise to show weakness at this early stage in the negotiations.

"Don't just stand there creating a draft, you wastes of space!" said the chief. "You two!" He indicated us with a wave of a cutlass that I was, frankly, rather impressed to see him lift. "Get inside. The rest of you lot, find something useful to do. Splice the main brace or scrub the poop deck or something."

"Ay, commodore!" bellowed the pirates in unison. They scarpered, leaving us to enter the chamber by ourselves.

"Shut the door!" shouted the commodore after we'd stepped over the threshold.

We did so.

"Thank you very much," said the commodore, now in an entirely more normal voice. "Won't you sit down?"

"I'm sorry?" Sarah said. She had been preparing to take a rather hard bargaining position and had been thrown off her stride somewhat.

"Sit down, sit down," said the commodore, rising up and scuttling around to one side of the table, where there were two chairs.

He pulled one out for Sarah who, after glancing at me, sat in it. I sat in the other as the commodore started working around the table.

"Can I offer you anything?" he asked. "There's some grog here if, for some unfathomable reason, you like grog? No? Can't say I blame you. I did have some tea, but I had to throw it out of the porthole because one of my crew nearly found it and I couldn't have had that, could I? Ha ha ha!"

"What's going on?" I asked Sarah.

"I'm sure we'll find out if we don't say anything stupid and let this person talk for long enough," Sarah whispered. I resolved to not say anything at all, for any reason.

"Goodness, where are my manners?" asked the commodore after locating three enormous metal chalices and emptying out their contents. "My name is Anthony Partridge, but the crew call me Commodore BloodBane." He crossed to a barrel that was in a corner and filled the three drinking vessels from it. "The crew think there's grain alcohol in here but it's actually water. Don't tell anyone," he said, passing us a chalice each.

"Look, what's going on?" I asked. Sarah kicked me under the table. That made me remember my resolution. I shut my mouth once more.

"What my colleague means," said Sarah, "is that I'm Sarah Wolfborn and this is Jay Blackhand. We're here to demand the return of our colleague, Oliver."

"Those aren't your real names, are they?" asked Anthony, perching on the edge of the table so as to be companionably near us but not so close as to be threatening.

"No," I said.

"Yes, they are," said Sarah at the same time, before kicking me again.

"It's okay, it's okay," said Anthony. "I should explain. I'm not a pirate by trade, I'm a businessperson."

"I've heard that before," said Sarah.

"As in, I used to work as a dogsbody for a firm of solicitors," said Anthony.

"But… " said Sarah.

"So, there I was," said Anthony. "I had been sent to collect the books of a firm my company was planning to merge with. I was there along with a few arachnids from the firm, as well as a bodyguard. These pirate chaps attacked and everyone except me was killed. It was quite a sticky situation, let me tell you. Anyway, I got the gun from the bodyguard and was just wondering if I should kill as many pirates as I could before killing myself or just cut to the chase, as it were.

"The pirate chief made my decision for me. She burst through the door to where I'd been hiding as I was holding the gun. She was a brute of an arachnid, but I got off a lucky shot that felled her.

"Now, it turns out that pirates run their succession rules on a dead arachnid's claws rule – whoever kills the boss becomes the new boss. So, they made me their chief."

"Just like that?" Sarah asked, incredulously.

"Ah, you're referring to my species?" Anthony asked with a twinkle in his eye.

"Well… " said Sarah, clearly thinking about denying it before giving in to the inevitable. "Yes."

"That's why I was such a beast to them when I was first graced with your company." He said. "The pirates all think I'm some sort of combat prodigy, that I'm dangerously insane and that if they challenge my rule, I'll massacre everyone on the base. It's worked so far but I won't be able to keep it up forever. I'm hoping to escape at some point, but that's for another day. Now, you came to talk about Oliver?"

"We did."

"Is he safe? Have you harmed him?" I asked, getting the most important questions out of the way.

"He's fine!" Anthony assured me. "He's in a cell. He was uncooperative because of the nature of his retrieval."

"Would you mind explaining his part in all... this?" Sarah asked.

"Of course! Would you like anything else before I start? I've got some roasted flightless bird, some fruit, some... I'm not even sure what that is, but it's delicious. No? Then I'll begin."

This is what he told us:

Oliver had come to his attention when a local warlord asked the pirates to assist with a coup she was thinking of initiating. Anthony had hired several of his pirates out, but he couldn't spare enough to make a real difference. Thankfully, Anthony's second-in-command knew of a middleman who could source some extra mercenaries, for a commission.

The mercenaries were found without trouble and were ferried down to the planet where they would be needed. The war started and the pirates got paid. Things didn't go well, unfortunately, and there was soon a call for new mercenaries. Anthony had asked around, and that was when the middleman suggested hiring his premium product: Yarl.

For some reason, Anthony kept referring to the middleman as Oliver. I decided the mystery behind that piece of misinformation was one to tease apart later. Sarah kept shushing me whenever I mentioned it.

The middleman said that he could get Yarl, the most dangerous slaughterbeast on this spiral arm of the galaxy, to the war zone soon. He was just waiting to arrange transport. Soon afterwards, Anthony had received word that the mercenary was on its way. The mercenary was to be delivered to the planet the following day. It never arrived, however, and that was when things had started to go sideways.

Anthony had asked his second-in-command to find out what was going on. She had taken a small flotilla to investigate. The thing was, as Anthony explained it, the pirates couldn't grasp the difference between:

"Find our contact and establish if there's a reason for the delay in deployment of the mercenary!"

And:

"We've been betrayed! Bring the traitor here for imprisonment and possibly torture if you're very good little pirates!"

The pirates had tracked down the *Cox* and were preparing for an all-out assault when Oliver had approached them. Apparently, he'd tried to explain matters to Anthony's second-in-command but he had used too many long words for the pirate to understand.

The middleman was brought back to the lair. Anthony had been too busy placating the warlord, who was currently very upset to be on the losing side of a war when she'd paid for the most proficient mercenary in several thousand light-years. Then we'd turned up.

Sarah and I exchanged a glance or two. I was wondering if it would be prudent to mention that we had Yarl with us, or whether that was information best kept secret. Sarah appeared to be thinking something similar. We never got any further than significant glances, because at that moment a pirate burst into the chamber.

Anthony immediately leapt off the table and started waving his cutlass around.

"Commodore!" said the pirate. "The mercenary is here!"

"Yarr!" cried Anthony in surprise. "Shiver me... never mind. That's good! We can get it down to the war zone without delay!"

"It's not in its chrysalis!" the pirate said.

"Oh," said Anthony.

"And it's slaughtering us left and right," said the pirate.

Yarl appeared to have lost patience with waiting for my signal and had started the attack early.

Chapter Thirteen

Jay and Sarah's Book of
101 Stair Jokes

Sarah and I both had matching looks of horror on our faces, which was genuinely impressive considering that our faces shared very few points of similarity. Our expressions were both twisted to such an extent that we looked neither human nor arachnid. We both looked like the only members of a new species: The Shocked-o-puss.

"Well… bullocks," said Anthony. I covered my ears before realising he hadn't said what I thought he'd said. "Sound the alarm!"

"We have, commodore!" said the pirate.

"Well, get out there and fight!" cried Anthony, glancing at us. He clearly wasn't quite done with our conversation.

"But I can't leave you here with these traitors, chief!" the pirate said. "They brought the mercenary here! They're here to kill you!"

"I know that, you scum!" roared Anthony, his voice so guttural it rattled the portholes. "I have them at my mercy! Get out or you'll get blood all over that lovely coat of yours!"

The pirate looked down at their coat and blushed. "I didn't think you noticed."

Anthony rolled his eyes. "Of course I noticed, it looks fantastic. Now, get out!"

The pirate fled the room. Anthony rounded on us. "You brought the mercenary here? And you let him out?"

"We expected you to be a great deal more hostile than you are… " Sarah said, weakly.

"Oh, *they're* hostile," said Anthony, waving his cutlass at the door. "*I'm* just trying to get out of here in one piece. I have no idea when my last backup was. I wasn't expecting trouble on this trip! I was just going to collect documents!"

"It's okay," I said. "We can explain to Yarl that it needs to back down."

"Oh no, you can't do that now," said Anthony. "My lot are all too drunk, belligerent or suicidally insane to back down from this sort of fight. We all need to get out of here, right now. Can I trust you?"

Sarah stood and moved so she was smell sensor to smell sensor with Anthony. They stared at each other for a long moment.

"Can we trust *you?*" Sarah asked. "You've carved yourself a pretty little niche out here. How many deaths are you responsible for?"

"Just one," said Anthony. "And I've already told you about that one. These idiots would have been running around, looting and killing, no matter who was in charge. I was just trying to organise them a bit."

"Organise them?" said Sarah, appalled. "You took a gang of murderers and you tried to make them better at it?"

"Look, what was I supposed to do? I had one chance to get out of there with my skin and I took it. Humans may get treated like dirt on my planet but at least the arachnids there *pretend* to be civilised. Here, they're under no such illusions. They wouldn't have just killed me. I would have considered myself lucky if I'd been eaten alive. There are a whole host of fates that I might have suffered, had I not taken control of the situation… "

Something exploded very close by.

"And do you really think *now* is a good time to be getting into this?" said Anthony, a note of panic creeping into his voice.

That was when the door burst open and two new pirates strode in. They were shouting.

"The base is going down, commodore!"

"We've got to get you out of here!"

Things turned nasty when they saw how close Sarah was standing to Anthony. They didn't like that at all. Before I could react, one was behind me with a gun to my back and the other was striding towards Sarah, raising a nasty-looking spinning blade contraption.

I forced myself to be calm. I breathed slowly. Time appeared to slow. I needed to do three things: I needed to assess the threats, I needed to assess my objectives and I needed to react.

First, my objectives.

Sarah's safety was my top priority. This was partly because I hadn't managed to shake my patronising mindset yet. Mostly, it was a case of honour and pragmatism. I had pledged to ensure that Sarah escaped this room alive. She also had more years of life left in her. Humans were not as long-lived as arachnids but my mindvirus meant that I was unlikely to see another three years, whereas Sarah had another sixty (or so) to go.

My second priority was safeguarding my own life. This was partly due to sentimentality and partly out of habit. I was quite attached to my life. It had been going for a long time. It would be a shame to end it now, before the conclusion of my holiday.

My third priority was Anthony's safety. His arguments just before things took an ugly turn had swayed me. Plus, I needed to get to the bottom of who this middleman might be.

My fourth priority was not hurting any of the pirates too badly.

There was a notable gap in how committed I was to these priorities. Priorities one and two were very important. Priority number three was an optional extra. It would be a pleasant surprise if I could get all three of us out unharmed. My fourth priority was buried so deep behind all other calculations, I immediately forgot about it.

So, what were the threats?

The pirate at my back had a firearm, which was pressing into my lower abdomen. This could mean one of several things; the fact that it wasn't levelled at my head was significant. The barrel pressing into my abdomen felt large, but I couldn't tell *how* large. It might be a rifle or some other large weapon. What further information did I have?

The pirate behind me had been running, its breathing rapid as it entered the room. There was also – what was that? The pirate's breath wafting over my shoulder smelled strongly of some sort of alcohol. Either they had recently been using mouthwash (which seemed rather un-piratical) or they were intoxicated.

The second pirate was calmer than the first. They hadn't shown signs of exhaustion as they entered. They only had the one weapon. The spinning blade thing that was less than a metre away from Sarah's head. I couldn't gather any other information in the time I had.

The third threat was only a possible one – Anthony. He had a cutlass and I wasn't sure if he intended to use it. If he *did* intend to use it, I wasn't sure who he'd try to use it on.

I turned my mind to how I should react. The pirate behind me was too close. I could turn and wrest the weapon from them. They were probably intoxicated and poorly trained. I had never excelled at close combat but even I could probably deal with an intoxicated, out of breath, untrained pirate. Once the weapon was mine, I could use it to dispatch the second pirate.

The only problem with that plan was Sarah. The second pirate's weapon was rapidly approaching her head. I wouldn't be able to wrestle the gun away from my pirate *and* dispatch the second pirate in time.

I had a backup weapon concealed in my suit; if I was quick on the draw, I could kill or disable the pirate charging towards Sarah. The pirate standing behind me would probably take a dim view of this. They would no doubt take any such attempt as licence to shoot me. I could attempt to dodge and shoot at the same time. My weapon needed only two claws to operate, leaving me six for ambulation and dodging purposes.

The trouble with this idea was that I would need to move fast enough to ensure my own safety, but not so fast as to risk compromising my shot at Sarah's attacker. I couldn't guarantee that I'd be able to do both.

I could attempt to disarm the pirate behind me whilst trying to shoot the second pirate at the same time. To do this, I'd need to stand on two legs, which wouldn't allow me to balance properly. My old drill instructor had repeatedly informed us that giving up balance in claw-to-claw combat was a shortcut to death.

I could throw myself to the floor and shoot the second pirate. This would get me out of the first pirate's line of sight but only for a second or two, and then I'd be in a really bad spot. I was starting to feel tense. I was losing concentration. What could I do?

Attempting to defuse the situation verbally was pointless, the second pirate was already swinging at Sarah's head. I could attempt to shoot the second pirate whilst jumping backwards *into* the first pirate. That would destabilise them, rendering them unable to shoot me immediately, but I didn't know how good their trigger discipline was. More than likely, the shock of the impact would cause them to fire by accident, which would be painful to say the least.

I needed to think. I wracked my brain for a path though the situation. The blades were descending towards Sarah's head. Every fraction of a second wasted meant that my plan would need to be even more perfect… and I hadn't even managed to come up with a workable outline. I needed more time, I needed more time.

I lost focus.

I felt time begin to speed up. I felt my mind stutter. I hadn't just failed to save one of us. Through inaction, I'd failed to save both of us.

That was when I saw Sarah's lower claw move. I traced the trajectory. She was going to move her body out of the way of the blade.

Had I the time, I would have slapped my forehead. Of *course* Sarah would dodge such an obviously telegraphed blow. I couldn't believe I had been so ridiculous as to not consider Sarah's actions in my planning. I had been, once again, incredibly patronising.

Self-recrimination would have to wait. Given this new information, my first plan would be just fine. I turned, twisting my body away from the gun pressed into my back. I brought a claw up behind me to catch the barrel of the gun and spin it with me, and scythed my two upper-left claws into the armed pirate's shoulders as I turned.

The pain wasn't enough to make the pirate drop the gun; he must have been truly intoxicated. I blocked two clumsy swipes with a free claw. I kicked into the pirate's abdomen as I bore down on the two claws I had buried in his shoulders. The pirate screamed and relinquished his grip on the gun, which turned out to be a long rifle.

I felt the rifle begin to fall to the ground, but I used the single claw I still had on its barrel to spin it around my body and into two other waiting claws. I located the trigger mechanism and shot the pirate in the thorax as he staggered away from me. Without waiting to see the rifle's effect, I turned, aimed and shot the second pirate in the head.

That pirate had just initiated a second swing after Sarah's well-timed dodge. My shot caused her legs to go limp. She staggered straight ahead, past Sarah, and collapsed, very nearly on top of Anthony. I turned again and shot the first pirate once more, just to be sure.

"Let's get out of here," said Sarah. She grabbed Anthony's claw and started to run. I followed.

Another pirate was running towards Anthony's chamber as we emerged. They were surprised enough by our sudden appearance to allow me to shoot them.

"Where are you keeping Oliver?" Sarah demanded as we ran.

"Three floors down, one module over," Anthony said. I drew in a breath as I ran. It was a long way to go. I tried to raise Bainbridge or Yarl on my communicator to see if they were closer than we were, but neither replied. An explosion rocked the corridor, giving a possible explanation as to why.

"We need to hurry," Anthony said. "I don't know how long this place will hold together."

"Oliver first," I said. Anthony turned and opened his mouth as if to argue. He paused when he saw my expression and nodded.

Anthony gently extricated himself from Sarah's grip and indicated the way to the nearest stairwell. We heard gunfire and running claws everywhere, but no pirates appeared, indicating that we were a safe enough distance from whatever trouble Yarl and Bainbridge were causing.

This all changed when we reached the stairwell. It was not often used, judging by the way it was decorated. It still looked like an ordinary stairwell, such that you might find in any space station across the galaxy. Elegant light fittings illuminated the burgundy carpet and the tasteful wall decorations. There was not a single skull or a pool of blood to be seen.

There were some obvious clues that this was the stairwell of a pirate base, however. Splashes of graffiti were dotted here and there, but they were rather half-hearted. They appeared to be there for the sake of completeness, as if the perpetrators had defaced every other location on the base so might as well tag this place, too.

It was an area that made me feel a little bit safer, being more familiar than the rest of the base. This feeling did not last long. A pirate was hurrying up the stairs from a lower floor, clutching a chest to their thorax. She paused when she saw us with Anthony and dropped her head.

"Commodore!" she said. "I was just... "

"Be gone from my sight, you worm!" said Anthony, who didn't stop, or even slow.

The pirate raised her gaze as Anthony passed and stared at Sarah and me. I heard a shout come from higher in the stairwell. Someone else had seen us.

"Commodore?" came the voice. "We need to get you to safety!"

Claws clattered down the stairs.

"Yes!" said the voice of the pirate who had until recently been either looting the base or engaged in legitimate wealth redistribution according to the pirate code. She started to follow as well. Two turns of the stairwell and both pirates were right behind us.

"Get rid of them," Anthony said over his shoulder. I turned.

"It's okay, we're escorting the commodore out of the base," I said. The pirates looked at me. They appeared sceptical.

I wasn't sure why. What about my five-piece suit, elegantly folded pocket handkerchief and my occasionally neat fur made me look anything other than piratical? The pirates were dressed differently from me, it was true. They adhered to a more raggedy style and their pocket handkerchiefs were stretched over their cranial regions, for some reason.

I couldn't afford for their scepticism to turn into suspicion. I decided to act. I pulled the trigger on my rifle. There was a click. The pirates looked down at my weapon. I fought the urge to do follow suit.

One pirate reached for a gun she had strapped across her thorax, the other raised a claw threateningly. I tossed my weapon aside and lashed out at the nearest pirate with two claws in quick succession. Before she could react, I wrapped two claws around her head and punched into her thorax with two more, skittering back down the stairs on my remaining four claws to keep the pirate off balance. The vicious looking gun she'd been holding up until that moment flew into the stairwell and was lost with a clatter.

My attack seemed to be working, the pirate was going limp in my claws, so I slammed her head into the stairwell wall and felt her stop moving entirely. The second pirate leapt forward, claws flying, but one of her lower claws became tangled in her fallen comrade's prone form, destabilising her. I still caught two blows in the head and one in the thorax as she attacked.

She lashed out at me again and again. I was able to block but not riposte, as she had a height advantage and was able to see where she was going. Things levelled out (literally) when I reached the flat turn in the stairway before the next flight of stairs.

I leapt away from the pirate, who let out a cry of triumph and charged at me. Believe it or not, this was what I had intended. I blocked the frantic flailing limbs of the pirate and grabbed hold of three of them. I wrenched the pirate to the side, using her momentum to my advantage. I scythed a lower limb at her legs and hurled the luckless individual towards the railing that separated the stairs from the stairwell. The pirate tipped over the railing, letting out a piteous cry as she fell.

I checked that all my bits were still where they should have been and ran to catch up with Sarah and Anthony; they had reached a door leading to the rest of the base, one flight below. Sarah had scooped up the fallen pirate's gun, and was hefting it experimentally. It was obviously heavy in her grip, but she was coping well.

"Did you have any trouble?" asked Sarah.

"None at all," I said. "Two pirates just had a plane to catch."

We stepped through the door and Anthony led us down the corridor beyond.

"What do you mean?" asked Sarah.

"Blast," I said. "I meant that they had a flight to catch."

"I still don't understand," said Sarah.

"Well, I had a fight with two pirates in a *flight* of stairs," I said, trying to get my breathing under control. "I thought it might be a good time for some wordplay to round things off nicely."

"Oh, I see."

We scurried along the deserted corridor in silence for a minute.

"You could have said they wanted to stop us, but you had to *step* on their ambitions to do so," Sarah said.

"Is that better?" I asked.

"It makes more sense."

I was planning to retort but another explosion rocked the station. A keening whine sounded down the corridor.

"That's the emergency evacuation alarm!" said Anthony. "We must hurry!"

We started to run.

"I wanted to watch you fighting just now," said Sarah, after a few moments of this. "But I didn't want to *stair*."

"You know what that fight proved?" I asked. "Sometimes it's both fight *and* flight. Of stairs."

"I'm guessing the pirates had a rough *landing*?"

"Yes, it was hy-*stair*-ical."

"Could you two please give it a rest?" said Anthony. "I can hear voices up ahead."

We skittered to a halt and, as my heartbeat slowed to a more normal rate, I found I too could hear voices. Or rather, one, very loud voice.

"Stop looting, you cut-throat dogs!" shouted the strangely familiar voice. The salt of the shipping lanes was in her voice and blood dripped from every syllable. "I'll splice your main brace if you don't avast the coxswain, you shark bait! Cutlasses!"

"What's she saying?" I hissed to Anthony.

"It's complete gibberish, but it's impressively piratical. Sounds like our new hire. A naja came looking for us a couple of days ago and asked to join up. Do you have any idea how rare it is for someone to ask to join? She must be a complete psychopath."

"Oh *no*," moaned Sarah. She stuck her head around the corner before pulling it back and rolling her eyes.

"What?" I asked, "who is it?"

"Megan."

"*Megan?*"

Sarah shrugged. "Megan."

Anthony looked between us. "You know her?"

Sarah spoke between gritted teeth. "We've met."

"Well she's in between us and the cells. We have to get past her, and we can't wait."

"I'm sure it'll be fine," I said. I stepped out into the corridor, to see it was, indeed Megan. She held a cutlass with the tip of her tail and was busy jamming it into the pedicel of a pirate who was clutching a wooden chest. The chest fell to the ground and spilled booty out onto the floor. At least, I assumed it was booty. It might have been plunder or something equally valuable.

"Megan! Good to see you again." I said.

Megan looked up. She twisted the cutlass out of the hapless pirate and waved it at me. "Good to see me? You, the person who found my company so unpleasant that you abandoned me because of a simple disagreement, are now saying it's good to see me?"

This was going less well than I'd hoped. "We're just passing through on our way to the cells," I said, approaching. I spread my upper legs non threateningly.

"We?" Megan asked. She peered around me. Her expression changed. Sarah must have emerged into the corridor behind me. "Oh look, you've still got your pet following you around. I hope you're happy, you little rat. We were having a great time before you ruined everything. I couldn't go home after you humiliated me. Look at me now! Pirates never have to deal with arachnids who change species every thirty seconds!" She flicked her tail so she was no longer pointing her sword at me. Instead, she aimed it resolutely at Sarah. "Heave ho, ye barnacle! Scuttle the black spot!"

Rage rose inside me. I already had more adrenaline coursing through my system than was healthy and I'd grievously injured two pirates who only wanted to help their commodore. I wasn't going to put up with any of Megan's nonsense when we had places to be.

"Get out of the way, Megan," I said, stepping forward.

Megan looked surprised, but swung her cutlass back to point at me. "Megan the pirate gives way to no landlubber! Shiver me crow's nest!"

I lost my temper. I lashed out with two claws, which Megan easily dodged. She riposted with her cutlass. I caught the blade between my leftmost upper legs and twisted it out of her scaly grip, sending it shuddering into the wall of the station. Megan lashed out with her tail, wrapping it around my lower legs. I stabbed a claw towards her throat, but found my legs whipped from under me. I crashed to the floor and fought to get free.

Megan towered over me. She opened her mouth, revealing her venomous fangs. She swayed slightly as I struggled to get free. She looked like she was picking her moment to sink her fangs into my flesh.

"Hey!" shouted Sarah from behind me.

Megan looked up, as did I. Sarah had raised the arachnid weapon she'd looted. It was enormous in her tiny human legs, and she was clearly struggling to keep it trained on Megan.

Megan chuckled. "What? What's the arachnid who thinks she's an attack helicopter going to do with that weapon? You can barely lift it!"

"I'm a human, not a fucking attack helicopter," said Sarah. She squeezed the trigger. The shot caught Megan in the face. She screamed and released me. I leapt to my feet and held Megan down whilst Sarah and Alison ran past her. Megan didn't seem to want to do much other than growl in pain.

Once Sarah and Alison were clear, I thought about saying something clever and cutting to Megan, but I couldn't think of anything, so I just ran to catch up with my friends.

We turned two more corners before Anthony announced: "We're here."

I would have been able to tell that, even without Anthony's helpful comment. This was partly because a brig is the sort of thing that's very difficult to mistake for, say, a sitting room. There are certain universal qualities to brigs. The security fields, for one. The trough system to carry away the inevitably-spilled bodily fluids, for another.

The other clue that we had reached the brig was that I could hear Oliver screaming for assistance. I tried to rush to his aid but couldn't get past the blasted door. I battered on it, feeling useless at my inability to tear through the metal door to rescue my friend. After a few attempts, I became aware that Anthony was trying to get my attention.

"Would you leave it out?" he said. "I've got the security hashsign."

Sarah laid a gentling claw on my thorax and I drew back, shocked at the speed my breathing and how thoughtless my actions had been up to that point. The security field allowed Anthony through. I could hear Oliver within. I made to follow but Sarah's meagre grip arrested my movement.

"I'll tell you anything you want!" came Oliver's voice from inside. "Just please get me out of here! I'll take you to the mercenary! That's all I wanted!" Strange. Oliver was playing along with their charade...

Anthony led Oliver out of his cell. When he saw us, he displayed a curious mix of emotions. Confusion was first, I think, but that was quickly followed up by maybe fear or relief? Or a combination of the two? Frelief? Relear? I could come up with a name for it later.

"I knew you'd find out sooner or later," he said.

"We really don't have time for this," said Anthony. "We need to run."

So we did. Anthony led the way, Sarah running to keep up. Oliver and I followed behind, lolloping along slowly in their wake. Occasional explosions or crashes rumbled throughout the base. It sounded as if the place was falling apart. Hopefully Bainbridge and Yarl would be taking that as their cue to leave with all speed as well.

Suddenly, and unexpectedly, Anthony skidded to a halt. "We're here," he said.

I looked around. The place was entirely unfamiliar. It certainly wasn't where we'd pulled up when we'd ferried over from the *Cox*. "No, we're not," I said.

"Don't be dense," said Anthony, tapping away at a data terminal. A hidden section of wall opened, revealing a short corridor, at the end of which was a shuttle. Not a boat, not even a motor vehicle; an enclosed space shuttle. This thing was designed to withstand combat, it wasn't open to the elements, only protected by an atmosphere field. It was a lifeboat.

We piled in. Thankfully, the shuttle was large, otherwise we'd have been sitting in each other's laps. Anthony said he didn't know how to fly the thing. Oliver started making noises about wanting to take over, but Sarah got in there first. She sat at the controls and manoeuvred us away from the base.

"Oh, hello… " said Sarah after a moment. I tried to peer over her head at the controls, but I couldn't get a clear picture of what was going on. "We've got company," Sarah said, after examining the instruments.

"More pirates?" I asked.

"Oh please, no… " Anthony moaned. "I can't drink any more grog. I hate grog. They always put lemonade in it and sprigs of mint and ice cubes, and they make out like it's this great summer treat but it's just this really sweet nonsense that isn't even *that* alcoholic."

"It's not pirates," Sarah said. "It's the police."

Oliver screamed.

Chapter Fourteen

On Liberty and the Pursuit of Long-Term Happiness

I sat in a break room, idly smoothing and re-smoothing my fur. My title – and, by extension, my status – had been enough to prevent my arrest. I was merely assisting the constabulary with their enquiries.

The police had, apparently, been drawn by a large number of explosions from an area of space they'd thought was abandoned. They had arrived in force, wondering if a new war was starting, only to find the pirate base and a large number of drunken pirates attempting to flee the area. They'd started arresting as many people as possible and taking every ship they could into custody, along with our shuttle. We'd then been ferried to a police station where the anti-piracy unit worked; the same anti-piracy unit I'd spoken to shortly before we discovered Yarl.

I'd been led past groups of pirates in irons. I'd been led past a kennel where Sarah and Anthony were being kept. Finally, they'd put me in what appeared to be a break room.

After a certain amount of boredom, the door clicked open and a police officer slid in. She was a naja and wore scale-paint instead of a cloth uniform. She sat down opposite me and opened a file. She began to read. I studied the backs of my claws for a while. Then I stared at the ceiling. Eventually, I said:

"Look, could you get my two friends out of the kennel? It's not very polite to keep them chained up in there with your hounds."

The officer looked up at me. "Are they people of consequence?"

"My friend Sarah once said something to me that I'll never forget," I said. "She got it from this old human television programme. I can't remember how it went, exactly, but it was something along these lines: To find an inconsequential person must be remarkable, for I have never done so."

"You seem very sure that they are people," the cop said. I suddenly felt less bad that I hadn't asked her name.

"I *am* certain," I said, fixing her with a stare.

"Very well," said the officer. She rose from her chair and stuck her head into the corridor. She called for someone called 'Jane' and held a whispered conversation with them. I waited, patiently.

"So, could you tell me," said the officer, returning to her basket-chair, "about the curious company you keep? A dogsbody for a law firm, a human rights advocate and a smuggler. Was there a reason you four were in the shuttle together or was it all a co-incidence?"

"Oliver is *not* a smuggler!" I said, shrilly. "He's one of my closest friends!"

"He can be both," the officer said.

"He could be, but he's not!" Match point to me, I thought.

The officer flicked her tongue, sceptically. She slid a dataslate across the table towards me. I looked at it.

Sarah once got me to read an article in some periodical or other about evidence. The article made the point that people, when presented with evidence that contradicts their beliefs, tend to double down on their false opinions, rather than change.

I read the testimony of the pirates who claimed they had been dealing with Oliver for years. I read the reports from the police on my home planet of Ranan who had tracked a smuggling ring to my home, only to conclude that they must have made a mistake somewhere along the way due to my name and social standing. Apparently, the police on Ranan were either very respectful of the aristocracy or extremely bad at their jobs. Or perhaps both.

I read the reports from Oliver's superiors during his tours of duty. Apparently, he had operated a black market for stimulants and body augmentations throughout most of his time in service.

I read about the arrests that had taken place over the last few hours in my home city of Tunsleworth. Once the pirates had started talking, other middle men and smugglers in the city had been revealed. They had been tracked down and arrested. They weren't *all* linked to Oliver... but most of them were. He had apparently been running his own little empire out of my home, using my respectability as a cover for his actions.

I thought about the various little favours I'd done for him in the past. There were always friends of his who needed help, or packages he needed to store in the flat until someone came to collect them. I'd even transported items for him on occasion. I hadn't asked what they were. Why would I? He was my friend.

There was all this information, there was all this *evidence* and... I had a choice. I could believe in Oliver, I could believe in my friend and see it all as... deception... or a conspiracy. I could see it for what I knew it to be... Or I could use my head, and understand that I had been lied to and exploited by someone I had known for most of my life.

This was what felt unreal to me... the universe as I *knew* it to be in my head and the universe as described on the dataslate in my claws directly contradicted each other. They were out of sync, they were wrong… and I had a choice as to which I trusted in.

I say I had a choice. I never had a choice. I had this overwhelming feeling, flipping through the evidence the police officer showed me… a feeling of the bottom dropping out of everything. I never consciously decided whether I would believe it or not, I just *knew* what my reaction was.

And… what genuinely scared me is that, in another life, had I made different choices… I knew that I might have believed in Oliver. I might have ignored the evidence on the table in front of me.

The thing about Oliver had been that… he was a wonderful chap to be around, for all of his little ways. I knew where I stood when I was with him, but he didn't like having other people around. I had needed to fight claw and fang to get Sarah into the flat. He hadn't liked it when I'd had chums round, which meant that when I was feeling sad or vulnerable, for the longest time the only voice of reason I'd heard was his.

And had I not had that wonderful human being, so strong in spite of… or maybe *because* of her vulnerabilities… had I not had Sarah, I might never have been able to see Oliver for who he was.

The officer very kindly left the room whilst I removed a speck of grit that had managed to find its way into my eye. Once she returned, I decided I should tell her everything. This took quite some time, and I found some parts of the story very difficult. Very difficult indeed.

Thankfully, the officer, whom I had thought a brute because of her treatment of Sarah and Anthony… was kind to me. She was patient, she was polite. She kept me stocked with tea and the occasional tot of something a little stronger when I needed it. The officer recorded our interview session and asked questions here and there. I answered them as best I could.

I found myself extremely tired by the time I had finished my story. The officer was understanding.

I added my digital signature to the recording and was allowed to leave, on the understanding that I didn't vacate the immediate area just yet. I was ferried, along with Sarah and Anthony, to *The Dancing Cox*, which had been towed to the police station along with the other ships the police had captured.

We didn't talk much in the shuttle. We were all very tired, I think. I enquired as to the whereabouts of Bainbridge and Yarl, but our driver either didn't know or was deliberately uncooperative.

When we reached the *Cox*, we found Bainbridge waiting for us.

I say waiting. He appeared behind me the moment the police escort disembarked. It gave me quite a start. Adrenaline in my system was not what I needed at that moment. I'd been looking forward to slipping into the dreamless. Sarah was a little shocked. Anthony nearly had a heart attack.

Sarah took Anthony off to show him where the hammocks were; or rather, their tattered remains.

"Did they hurt you? Are you okay? What did you tell them?" asked Bainbridge, his voice rather tense.

"No, maybe and everything," I said.

"What did they tell you?" Bainbridge asked, after a long exhale.

"About what Oliver has been up to for the last… " I waved a few claws. "… However many years."

Bainbridge thought about this.

"I'm sorry, Jay," he said, eventually.

"I'm not sure I want to carry on with my holiday," I said.

Bainbridge looked up at the glinting stars. "See how you feel in the morning, old salt," he said, "but we've vanquished pirates and unmasked a smuggling ring. You never know, things might actually be calmer and more relaxing from this point."

His words held merit. I didn't really feel... I didn't have a coherent emotional reaction to anything that had happened. There were too many emotions sloshing about the place. I asked him if he'd been released from police custody and he found this amusing. I'm ashamed to say I was rather irritated by the chap's giggle.

Bainbridge explained that he had been enjoying himself, terrorising pirates, when the cops showed up. He'd surrendered to the police and then he had discharged himself from their custody as soon as they'd reached the station. He had dropped in on Yarl on his way out. Yarl was securely restrained, and Bainbridge had asked it if a breakout was in order.

Yarl had pondered this question. It appeared to be considering its choices: to escape prison, and try to return to its life before it got involved with The Lower Biggleswade Alcohol and Crumpet Society, or to see what charges were to be levied against it, and face them, in the hope that a brighter future was waiting up ahead.

I nodded at this news, glad that everyone had made it out in one piece. Still, I was exhausted. Sleep was, I decided, the one thing I really needed. I asked Bainbridge if he minded my turning in for forty winks. He bowed and told me that I deserved a rest. He said that he needed some time to himself, as well. He hadn't yet completed his daily therapy and, after his experiences on Dessan... well, it wouldn't do to miss today's session.

We parted company. Bainbridge scuttled below deck to find somewhere quiet and I attempted to catch forty or so winks. Naturally, sleep would not come.

The hammocks didn't help. They were more the consistency of cheese wire than sturdy cloth after their encounter with Dessan's debris field, so I attempted to sleep on the deck. This did not result in success. I could not get comfortable and, when I found a position that was at least not dreadfully uncomfortable, my head just wouldn't settle.

The sound of humans sleeping was relaxing, at least. Sarah and Anthony had taken the blankets from Sarah's pack and created an impromptu cocoon. They slept together, soundly. I must have drifted off eventually. My dreams were confused and fitful.

I awoke to the sound of ships approaching the police station. I rose and walked to the port side, which boasted the most complete view of the station. The station was a space base not unlike the pirates' lair. It was considerably less ramshackle, but made up for this by being painted the horrifically ugly universal police colours of salmon pink and whitewash.

The main complex gave way to a shuttle landing pad, open to the vacuum but protected by an atmosphere shield. I could see several figures in police uniforms waiting there, with a few dozen pirates in irons lined up along one wall. Off to one side, guarded by two officers each, were Oliver and Yarl.

As I watched, the pirates were herded into a large craft painted in police colours. It must have been one of the craft that woke me. The pirates were being transported to the nearest law court for trial, it would seem.

Presumably, Oliver and Yarl would soon be loaded into the same craft, or one much like it.

I needed to say goodbye. Not to Oliver; I couldn't face Oliver, not now... but it would be the height of bad manners to let Yarl leave without saying goodbye. I had only known it a short time, but I had enjoyed its company.

I took the skiff over to the police station. I was waved down by a nervous patrolman, possibly worried I was attempting some sort of breakout. I explained my business and he allowed me to proceed as long as I tried nothing funny. I assured him that my intentions were the least humorous I'd ever known them to be.

Yarl and Oliver were standing fifty or so metres apart. I approached Yarl, being careful to avoid Oliver's gaze.

"I see you made your decision," I said. I didn't really know how to begin a conversation such as this.

Yarl grinned. "What decision?"

"You've decided to pay for your crimes?" I said.

"What crimes?" it asked.

I thought maybe I wouldn't miss this chap that much, after all.

"Those massacres you committed for the selection committee of The Lower Biggleswade Alcohol and Crumpet Society?"

"Oh," said Yarl. "Ooh yes. That. I say, I knew there was a reason I had these on."

It showed me the restraints that bound its various legs together.

"These officers," Yarl said, indicating the heavily armed police standing around it, "went over things a few times with me. Apparently, I'm one of the most wanted beings in this area of the galaxy. Well, I mean, can you imagine? That came as something of a shock."

It chuckled. The police officers shifted their grips on their weapons.

"But they were very nice," Yarl said, "and explained that I would have to go to prison for a bit but I would get psych… psyk… some sort of help."

I didn't know if I wanted to cry or not.

"Yes, yes, I know what I meant to say!" said Yarl. "When I'm out after all this prison and medical stuff is over, we can have another holiday. Would you like that? A slightly longer one? With fewer massacres?"

I smiled and nodded. I didn't want to mention that, chances were, I would be dead by the time Yarl was out of whatever prison they put it in. I didn't want to spoil its mood. "I would very much like that," I said, my voice cracking.

They led Yarl away. I watched it go. Oliver followed not long after.

The thought that I should say something arrived in an unhelpful way. It needled its way into my consciousness. I stared at Oliver's back as he was led towards the transport.

I knew I had to say something to sever our relationship. I needed to draw a line under… whatever that thing was that had existed between us. I called for his guards to wait. They obliged, and I scampered up.

Oliver glared at me.

"Oliver," I said.

"What?"

"I need you to move out of the flat," I said. "I'll have your things sent on."

Oliver stared at me for a long time, then shook his head. "Let's go," he said to his escorts.

I thought about offering to write a reference for his next place of residence. The poor chap had experienced problems finding lodgings in the past, after all… but I refrained. I was attempting to sever connections with the scoundrel, not give him a reason to intrude back into my life.

Besides, his next place of residence was most likely prison. I didn't think you needed a reference to get allocated a prison cell. I watched the shuttle depart and went to ask the desk sergeant if Anthony, Sarah and I were free to move on. They didn't know so they fetched the officer who'd interrogated me, who informed me that we were. The officer confided that they had been thinking of charging Anthony along with the rest of the pirates. They'd refrained, however. Given the mitigating circumstances surrounding his actions and the complications involving his species, it was deemed best to just ferry him away from the station with as few questions as possible. Less paperwork for the police, no unpleasantness in a courtroom for Anthony.

Chapter Fifteen

There Are Emotional Sections
In This Chapter

I found my thoughts clouded when I returned to the *Cox*. The distractions of the past few days had melted away, leaving me facing my approaching death and the breakdown of a relationship I had treasured with little to distract me. That being said, I was not supposed to be distracted. I was supposed to be coming to terms with my condition. So far, I had been doing precious little in the way of coming to terms with anything, whilst allowing myself to be distracted far too often.

It was about time I faced up to some of the things I'd been maintaining stolid ignorance about. I found a deckchair, sat at the bow of the *Cox* and started to do some serious thinking.

Thinking can be tough when, like me, you're prone to getting muddled... but after an hour or two I felt I was getting the hang of it.

I don't feel comfortable detailing my precise thoughts as I sat watching the stars. Suffice to say, I thought a lot about death and what to do with the fleeting time I had left. Occasionally, Bainbridge or Sarah would approach to ask if I needed anything, but for the most part they assumed I wanted to be alone with my thoughts. This was fortunate, as I didn't know how to frame that particular sentiment without appearing rude.

After a few hours, I felt the engines kick into life. I didn't know where we were going. I didn't really care. Onwards to Newbury Towers, I suspected. Bainbridge had people he needed to see there, after all.

Much later, when my brain finally became bored with thinking, and ennui gradually gave way to hunger, I learned what had transpired during my trance:

Bainbridge, Sarah and Anthony had discussed what would be best to do with the ex-pirate. For his part, Anthony was confused and emotional. Sarah suggested a few courses of action. So did Bainbridge, but Bainbridge's ideas were less constructive and mostly involved causing damage to people or property for therapeutic reasons.

Anthony's reactions to the various plans were muted. He appeared to be withdrawing into himself. Only one suggestion from Sarah elicited a positive reaction: they should find him a supportive group of humans that could help get him back on his claws. Sarah, being Sarah, knew groups like this across the galaxy. Such groups could look after Anthony until he was well enough to travel. Once he was recovered, he could decide if he wanted to return to his old home or start afresh on this new planet.

Anthony accepted this plan, so Sarah and Bainbridge spent an hour trying to locate a nearby planet that had such a group, but also wasn't an unentertaining backwater or likely to get us involved in another complex murder plot.

A planet was selected and vetted by all three parties. There had been several possible candidates, but one was chosen that was on the way to Newbury Towers, so we didn't waste too much time buzzing about. Anthony insisted he didn't want to be a bother.

The chosen planet was called Colin. The reason behind its name was lost in the fog of history, but it was generally theorised that the first settlers hadn't been able to think of a good name. Someone had suggested Colin and everyone, to their shame, had accepted it as a compromise. Now that the name had been in place for millennia, it was practically impossible to change it.

It was a great deal less provincial than Dessan, the last planet we'd visited. This was mainly due to the famous University of Colin, the institute that had educated Colin Desabio, Colin St John and, of course, Colin Trout.

The university didn't *only* accept Colins. That would be ridiculous. It was just that people called Colin tended to do extremely well when attending that particular university, for some reason. I had a distant cousin – now named Colin – who changed her name specifically to increase her chances of being admitted by that institution. Such tactics weren't unusual. The university assured its applicants on all promotional material: 'Whilst we do accept students with names other than Colin, legally changing your name prior to application as a show of commitment is, quite frankly, the least you could do'

Colin was about half a day's travel away, so Bainbridge fired up the engines, pointed the *Cox* in roughly the right direction and set off.

The next hour passed with little drama, which should have been cause for suspicion. As the first hour bled dry and the second hour started to make its presence known, Bainbridge was compelled to walk past the cupboard that Sarah was hiding in.

The little scamp had attempted to sneak past Bainbridge and had secreted herself in a hidey-hole, the better to leap out at him and shout 'boo'. This was far from the most inspired prank Sarah had ever pulled, but she hadn't felt there was time for any of her usual intricate preparations.

Sadly, Bainbridge was aware of her attempts at stealth and humoured her for a short while. He then became concerned that her body would resent being folded into such an exposed space for any great length of time. He strolled past the cupboard, making as much noise as he could.

Sarah leapt out at Bainbridge and yelled 'boo'. What happened next depends on who you believe. Sarah described Bainbridge leaping ten feet into the air and yelling fit to burst. Bainbridge told of how he stared at Sarah, then remembered that he wasn't supposed to know she was there, and said something along the lines of 'aaah, you got me'.

Coincidentally, it was around that time that my dataslate started receiving calls. The slate was still in the hiding spot Sarah had found for it. She had agreed to look after my dataslate because I was supposed to be spending time with my thoughts and my friends, not the data waves.

The first call my slate received since setting off went unnoticed, as Sarah was in the process of leaping out at Bainbridge. She was in no position to hear the slate; I was later informed that she had hidden it in a plain envelope, which was taped halfway up the hull at the stern of the *Cox*.

The second call did manage to get Sarah's attention. It was for this very reason that, some hours into my reverie, I was interrupted by Sarah storming up to me, yelling: "There's a *cure* for your mindvirus?"

"Oh," I said, rising.

"You have been going on and on about how you're dying," Sarah bellowed, "for *days* now... and you didn't think it was worth mentioning that you might not be? That you could seek treatment? What the blue blistering blazes is wrong with you, Jay?"

I started to answer, but Sarah informed me that her question had been purely rhetorical.

This is what had occurred: Sarah had heard my dataslate receive a call. She had asked Bainbridge to fetch it from its hiding place. This done, she unlocked it to see who was calling. It might, after all, be important. She saw that the call was from my doctor.

Had this call taken place on another occasion, Sarah might have ignored it and simply told me when she next saw me. As she explained it, though, she was worried about my state of mind. She had never seen me this deep in thought for this long. I usually gave up on thought after about thirty seconds, unless I was supposed to be developing some sort of strategy.

She called my doctor back, explained what state I was in and why this was the case. The doctor asked if I had been taking my medication. It was news to Sarah that I had medication to take. This was because I'd never picked the stuff up.

The mindvirus, you see, was curable. There was medication that could fix it. The medication would cause serious side-effects and was not guaranteed to succeed, but it was successful in the majority of cases.

Sarah asked me why, for the love of God Empress Patricia Wilberforce IV, I wasn't taking it.

I held my head in my claws.

"Because," I said, "I haven't decided if I want to take it yet."

Sarah Frowned. "Oh?"

"The doctor sent me on this trip so I could come to terms with my condition," I said. "Part of that was… I wanted to see if I could think of a reason to carry on."

I waved a claw. Sarah appeared to understand what I meant. "Oh, Jay…" she said. I sat down. She sat down on the deck next to me. I had really hoped to keep Sarah from discovering the reason for my ambivalence about remaining amongst the living. I did not feel strong enough for this conversation. I barely felt strong enough to admit the reason to myself. Nevertheless, Sarah had found out. I suspected I needed to confide in her now, or never at all.

"During my first tour," I said, keeping my eyes on the deck of the ship, "I was tasked with choosing a location for an ambush. There were several possible locations, but the one I considered most useful was a small planet in the inner circle of the solar system we were in.

"The planet was mostly inhabited by arachnids, but one continent had been given over to a human colony. That is where I decided we should stage our ambush."

Sarah stroked my back. I heard her tiny mouth open to speak, but I pressed on. If I didn't finish this story now… "We needed to clear the area for our troops to operate in," I said. "So, I ordered that the humans be exterminated."

I felt Sarah's tiny human hoof or hand or whatever it was called freeze where it had been stroking my back.

"I had only seen humans as feral wildlife. I thought this was a move equivalent to pest control. You know how some poor families need to drown kittens because they can't afford to keep them? That was what I thought I was doing… disposing of creatures that didn't really matter if we could save *real* people."

I spat that penultimate word.

"Do you know the worst thing? Other than the thousands of lives I took? I felt sorry for them. I thought it was a shame. I didn't go any further than that. I didn't feel sorry for the creatures I'd annihilated, then go and find out if I should have taken another course of action. I mused that life could be cruel sometimes and carried on with the campaign. It never occurred to me what I had truly done."

Sarah's hand was no longer on my back.

"And then I met you," I said. "And I met your friends. And I started to question everything I'd believed in up to that point… and then I felt the guilt start to take hold of me. That was when I knew what I had done out of pure, malicious ignorance. Out of the unthinking assumption that *of course* humans don't matter. Everyone knows that… .

"And that was when I started looking forward to the day I would die, not just because I won't have to feel this guilt any more, but because I don't deserve to remain on this plane of existence after what I have done.

"I thought about making amends but whenever I tried to think what that might mean, I ran up against this wall of thought that said, 'You cannot make amends for what you did to that colony. You *murdered* ten thousand, three hundred and ninety-two thinking, feeling people.'

"That is why I love my mindvirus. It will cause me to just slip away. I don't need to think about it. I'll just slowly start to disappear. A month from now, I won't be able to work. Six months from now, I'll forget who my friends are. A year from now, I won't even remember my own name. It'll all just be taken away from me and I won't have to feel this anymore. If I'm dreadfully lucky, one of the first things to go will be the memories of that massacre.

"It's that, or try to fight it. Try to face up to what I have done, try to do something to make up for things. I don't know if I'd be able to do that. I'm not strong like you or Bainbridge. The drugs will be painful… and the end result is the same, whatever I do. And overall- I don't deserve- I don't think I d-… I don't *know*."

I flopped a claw about to try to illustrate my point, but I'm not sure if it had the desired effect.

"Do you have an opinion on the matter?" I asked, as Sarah had been very quiet for some time after I finished talking. She sniffed.

"I had no idea," she said, eventually.

"I haven't been able to tell you," I said.

"Do you know the number of human deaths I caused before finding myself?"

I tried to look at her, but I couldn't. I tried to answer her, but I couldn't.

"Roughly three hundred. They were mostly the result of collateral damage. I didn't keep a full count. We've all done terrible things, Jay. I won't say the deaths weren't your fault, because we both know they were... but our upbringings were more at fault. How did humans come to be seen as nothing but animals? Who first thought and said that? Who unthinkingly repeated it? Who had so little empathy that they classified a clearly intelligent species as vermin, simply because they dress untidily, have some unfortunate habits and smell a bit?"

She sniffed. I saw her round on me in my peripheral vision. "*And*, by the way, you *have* been making amends. You invited me into your home. You put me in touch with my charity. You've supported us financially and by challenging the attitudes of your friends who think as you used to. Every time you have stood up for the good name of humanity, you have chipped away just a little at our reputation amongst the other species. It doesn't excuse what you did but you *are* trying.

"There's no absolution for your actions... but you have a choice about what you do from now on. You can make the universe a better place, or you can abandon it as it is now."

We talked. It was a difficult conversation. Both of us felt in the dark to an extent when it came to discussing this particular topic.

Slowly, Sarah gave me her opinion, which was that she felt the universe was a better place thanks to my presence.

I didn't know if I agreed or not, but it's useful to have someone else's opinion on the matter.

Sarah did raise a fair point, though. It was this:

If I did not wish to carry on, it would be better to actively decide that this was the correct course of action. If I continued on my current course, I would likely dither for long enough to have the decision made for me, whether it was the correct decision or not. The default position, she assured me, should be that life was worth living.

I quibbled mildly at this point, but she assured me that *my* life was certainly worth living. I didn't feel the need to argue strongly. I could, she reminded me, always stop taking my medication if I felt that was the right thing to do. Otherwise, she would count it as a favour if I started taking them.

She said she felt no betrayal about not being told what had transpired during my first tour. She completely understood my silence. She told me that she loved me, and that I needed to remember that.

She pressed my dataslate into my claw. This was a surprise, as I hadn't even particularly wanted the thing, but I saw that Sarah had dialled my doctor's number. I spoke to her. She informed me that a supply of medication would be ready for me when I reached Colin.

I could always stop taking it if I wanted to.

We arrived at Colin several hours later. I was feeling a little less wretched, having chatted with Sarah for some time. It was getting late in our personal days. We had all been awake for at least twelve hours. Because of my disturbed sleep, I was carrying something of a debt in that regard.

We decided it would be best to drop down to Colin now, rather than take any rest. This was mostly due to the fact that our bedding was still unfit for purpose. Our lives would be improved significantly by a night in a real bed. If our night's sleep could be counted on to not be interrupted by screams every five minutes, things might be said to be perfect.

There was a certain amount of buzzing about in preparation for our trip down to Colin. I stayed watching the stars for the most part. Organisation is one of those things I'm very happy to indulge in, but not when in the middle of an existential crisis.

Eventually, we all piled into the skiff and I was caught up on the Grand Plan, if that's not overstating things too much. It had been decided that Sarah would take Anthony to her contact at the human support group, whilst Bainbridge and I shopped for new hammocks and bedding. We'd then meet up to find a place to rest our weary heads. On reflection, the term Grand Plan was rather fitting.

Sarah dropped us off in the largest city we could find, reasonably near to the University of Colin. Students probably needed bedding, we reasoned, even the ones that weren't named Colin.

The city of Colinsberg was quite pleasant, really. Bits of it were decently modern, but the area we found ourselves in boasted cobbled streets and buildings that were a few hundred years old if they were a day. It reminded me of the town where I'd attended university.

Bainbridge and I waved as Sarah shoved off with Anthony to take him to the community that would assist with his recovery. We then set out to look for a shop that might be able to replace what was damaged during our stay on Dessan.

The first few shops we tried all sold incense, fancy dress costumes and forms that would allow you to legally change your name to Colin. It was because of this that we moved a little further away from the university.

To our surprise, we came across a promising looking shop not long after making this decision. It was squeezed between a shop that sold alcoholic stimulants and an emporium dedicated to the sale of deodorant.

The sign on the door indicated that the shop was open, although the windows were dark. We could make out bedding in the gloom, though, so we walked in. I briefly wondered if we had stumbled upon an intimacy club or something equally ghastly, but I was thankfully wrong.

An entire wall of the shop was lined with bedding of different sorts. Hammocks hung from the ceiling. There were also shelves dedicated to candles, cushions and other homely comforts but those weren't relevant to my mission, so I paid them no mind.

What did demand my attention was the shop assistant. She popped out from behind the polished wooden counter as soon as the bell over her door rang. She held in her claws three extremely potent-looking firearms. Bainbridge and I glanced at each other and slowly raised our claws.

"You," said the assistant. "What are your names?"

Well, this was good news. She wanted to be introduced. It's rare to shoot someone you've been introduced to. It's not polite. I replied that my name was Jay, and Bainbridge said that his name was David T. Suffolk.

"Neither of you are called Colin?" asked the assistant.

We assured her that we were not called Colin. The assistant exhaled and lowered her weapons.

"They're everywhere," she whispered, the dread in her voice chilling us to the flesh.

Bainbridge's eyes met mine, and I asked, "Have you worked here long?"

The assistant laughed. "Only a week. A week I've been surviving. Living off my wits. They won't get me. They won't make me one of *them.*" Sudden suspicion clouded her features. "Wait. How did you get through? Are you infected?"

"No," Bainbridge said.

"What," I said, before the assistant could say anything else, "do you think is happening here?"

The assistant explained that her uncle had worked in the shop until a week ago. Sadly, he had died and left this shop to her in his will. She had only worked here for a few days before she noticed something odd. Everyone appeared to be called Colin, and even people who weren't would turn up later calling themselves Colin. She naturally suspected foul play. She had, she reported, been hiding in her shop for the last thirty hours after her uncle's assistant came into work, suddenly calling herself Colin. The memory of this incident made her shudder.

"You are worried that proximity to the Colins will convince you to change your name?" Bainbridge asked.

"Worried? *Worried?*" cried the assistant. "I've seen it happen! I had someone come into the shop on my first day, she was called Anna. Two days later I see her again and chat to her... she's suddenly called Colin! There can be no escape!"

"Fantastical as your theory is," said Bainbridge, "I'm afraid that the truth is far more mundane."

We explained about how people would change their names to be favoured by the university.

The assistant raised her weapons again. "Do you think me a fool?" she demanded. Bainbridge passed her his dataslate. On it, he had queued up the history of the University of Colin that we had read before dropping down to this planet. The assistant read it.

"Oh, I do feel silly." She laid down her weapons on the shop counter. "I mean… this might be a trick?" she said, hopefully.

"Come now," said Bainbridge. "What is the more likely explanation?"

"Our explanation doesn't seem particularly likely," I muttered in Bainbridge's ear. He shushed me. The assistant agreed, reluctantly, that she was possibly not in danger of becoming a Colin.

With that out of the way, all that needed to be done was to replace our hammocks and bedding. This was done with some care but, as we were the only customers present, it took barely five and twenty minutes.

We emerged into the blazing sunlight with our packages tucked under our legs. This made walking both difficult and undignified, so we found a student that didn't look busy (amazingly, we had no difficulty with this) and slipped them a few quid to carry the packages for us.

Without our boat we had no way to get our purchases back to the *Cox,* so we decided then was as good a time as any to locate a place to rest for the night. We shortly found an inn that looked promising thanks to my tactic of wandering aimlessly, rather than Bainbridge's proposed 'evidence driven' approach. Our student was grateful to gift our packages to the girl in a porter's uniform before grimacing and scuttling off. We followed the porter inside.

The interior of the inn was pleasant, the plentiful windows keeping it from being too dark. Stuffed creature heads lined the walls but, in deference to a modern distaste for such things, someone had placed silly hats on each one, which made the atmosphere rather jolly.

I felt my mood lifting as I looked around for the reception desk. Bainbridge spotted it first and stalked up to it, the receptionist looking nervous as he approached. He glanced at her name display and then locked eyes with her.

"Ursula," he said.

"Good afternoon, sir. How may I help?"

"Are you running any sort of Live Action Roleplay?" he asked.

"No sir," said Ursula.

"Okay," said Bainbridge, thinking. "Have a group of strangers gathered here on this night, all with a mysterious past? They won't have met each other before, but they'll all have been invited by the same person."

"We've only got two other people staying here," said Ursula. "And I think they're here to visit their children at the University of Colin."

"Are either of them potential murderers?" Bainbridge asked.

"We're all potential murderers," said Ursula, nervously. "It's the Arachnid Paradox. Each of us is the epitome of both virtue and vice, it is only circumstance that allows us to rise above our worst instincts."

Bainbridge blinked "Good enough," he said. "Three rooms, please."

We were shown up to three decently-sized rooms on the first floor. The porter stashed our purchases in Bainbridge's chamber, whilst we attempted to find out whether Sarah was finished settling Anthony in. Sarah didn't answer her communicator, which Bainbridge seemed oddly pleased about.

"Shall we get some dinner, Jay?" he asked, leaning against the doorframe to his room.

I hadn't realised I was hungry until he raise the subject. I had thought to spend the next hour or so crying in my room, but eating was probably a more sensible way to pass my time. I remarked that his timing was excellent. He grinned. We both retired for a few moments to freshen up. I scuttled downstairs to find Bainbridge in conversation with Ursula about local eating houses. Five were recommended, and Bainbridge suggested we try the one that didn't have the word 'Colin' in the name.

That was how we found ourselves eating traditional arachnid cuisine in a charming rooftop restaurant overlooking the city. The drummond and pigmato soup was excellent, as was the view. The fish and the wine that came with it were stunning. With each mouthful, I was able to put my conversation with Sarah further and further from my mind. I was able to relax and enjoy the food, the view and the company.

The only thing that made the evening less than fantastically enjoyable was Bainbridge's behaviour. The chap was acting a little… oddly. He mentioned several times that he'd really enjoyed being on holiday with me. Once we'd finished the fish, he complimented me on the things I'd done with my head-fur. As we selected what coffee and plugnuts we wanted to round things off with, he mentioned that I had done sterling work getting Sarah out of a sticky situation on the pirate base.

There was other conversation happening around such points, but those were the ones that stuck in my mind. As the bill arrived, I decided that I needed to find out what was going on.

"Look here," I said, "why are you being so nice to me?"

Bainbridge suddenly looked hunted, like he had been caught divulging something he was supposed to be keeping secret. Then, it struck me. I was suddenly very angry.

"Sarah told you, didn't she?" I growled.

Bainbridge's eye-fur shot up.

"I think that's a little much. I had been keeping both my past and my response to my condition private for good reason. I don't appreciate being patronised by *you*, young Bainbridge. I'm sure you have the best of intentions for trying to cheer me up but if I choose to live, it will be for my own reasons, thank you, not because someone felt they needed to compliment me into a longer life."

Bainbridge looked suitably chastised. I studied the bill, furiously.

"I'm not entirely clear what you're talking about," said Bainbridge, after a while.

I glared at him. "Please, do not treat me like a fool," I snapped.

"No, really!" he said. "Sarah hasn't told me anything! Wh-what… "

I narrowed three of my eyes. "So why," I said, "have you been so nice to me all evening?"

"Well… " Bainbridge said, before trailing off.

"What?" I demanded.

"If you must know," he said, "I was working up to asking if you felt like you might enjoy going for dinner again, once the holiday was over. Just us. The two of us. No-one else."

"Oh," I said.

"Sorry," said Bainbridge.

"No!" I cried. "No, no, no, no… "

I had to think quickly but I can't really do that outside of a combat situation, so I decided to stall by making a sort of 'errr' noise.

So, it seemed that Bainbridge was attracted to me. Had he always been, or was this a spur of the moment thing? No, I couldn't think about that, that didn't matter. The 'errr' noise was already proving difficult to maintain, my mind straining as it was to process Bainbridge's information.

Was I attracted to Bainbridge? Maybe. He was a good-looking arachnid, although I was generally not the sort of person who noticed such things unless they were brought to my attention. Did I enjoy Bainbridge's company? Yes. Would I enjoy more of it?

Probably. Were there other things I was supposed to consider when deciding whether or not to walk out with someone?

My thoughts were making me sound like someone who had only read about relationships in books. I have had relationships in the past. You don't get to my age without having the odd... Well, I mean, there was Roger, he had had been very nice. There had been Tara, she'd been lovely. I had walked out with Alice, Amin and Rafik for a while. That had been perfectly delightful, but it ended, as everything must.

I shook myself. I had no intention of justifying my entire romantic history to myself. Why had I even brought it up? That wasn't important. What was I going to do about the matter in front of me?

My problem was, I tended not to notice whether or not someone would make a good romantic partner unless they made their intentions very clear and I didn't immediately panic and run away. A, A and R, for example, had sat me down at a party and explained why they thought I'd make a great addition to their relationship. It took several hours for me to work out they were inviting me to join them, rather than wondering out loud if I knew anyone *like* me who might be interested in a relationship with them. Thankfully, they were very patient with me.

Okay, things were starting to get really bad. I was running out of breath and the 'err' noise was starting to sound more and more desperate.

What were the questions I'd asked myself earlier? Attractiveness, enjoyable company and the prospect for more of the same. Was I ready for a relationship? I was dying. But I might not be, depending on what I decided to do about my medication. Blast, I hadn't picked it up. Sarah would be cross. The dying... well, that was for Bainbridge to decide if it was a problem. Would I appreciate some intimacy? Probably. It had been a while. I would have blushed thinking this, had my fur not already been colouring from the lack of air.

There was one other thing. If anyone would understand the guilt I was feeling due to the events of my first tour of duty, it would be someone who had spent time in the Special Operations Unit. If I wanted understanding, understanding was staring me in the face.

I had maybe a second or two of air left before I had to breathe. I hadn't panicked or run away. I couldn't think of a reason not to walk out with Bainbridge at least once and there were, in fact, several reasons why it might be mutually beneficial.

With the last fragment of breath at my disposal, I changed the 'err' noise into a 'yes'.

"Sorry, I'm confused," said Bainbridge. "What does 'no no no no no err yes' in response to an apology mean?"

"It means," I said, leaning forward slightly, "I would be delighted to see you again after the holiday. Just us." I was then treated to the frankly improbable sight of Bainbridge blushing.

I sat back and thought for a moment. This evening had been wonderful, and it had just taken an unexpected turn. I felt like I had to ruin it.

"I must apologise for overreacting," I said. Bainbridge was about to wave this away, but I pressed on. "Would you like to know what I thought Sarah had told you?"

"Not if it's none of my business," said he.

"If we are to see each other again," I said, "it might become your business."

"Then, if you're happy to tell me... please, tell me," said Bainbridge.

So, I told him about the cure for the mindvirus and the decision I was yet to make. He didn't ask for the reason behind my indecision – he was a gentlenid – but I told him anyway. At the conclusion of the story, I thought he might have wanted to reach forward and take my claw. I wouldn't have minded if he had… so I found myself leaning forward and taking his.

We went for a walk after dinner. We found a place to watch the sunset. It glistened on the glass panels of the university and bathed the hills beyond in a warm orange light. I felt calm. I did not feel peaceful, but I felt that peace might one day be an option.

"I feel I should tell you something," said Bainbridge.

I'd ruined everything. I *knew* I shouldn't have told him about the mindvirus. Why did I always do this? What was wrong with me? Everything. That was too broad. I started to make a list.

"No," said Bainbridge. I had apparently not been able to keep the look of blind panic from my face. "Sorry, I meant… look. I've been wanting to talk about something, because… we're getting close to Newbury Towers and… I don't know what's going to happen when we get there."

I tried to wrestle my heart rate down to a less terrifying level.

"Please continue," I said, attempting to sound like a suave individual rather than a panicked one.

"Did I tell you about how I joined the Special Operations Unit?" he asked.

"As I recall, you said you were persuaded to, and it seemed like a good idea at the time."

"Ah, yes," he said. "I should really give you a little more detail one of these days but as I might have said, it's a long story and not exactly necessary for the current conversation."

I wondered why he kept bringing it up if he wasn't going to actually tell the story, but I didn't say anything.

"The thing is… the thing is… " said Bainbridge, before sighing and hanging his head. "The thing *is*… I was not a very good person before I joined the Special Operations Unit."

"Oh, come now… " I said.

He held up a claw. "I mean it, Jay. My behaviour left my relationships with my family rather strained. You see… my father, Sir Arthur Lusitania, had been wounded in combat rather badly. He had, as such, spent much of his life in and out of many different medical facilities. This left my upbringing and the running of the Lusitania estate largely in the claws of Sir Angus Possingthrut Woebuston Wermacht IV, Sarah's uncle."

"Oh, my dear chap… " I said, not really knowing if I should be saying anything at all at this point.

"I was hedonistic," said Bainbridge. "I was selfish, and I was a cad… but that was then, and this is now. The thing that worries me, Jay… the thing that really scares me is what's going to happen when we reach Newbury Towers. What, when you get right down to it, is going to happen when I see Sir Angus Wermacht or my father? Are they going to see me, or the cad I once was?"

I didn't know what to say to this. "If they see what I see, they'll be proud of you."

I really was a colossal idiot. Why, when given the opportunity, had I not come up with something insightful? Something that might actually *help* in this situation? Why had I said something so trite, something so *utterly* useless, that it would make any sane person shake their head and wonder why they had bothered asking in the first place?

It transpired that, for the purposes of that conversation, Bainbridge did not qualify as a sane person. I found his claw gripping mine once more.

Bainbridge's data panel blipped. He swore and slapped at it, trying to shut it up before it ruined the moment.

"Who is it?" I asked.

He glared at the readout, then frowned. "Sarah. She's calling back."

He answered it. He exchanged a few words with Sarah. A look of anger flashed across his face before he rolled his eyes and smiled.

"We'll be right there," he said.

Chapter Sixteen

The Mysterious Anthony Partridge

At around the time Bainbridge and I had been purchasing bedding, Sarah and Anthony had touched down in one of Colin's smaller cities: Lotus. Lotus had a high human population, due to a series of protection acts passed by the local government.

Sarah and Anthony had spent a few hours getting used to the city. Anthony needed to make sure this was a place where he might conceivably feel at home, after all. They wandered the city, bought a few pastries from a pastry shop, purchased some meaty snacks from a meaty snack dispenser and generally had a pretty decent time of it.

Sarah had been intermittently checking in with her group of human contacts. Many of them had jobs and other commitments they couldn't drop at a moment's notice to meet a new member. Sarah and Anthony discussed matters and established a time and a place to meet with the group.

The meeting place was an inn on the edge of town. It overlooked the sprawling hills that bordered Lotus. The star that illuminated the city slowly set as the meeting time approached. Sarah checked her vox-o-matic at some point, around the time Bainbridge and I were watching the sunset, and saw that Bainbridge had tried to call her.

She rang him back and explained the situation. She said that if Bainbridge and I wanted to say goodbye to Anthony, we'd best drop by, as it would soon be time to part ways.

We arrived at the inn shortly after several humans who were part of Sarah's network, and found Sarah surrounded by humans in the public bar. We greeted our friend and were introduced to her fellows.

Anthony wasn't there; Sarah explained that he had slipped away to wash his claws. Sarah's friends had spent a short while getting to know Anthony and were full of praise for him. Bainbridge and I purchased refreshments from the barkeep and joined the group. Every so often, a new human would arrive and we were introduced to them.

The company was most pleasant. I've spent time with Sarah's human friends before and I found them to be charming, intelligent, witty and generally delightful people. Some of them did smell a *bit,* but nowhere near as badly as I expected; honestly, it was hardly noticeable after a while.

At one point, I noticed Bainbridge and Sarah murmuring to each other. Sarah caught my eye and grinned wolfishly at me. I grinned back, not really knowing what was going on. A few moments later, Sarah approached me and embraced me, causing her friends to cluck a little.

"You two are going to be great," Sarah said.

I thanked her, trying to think what she could mean.

I then worked it out. I hugged her back.

The sun had set by the time Anthony's absence was commented upon. Watches and data panels were checked, and it was agreed that he had, indeed, been gone for quite some time. Sarah announced that she would visit the water closet and check to see that he was okay. He might just have been nervous about meeting a large group of new people.

She was gone for a few minutes before she returned, chewing her lip.

"He's gone," she said.

"Eh?" I asked.

"He's gone. He's not there. He's vanished."

"We need to look for him," said someone.

"Where would he have gone?" asked someone else.

We brainstormed. We drew up plans. We split into teams.

The humans that knew the city left to do what could be done there. They visited police stations, hostels and shelters – anywhere a human might go if they needed help. Anthony might have been in trouble. He may have been attacked. Some of our group even visited the local medical centres to see if he was under their case.

Bainbridge, Sarah and I, not knowing the city of Lotus, were tasked with sweeping the hills on the outskirts. We started from the back garden of the inn. From there, the dark, dark landscape stretched out before us.

We each set off in a different direction, checking our data panels to confirm our positions and bearings as we did so. Nobody called anyone else except for the occasional check-in. We needed to keep the airwaves open, in case Anthony was found and needed immediate help.

My night vision was tolerable at close range so I felt confident that I would be able to spot Anthony as I searched, even at this time of night. This changed when I reached the crest of the hill.

Darkness stretched out before me. The few hundred metres I could see ahead of me were comprised mostly of scrubland. Deep purple grass waved in the breeze. I needed to venture into the dark-ness, or my search would be inadequate.

I trundled through the scrubland on the other side of the hill, satisfying myself that there was no sign of Anthony or his passage. This done, I turned my attention to a small patch of woodland that covered the western slope of the hill.

I might have been only a few metres from Anthony and still missed him, thanks to the thickness of the vegetation. At one point, a bear (or possibly some sort of large marsupial) dropped out of a tree onto my head and attempted to bite through my skull. I lifted it down, as gently as possible, and tossed it into a clearing.

The creature roared adorably and appeared a little confused by my complete lack of surprise or fear. I roared back, companion-ably, which caused it to scamper up the nearest tree. I worried that I might have frightened the poor thing.

Another hour passed before I had to admit defeat. I trudged back to the inn, Anthonyless, to see what progress my compatriots had made.

None, was the answer.

Bainbridge and Sarah returned soon after I did, similarly empty-handed. We conferred with Sarah's friends and found that Anthony was nowhere to be found in the city, either. He had simply vanished.

We pondered our next move and discussed what all this could mean. It was seeming less and less likely that something had hap-pened *to* Anthony. There were no signs of a struggle in the wash-room or anywhere around the inn. No-one had reported anything suspicious to the police. It seemed that Anthony had simply chosen that moment to… leave.

As Sarah aptly summarised, the following four possibilities were most likely:

The first: Anthony had felt tremendous guilt and shame about his life with the pirates. He had fled the group in order to take his own life.

The second: Anthony had felt overwhelmed by the group's generosity, feeling he was undeserving of it. He left the group to forge his own life without imposing on others.

The third: Anthony felt that the group was imposing on his life. He hadn't needed other people, and felt that he should leg it and forge his own path.

The forth: Anthony had massively understated his role as commodore of the pirates. He had manipulated us from the moment we first met him. Seeing which way the battle between his people and Yarl was going, he used us to get him off the base and trusted that we would speak favourably of him to the police. To his surprise, he wasn't charged. He then made his escape at the first available opportunity, and would either start a new life or find a new group of ne'er-do-wells to integrate with.

There was no real solid evidence for any of these ideas… but none of them sounded like a particularly pleasant outcome. There seemed little to be done when everything was set out like that. Sarah's friends told us that we had better be on our way.

Sarah objected, saying we could continue to help in the search. Bainbridge and I agreed vigorously, but it was pointless. Where would we start? It very much appeared that Anthony did not want to be found.

Sarah was very quiet as we flew the skiff back to Colinsberg. She was grateful to find a room waiting for her and excused herself from our company, assuring us that she needed nothing. She was simply extremely tired. Bainbridge and I exchanged a few sad words before retiring for the night as well.

I lay awake for some time, thinking about Anthony all alone on a strange planet. There was more we could have done to find him…

but it wasn't our place to do so if he did not want to be found. It was in the claws of the police and Sarah's friends, now. Hopefully he was alive, safe and... happy with whatever choices he'd made.

Sleep did come, eventually. Despite the wonderful comfort of the bed, it was fitful.

Sarah, Bainbridge and I breakfasted at the inn after sunrise. It was a muted affair. Anthony's fate weighed heavily on our minds, but we were still of the opinion that there was nothing to be done. To change the subject, I mentioned to Sarah that I had neglected to pick up my medication. She rolled her eyes.

Once breakfast had been sufficiently consumed by our various mighty jaws, Sarah took me by the claw and led me to the nearest pharmacy with Bainbridge in tow. I nearly got distracted a few times by shiny objects or people who looked like they might not be called Colin, but Bainbridge kept me on track with the application of a claw to my upper thorax.

The pharmacist checked her local network for the prescription from my medic and raised her eyebrows at the drug I was to be dispensed. The shop was empty apart from the three of us, so she flipped the sign on the door so that it read 'closed' and sat us down in an adjoining room.

The expression she fixed me with was extremely serious. My face immediately wanted to crack into a smile.

"The near future," she said, after we'd all been formally introduced, "is going to be tough. I'm glad you have friends with you."

She pinged an information packet to Sarah and Bainbridge's dataslates, after establishing that I didn't have mine with me. She asked us to look at the list of side-effects. They were listed in categories from very rare to likely. The very rare side-effects sounded extremely nasty. Apparently, my blood might decide to leave my body by any means necessary if things went badly wrong. The likely side-effects didn't sound like a picnic, either.

There were words listed that I had never seen before. Most of them consisted of more than four syllables. Of the words that I did understand, a few stood out: Convulsions. Photosensitivity. Severe allergic reactions. Sedation. Anxiety.

"Some people don't react at all badly to this medication," said the pharmacist, in a way that I suspect was supposed to be comforting, "but I must advise that, once you start taking it, you shouldn't discontinue the treatment without speaking to your doctor first. The first few days are going to be the most intense and, if you give up during that period, it's unlikely you'll want to try again."

I swallowed. Sarah took my claw. On the other side of me, Bainbridge took another. I felt a slight thrill. I nodded at the pharmacist.

I was given several packets of pills, along with a rather nice box with lids marked with the days of the week to keep them in. I was also given several emergency contact frequencies in case anything went wrong, as if I wasn't already nervous enough about taking the pills.

I must have been in quite a state by the time the pharmacist was done with me, because Bainbridge and Sarah put their heads together for a few moments before purchasing a significant number of glucose-based treats sold at the pharmacy counter. These were then pressed into my claws.

I was initially outraged at how my friend and my... potential partner were treating me, as if I were some sort of child, but I felt a tear on my cheek and inserted a flavoured glucose treat into my mouth. To my surprise, it did make me feel a little better.

I put the other fifteen into my mouth as well.

We bade our farewells to the pharmacist, although mine was a little muffled. We then returned to our inn, where we gathered the purchases Bainbridge and I had made yesterday. The porter ferried them downstairs for us while we purchased vittles from the inn's kitchen, enough to get us to Newbury Towers.

This done, Sarah went to fetch our boat so we could head back to the *Cox*. Bainbridge was very sweet and distracted me with embarrassing tales from his youth. Before long, we found ourselves back on board ship. I helped Bainbridge string up our new hammocks whilst Sarah pulled us out of orbit.

"What are you doing?" I enquired, after Bainbridge fumbled his end of the first hammock for the fifth time.

Bainbridge looked up at me. "Last time we tried something like this, I lost a leg. I'm being careful."

I pointed out that these were hammocks, not energy fields. The likelihood of injury was much lower. That was how we wound up, ten minutes later, with three of Bainbridge's legs lashed together by hammock rope. I still have no idea how that happened.

Sarah emerged from the bridge after I'd cried for help, unable to free Bainbridge by myself. We worked together and eventually extricated the poor chap from his predicament.

"Perhaps," Bainbridge said, "we should read the instructions."

I waved this away, saying that we didn't need instructions.

Bainbridge massaged a part of his leg where the blood supply had been cut off during his imprisonment. "I think we do… "

So, we read the instructions. I couldn't make head nor tail of them, but Sarah and Bainbridge explained patiently what needed doing step-by-step. Before long, we had one hammock strung up properly. We then realised it was upside down. A few more instances of trial and error later, we had three glorious-looking hammocks in place.

By then it was time to eat, so we finished off what supplies we had left on the boat, saving the provisions we'd purchased from the inn for that evening.

Then, after encouragement from my two companions, I took the first of my medication.

This is fine, I thought. *Nothing appears to be happening.*

I joined Bainbridge and Sarah on the bridge, and even took control of the lines as I hadn't piloted the *Cox* in some time. We pulled away from the planet of the Colins and I pointed us in the direction of Newbury Towers. I then realised that, thanks to a bend in the course of the shipping lane, this would send us careering out of the lane and into an asteroid field. Not wanting to deal with space debris again, I adjusted our heading.

Bainbridge and Sarah stayed with me on the bridge as I piloted. We chatted about this and that, although certain topics were steadfastly avoided. Anthony, for example. The amount that he didn't get mentioned fairly took my breath away.

Still, the medication didn't appear to have any adverse effects. Well, hardly any. After an hour I started to feel a little delicate, but it came on so gradually that I barely noticed. I'd wince whenever voices were slightly raised or the control panels sounded an alert, but nothing more.

After two hours, I abandoned my piloting duties, as the lights on the control console were giving me a headache. I returned to my hammock to lie down.

At the third hour, I had to run to the starboard beam to be sick.

Things got worse from that point on.

I felt groggy and disorientated. I felt sick to my stomach. I had serious difficulty sleeping. My mouth was dry and left with a lingering, unpleasant taste. Water was disagreeable to drink as a result, so I drank nothing but sweet tea.

I was unable to bring what remained of my mind to bear on things. I quickly became too bored to enjoy watching the stars as we sailed through them, but I lacked the concentration to be able to read or converse with my friends. I quickly became certain that this was how I would feel for the rest of my days.

Sarah and Bainbridge were amazingly supportive. On the second day, after barely getting any sleep and being entirely fed up with feeling like my brain was dribbling out of my hearing sensors, I decided I would cease my course of medication.

Bainbridge and Sarah encouraged and wheedled and threatened me into taking my next dose, and the one after that.

At the risk of stating the obvious, I did not enjoy the rest of the holiday. I mainly felt guilty, like I was making things worse for Bainbridge and Sarah. Sarah had returned my data panel to me on the second day because I desperately needed something to pass the time. She took it away hours later, as I kept looking up things that she and Bainbridge could do for entertainment on the way to Newbury Towers.

I was repeatedly told to stop worrying about them. The purpose of the next few days was to get me through the worst of my medication's side-effects. I felt extremely embarrassed, because I was ruining their holiday and partly because I did not know what I had done to deserve such good friends.

Sarah and Bainbridge did stop off at a few points of interest. One planet we passed had a highly-recommended science museum. There was also a space station near the lane that had been operational for thousands of years. Bainbridge and Sarah dropped in to see both, leaving me on the ship. They made certain I had my communicator in case I needed anything, and were sure to not take too long, despite my assurances that they could take as long as they liked.

I felt a little better on the fourth day. My head felt clearer and I had stopped evacuating the contents of my stomach at every available opportunity. I had hoped the side-effects would vanish from me like snow in the sun, but they seemed to be taking their sweet time about it.

Still, improvement was improvement. I was no longer dreading every single dose of medication, meaning Bainbridge and Sarah didn't need to spend half an hour getting me to take the things every single time. In fact, by the time Sarah let out a cry to let us know she had spied Newbury Towers on the horizon, I was feeling almost arachnid again.

Chapter Seventeen

Bainbridge Lusitania

Newbury Towers turned out to be quite a pretty country house orbiting some grounds and overlooking an asteroid belt that was home, apparently, to a set of humans. Sarah parked the *Cox* in orbit around the house and we all piled into the skiff. This was my first time off the ship in days and it caused me to feel quite queasy.

Sarah had wired ahead to let her cousin Gertrude and Uncle Angus know our expected arrival time. They were both standing on the steps of their house, waiting for us.

Sarah beached the skiff on the driveway, leapt out and ran up to hug her uncle and cousin. Bainbridge helped me out of the skiff and we both followed. Bainbridge seemed hesitant. I understood things between him and Sir Angus Wermacht – Uncle Angus – had not ended well when they'd last seen each other.

As Bainbridge approached, he nodded to Gertrude and then, hesitantly, he extended a claw to Sir Angus. The older arachnid looked at Bainbridge for a few moments and then embraced him, ignoring the outstretched claw. He whispered something into Bainbridge's hearing sensors. I saw the hug tighten.

I approached once the two had separated. Sarah introduced me and I bowed. We were shown inside to the morning room, where Gertrude and Sarah made light conversation. Sir Angus, for his part, said he needed to speak with Bainbridge as a matter of some urgency. He apologised for breaking up the party at this early stage. We, naturally, thanked him for his consideration but assured him that it was fine.

Gertrude persuaded us to spend the next hour recounting our travels thus far. We told her about the murders on Dessan, Yarl and the planet Colin. I was just telling the story of the attack on the pirate base, when Bainbridge and Sir Angus re-entered the morning room. Bainbridge looked like he had been struck by a trolley bus. I thought about asking if he was quite well, but decided now was not the time.

Before the conversation could get into its stride again, Bainbridge wondered out loud if we'd like to come and visit his family estate. Sarah and I looked at each other. After all, we'd spent all this time getting to Newbury Towers, it seemed too soon to be moving on. Bainbridge's expression begged us to acquiesce, so we mentally shrugged and agreed that it sounded like a fine thing to do.

Sir Angus asked a servant to fetch a car that could transport three gentlenids and a human, before buzzing off somewhere on his own.

"What's going on, B, old chap?" Sarah asked, once her uncle was out of earshot.

Bainbridge looked from the floor to me, to the floor, to Sarah and back to me. He relayed what had passed between himself and Sir Angus Wermacht with an expression that hovered between despair and relief:

Bainbridge had followed Sir Angus into a study decorated with portraits of gentlenids posing next to architecture. A huge desk dominated the room. It was fully three times larger than it needed to be, and it left precious little room for anything else. A chair had been squeezed behind it, whilst a stool had been propped in a corner by the door.

Sir Angus offered Bainbridge a drink from one of a number of decanters that occupied one tiny fraction of the enormous desk. Bainbridge asked for water. Sir Angus blinked at this but nodded and filled a tumbler. He waved at the stool. Bainbridge sat, Sir Angus squeezed around his desk and contorted himself into the chair.

"My boy," said Sir Angus, "I'm afraid I have bad news."

"It is my father," said Bainbridge.

"You know already?" asked Sir Angus, shocked.

Bainbridge sighed. "No. But there are few reasons why you would ask to speak to me like this," he waved, indicating the situation the two gentlenids were in, "and the most likely is that my father's health has worsened."

"I'm afraid so," said Sir Angus. "He has deteriorated over the last month."

"Did he get my letters?" Bainbridge asked.

Sir Angus smiled. "He did. The old boy was thrilled upon receiving them."

Bainbridge allowed himself a smile in return. "I am glad."

"Of course, he wanted to write back… " Sir Angus trailed off.

Bainbridge shook his head. "I am glad that he couldn't," he said. Contact with Special Operations officers was generally not allowed unless in an emergency, due to the secretive nature of their work.

Sir Angus raised an eyebrow at this last statement of Bainbridge's. Bainbridge shook his head. "Sorry. I meant… I had this idea that when we saw each other for the first time after I left the Special Operations unit… we would… well, we'd reconcile and music would play, and it would be wonderful. I dare say I imagined that we'd run into each other's arms or... something. Is that a thing fathers and sons do?"

Sir Angus looked a little baffled and shrugged. He only had a daughter, after all.

"Well, anyway," said Bainbridge, "that thought kept me going and... if I'd had letters from him... I don't know. It would have... I don't know."

There was silence for a few moments.

"He wanted me to tell you a great many things," said Sir Angus, "many of which he will now be able to tell you himself. There is one thing he wished me to tell you as soon as I saw you, however."

Bainbridge looked puzzled.

"He wants you to take over the running of the family estate."

*   *   *

Sarah and I gasped two or three times apiece at this news. Bainbridge nodded, appreciatively, at our shock, but didn't say any more. A servant pulled up with a car moments later. Sir Angus returned from his errand, his eyes looking a little red, shortly afterwards. We piled into the car and set off towards the Lusitania estate.

Our destination was one star system over from Newbury Towers but Sir Angus was an excellent host; he filled the journey by relating interesting facts about the local area, many of which Gertrude, Sarah and Bainbridge had heard before, but I was riveted. He detailed the history of the human village that Newbury Towers oversaw. He explained how the roads in this area linked up with the shipping lanes. Then, as we approached the Lusitania estate, he invited Bainbridge to divulge a little family history.

It transpired that Bainbridge's great-grandmother had been named a countess after an especially successful campaign against a collection of flesh-eating monstrosities that sought only to breed and consume. These creatures had managed to tear a hole in the very fabric of reality, leaving behind a portal to another dimension.

I was shocked by this. I had no idea that the existence of other dimensions had been verified, let alone rendered accessible. Bainbridge was quick to correct me. It had transpired that the existence of only one alternate dimension was proven. There might possibly have been others but no-one was keen to find them given the only one that had been discovered thus far was so utterly ghastly: It was a dimension of warlike beings who sought only to conquer and control. Apparently, in spite of this, they weren't particularly pleasant people. Bainbridge said they were rather uncouth.

The denizens of this uncouth dimension used flesh-eating monstrosities as attack dogs, which was rather cruel to the poor things, not to mention whatever they ended up eating. They also had a habit of targeting locations used to store the backups of our arachnid consciousnesses, meaning that if we tangled with them there was a real chance we might die permanently. This wasn't only dangerous; it was rude.

Bainbridge told us how the Lusitanias, after being ennobled, had been charged with guarding the dimensional tear. They'd built an estate around the tear's location and, every fifty years or so, they'd lead the charge when it opened and started spilling uncouth creatures into our reality.

It was one of these encounters that had wounded Bainbridge's father. The impolite monstrosities were driven back, but at considerable cost. Bainbridge had been only young when the attack occurred, so he had been evacuated to Newbury Towers for safekeeping, Sir Arthur Lusitania and Sir Angus Wermacht being old pals.

Things went a bit wrong from that point. Young Bainbridge was an only child and Sir Arthur's partner, the Countess Lusitania, had been permanently killed in the last attack. This left Sir Angus to raise Bainbridge whilst Sir Arthur recovered.

The Lusitania family estate had been essentially shuttered since the last attack. There were a few staff on site to monitor the dimensional tear in case it reopened without warning, but otherwise, apart from brief periods when Bainbridge's father was able to live there, the place was quiet.

The estate appeared deserted as we pulled up to it soon after Bainbridge finished his story. The enormous arched windows were shuttered. The monuments that lined the driveway were covered in debris-resistant sheeting. The massive polyninium alloy doors didn't look like they'd been opened in my lifetime.

We stepped out of Sir Angus' car and gazed up at the mansion. It was a little foreboding. Newbury Towers had been a perfectly nice country house with all the features you'd expect of such a joint. It seemed that when the Countess Lusitania was having this estate constructed, she felt that its design should match the gravitas of its purpose.

I swayed a little as Bainbridge approached the steps leading up to the doors. I thought I must be overawed by the historic occasion. This was the first time in his adult life that Bainbridge had set foot on his family's estate. He was taking on a momentous responsibility. It was admirable. It was noble. I felt my heart beat faster.

Sir Angus had followed Bainbridge, careful to stay just behind him. He reached a claw forward as Bainbridge reached the top step and spoke to him, quietly. Bainbridge regarded Sir Angus' claw and took what was in it. He reached out to the door and it swung inwards. My vision blurred.

Bainbridge took over the Lusitania estate. He borrowed a maid and a valet from Sir Angus for a few days until more permanent help could be sought. He threw open the shutters and let the galaxy know that the Lusitanias were, once again, defending them from interdimensional impolite invaders.

He went to see his father, who was being cared for at the local medical facility. There were tears, there were reconciliations. His father told him that he was proud of his son.

Bainbridge continued with his recovery programme. It was slow going, but he chipped away at it for an hour every day. On some days that wasn't enough, and he would need to go for long walks in the peace of the Lusitania estate. On some days, he felt like he would be able to leave his memories of the Special Operations Unit behind.

Sarah should have returned home, but she said she had things to attend to on the Lusitania estate. I say things. There was only really one thing: me. I hadn't witnessed Bainbridge hiring his staff. I hadn't been there for him when he'd visited his father. I hadn't seen the transformation of the Lusitania estate from fortress to Bainbridge's new home, because I'd been in bed nearly the entire time.

As soon as Bainbridge had first opened the doors to what was now his home, I collapsed. Apparently, I hadn't recovered from the side-effects of my medication as completely as I'd thought. The travel, first to Newbury Towers and then the Lusitania estate, had been too much for me.

I spent the majority of the month that followed in bed, wishing to either recover or just die and get it over with.

I had been warned that the side-effects of my medication would be nasty. I had been warned they might render me unable to do much of anything. What I hadn't been warned about was how *tedious* that would be.

I likened it to being stuck in a waiting room for an appointment and unable to leave. I quickly exhausted every available entertainment, and the tedium set in. Then the tedium gave way to boredom. Then things *really* got bad. I wanted to go back home but I was repeatedly informed that I was not well enough to leave. I risked making things worse by subjecting my mind and body to the rigors of travel. So, I imposed on Bainbridge's hospitality.

I didn't *want* to impose on Bainbridge's hospitality. What I wanted, more than anything else, was to return home. This was not just because I was homesick, although that was part of it. It was mostly because Bainbridge was being wonderful. He was coming to see me whenever he could be spared from his duties revitalising the estate. He kept me entertained and prevented me from slipping into a boredom coma.

I did not want him to see me like this. The plan had been to finish the holiday and then walk out together, to get to know each other a little better. As things stood, he was getting to know the wrong side of me. He was seeing me at my worst. I was barely conscious a lot of the time. When I was awake, I was petulant and snappish because I was so bored.

I didn't want him to see those parts of me. I wanted him to see my better qualities, like... Well, the matter is moot anyway, as there weren't any qualities that were less than awful during Bainbridge's little visits.

I wasn't really getting to know him, either. All I had discovered was that he was loyal, loving and kind, which I had pretty much already gathered. It all felt so massively unfair. Were our situations reversed, I would not have minded so much. I could have mopped his brow and caught occasional glimpses of his muscled legs whenever he passed a claw over his eyes. It is much better to care for someone than to be a burden on them, in my opinion.

Slowly – and yes, blissfully – I recovered. After what seemed like an eternity, I was strong enough to spend more time out of bed.

I was able to sit in the chair in my room. Then I was able to take one meal per day in the dining room, rather than one per week. Soon, I was eating two meals a day. Then three, then four, then five as my appetite increased. I then dropped back to three, as I returned to a healthy weight after my incarceration in that pillowy prison.

Shortly thereafter, I was able to stroll through the grounds for brief periods. This resulted in a pleasant surprise. One morning, as the larks were singing and the carnivorous plants were snapping the morning chorus, I went for a stroll, only to come across Yarl doing strange, alien stretches on a yoga mat.

"I say, hello there!" I said. My voice was still weak but it was getting stronger every day. "I thought you were going to prison."

Yarl started, turned to look at me and then howled in delight. It ran towards me and snuffled at my thorax. "You're up, you're up! How wonderful!"

"Yes, yes it is," I said, easing two of his three heads away to a more socially acceptable distance. "It's lovely to see you too, Yarl. But prison, Yarl, why aren't you in prison?"

"Oh, but I am!" Yarl tapped at three thick, electronic collars that adorned its three armoured necks. "Bainbridge put in a plea with the magistrate for me to serve my sentence on his estate, crushing the enemies of arachnid society." A laugh burst from one mouth, and a burst of flame burst from another. This mouth, thankfully, was pointing skywards at the time.

This made me frown. Not the flame, the flame was perfectly pleasant. Bainbridge's actions, however were a little…

"You think he's throwing his weight around to get me a lighter sentence, don't you?" Yarl said, grinning expansively. "I said the same thing when the magistrate told me about the request. The thing is, there's a word you arachnids have. It begins with an R and ends with an 'ation'. Can't get the hang of it myself, but apparently if I spend time serving the community and spend time with one of your head shrinking people that's more useful than just sitting in a prison cell."

"Rehabilitation?"

"That's the word! Rehamilton! Yes! Anyway, it's brilliant. I've crushed more than fifty invaders with my mighty jaws and I'm learning about self-destructive thought spirals." Yarl thumped its chest and belched flame towards the sky again.

I swayed slightly at this, before swaying slightly more.

"Jay. Jay!" cried Yarl. "You should go back to bed. I'm sorry if this has all been too much for you."

I smiled at it and nodded. "It was lovely to see you again, Yarl."

I went on a little walk every day from that point on. I chatted to Yarl whenever I saw him, but I was careful to only stay out for as long as my body could take.

Two more weeks passed. At my request, Bainbridge and I started spending less time together. He'd looked extremely hurt when I first asked him to maintain some distance, but he understood once I explained the reason.

I continued to take my medication. I had weekly conversations with my doctor to make sure I was surviving to the best of my ability. I still hadn't made any permanent decisions about my future, but I felt no urgent need to do so.

I had been spending less time with Bainbridge in order to separate myself from him during the final stages of my recovery. I needed to draw a line under my immediate recovery. I wanted the next time he saw me to be a joyous occasion.

Sarah and I talked at this point, and we agreed that she could leave me in the capable hands of Bainbridge's staff. He had built quite a crew in the month I had been bedridden. Besides, Sarah had a task she needed to take care of herself.

She had been working remotely, via the datafeeds, when not caring for me. She'd been brokering deals between human-relief organisations, as well as bullying district governments into setting up human sanctuaries in their cities. In her spare time, she'd been trawling the feeds for news of Anthony Partridge. Finally, she'd found something.

Sarah told me that a new group of pirates had sprung up on a base near the tomb world where we'd initially parted ways with Megan. Their leader was a human. Small, seemingly defenceless and utterly without mercy.

It *might* not have been Anthony, but it sounded dreadfully like it was. Sarah had reached out to the anti-piracy task force and had negotiated her way onto the strike team that was preparing to take down the pirates once and for all. I told her to get in touch if she needed a strategic consult. She hugged me and said she would. With a wave and a smile, she was driven to the local enforcer base by her cousin, Gertrude. My recovery continued until – *finally* – I considered myself ready to venture away from the estate. I borrowed a car and drove to the nearest planet, a nice little place called Tippily. I touched down, parked the car and went to find a river. It wasn't a patch on the river back in Tunsleworth, but it was nice enough. I watched the water flow for an hour or so.

I didn't feel weak, I didn't feel nauseous. I didn't feel like I was going to faint at any moment. My claws didn't drag along the ground when I walked. I didn't need to support myself on nearby objects to avoid falling down.

That night, when I returned to the Lusitania estate, I sent a message to Bainbridge's data panel asking if he would join me for a meal on the morrow.

The following morning, I borrowed a car again. I dropped down to Tippily to purchase a new suit. I had my fur professionally dishevelled and paid a nice young chap to sharpen my claws with a belt sander.

The fated hour rolled closer, as hours do if you're not watching them closely. I worked through possible disaster plans in my head. With this relaxing activity out of the way, I started to worry. Questions beginning with 'what if?' plagued me. What if my recovery was set back by the evening? What if Bainbridge realised he'd made a mistake and didn't want to spend any further time with me? What if, what if, what if…

My tablet pinged. I reached down and saw a message from Sarah. 'I'd wish you good luck for tonight' it said, 'but you don't need it. You're going to be wonderful.'

The smile that spread across my face would have blinded anyone who happened to be in the room with me. I checked the time and dressed myself in a simple, elegant evening suit. I still felt butterflies in my stomach. I should have known that having butterflies for lunch would come back to haunt me. To settle myself I re-read Sarah's message. I nodded to myself and lay down my tablet on my bedside table. It was time, and I didn't want to keep Bainbridge waiting.

Printed in Great Britain
by Amazon